D1482249

More praise for
TEMPTATIONS

"Part thriller, part mystery, and part spiritual autobiography . . . Paul Wilkes asks the important questions, and identifies the essential issues in a seemingly limited setting of a monastery. . . . [He] brings together his considerable journalistic skills with a keen interest in and understanding of contemporary Christian spirituality."
—*Greensboro News and Record*

"Readers familiar with the elegance and style that distinguish Wilkes' writing will not be disappointed by this gracefully told and sensitive novel."
—*Worcester Telegram & Gazette*

"Against four seasons of powerfully evoked rural Vermont scenery, Wilkes follows Joseph's inner journey. . . . [He] doesn't flinch from the hard questions of sprituality in the modern world, and his gracefully written novel leaves its mark on the reader's mind.
—*Publishers Weekly*

"Paul Wilkes [is] gifted with eloquence, understanding, and common sense."
—*Commonweal*

TEMPTATIONS

Paul Wilkes

BALLANTINE BOOKS • NEW YORK

Copyright © 1993 by Paul Wilkes

All rights reserved under International and Pan-American Copyright Conventions. Published in the United States of America by Ballantine Books, a division of Random House, Inc., New York, and simultaneously in Canada by Random House of Canada Limited, Toronto.

Library of Congress Catalog Card Number: 92-50510

ISBN 0-345-38642-6

This edition published by arrangement with Random House, Inc.

Manufactured in the United States of America

First Ballantine Books Edition: May 1994

10 9 8 7 6 5 4 3 2 1

To the memory of my parents,
Paul and Margaret Wilkes

To love Him truly you must love change,
    and you must love a joke,
        these being the true inclinations of His own heart.
                                            —ISAK DINESEN
                                            "The Dreamers"

The Years Before

I WAS born to Eastern European parents who never quite mastered the curious language Americans spoke. When we realized that there were classes in America, we called ourselves lower-middle, which of course we were not. My father was a steelworker, too heavy a drinker for his infrequent pay stubs in an industry that had died decades before but lingered on, like him. My mother always worked, regardless of whether she was pregnant or had to care for small children. She was a domestic, she told us, and that had a nice American ring to it—that is, until we found she was no more than a cleaning lady.

They were religious people, my mother and father, who never owned their own home, never bought a car new, but readily made any sacrifice necessary for their eight children to receive a Catholic education. There was really no premium put on education per se—the way for instance that Jews treasured learning—but the Catholic part meant everything. My parents couldn't provide, then launch us into the world with material possessions or good contacts, but they could send us forth solidly Catholic, which to them meant far more.

From kindergarten through as many years of high school as each of us could withstand, dressed in plaid jumper or pressed trousers, white shirt and tie, we were educated by nuns, brothers and priests and by the occasional dedicated and underpaid layperson who taught in Catholic schools in those days. The message was clear and consistent: your life must add up to more than the sum of your accomplish-

ments, status, place, or wealth. You must give yourself over
to something beyond, something bigger. It was perfect
Catholic theology and, for the blue-collar families of my
time and neighborhood, it was practical—we might not
amount to much in the eyes of the world, but in God's eyes
we always had the potential to excel.

A Catholic education was certainly intended to transcend
the mere mastery of various subjects; it was a preparation
for life itself, a template for everyday decisions, a mantle
never shed. But in the rapidly changing world of the 1960s
and 1970s it didn't work out that way for most Catholic
families.

My sisters and brothers wore their religious beliefs
lightly, with comfort, like a well-broken-in jacket that could
be put on for life's storms or laid aside when the weather
of the soul cleared. Once they had left home, they attended
Mass at their convenience; rarely did they speak of their
Catholic upbringing or talk about living for something beyond their daily needs. They married, had children, and
generally made a peaceful accommodation to the world.
Not me. I was the only one, it turned out, Catholicism
wouldn't let loose.

In school, like many boys, I had thought I might become
a priest, but that was before my hormones—late to kick
in—informed me that a life of blessed celibacy was not so
blessed. In my senior year our class took an intelligence
test; no one was more amazed than I, the son of a man and
woman who had gone no further than the sixth grade, when
a full scholarship to Columbia University in New York City
was offered on the strength of my score. Had it been from
Notre Dame it would have counted for much more in my
family's eyes. While at Columbia I wrote stories for the
Spectator, then worked for small newspapers in Rockland
and Westchester counties, and eventually began to write for
national magazines. A story led to a small book contract. It
was hard for me to believe, coming as I did from a family
that had so much difficulty with the written word, but my

career took off, and after the first three books I found myself considered a somewhat accomplished nonfiction writer.

My genre was the "lived experience" kind of book—I had lived in and written about a neighborhood poisoned by a toxic-waste dump, spent months with blacks in South Africa, with the enormously rich on Florida's Gold Coast, and gone on to write about a family of rebels in Afghanistan, a noted transplant surgeon, and a young mother whose three small children were dying of AIDS. I appeared on a *Time* cover related to a story entitled "Today's Promising Young Writers," which said, "He has the uncanny ability to enter the mind and soul of his subject and to reveal such telling truths that we forget we are reading a book and not listening to an old trusted friend." An example of newsmagazine hyperbole, to be sure, but it still felt good.

I lived in New York and for ten years Felice Benjamin and I were a couple. Felice came from a moderately wealthy Seattle family, and was a talented though unacclaimed landscape painter who dealt primarily with murky pastels, work that got respectable reviews but never sold well. We loved each other but, being children of our day, had decided that marriage was an unnecessary encumbrance. We owned a brownstone on the Upper West Side, a summer home a block from the ocean in Amagansett, and individually and as a couple were quite popular. But as my writing became better known our relationship began to suffer. Felice, in my absences or distractions, grew more and more prone to the indiscretions of which she rightly accused me.

As a once-again-unattached man in New York, I began to devote still more time to a hedonism that could now flourish unchecked. But, oddly, my Catholicism was ever with me. I rarely missed Sunday Mass, and this required some doing and some inventive excuses in the places where my Saturday nights took me. On my shelves, alongside the books that were currently being discussed on the party circuit, were Bernanos's *The Diary of a Country Priest*, Augustine's *Confessions*, a translation of the *Summa*

Theologica, and volumes by contemporary saints like Dorothy Day, Jean Vanier, and Danilo Dolci. I lived a life of wonderful self-indulgence, winter vacations at will in Utah or Anguilla, "A list" parties on both the West and East sides, and yet I was never entirely comfortable in that world. The reason for this could be that catchall—Catholic guilt—but I knew that, delightful as they could be at times, I did not belong in these places, with these people. I knew there was another attraction, something else. Accomplishment, fame, money—these were not the measure of a man, a Catholic man, anyhow. My Catholic upbringing and education weren't about to release me. I tried, tried desperately, to be generous to friends on hard times, gave to various charities; I never rolled up my window against the windshield washers, handing each a bill and talking to him until the blasting of car horns behind urged me to move. But, again, I knew I was giving out of my abundance, which, of course, is not giving at all. When I was alone, I knelt down to pray each night, but the examination of conscience and determination to change my ways were quickly dissolved by the next day's adventures.

Now, I knew mine was not a unique angst and that life had not dealt me a bad hand. After all, cocktail parties are meant to be no more than a cracker on the way to a meal, acquaintances encountered at such places are not intended to be real friends. But I realized I was increasingly surrounding myself with people, going to events, making conversation that, while each involved me for the moment, dug the hole still deeper.

On a fall morning some five years ago, I was in the basement of the building I lived in doing my laundry. I was orderly about such things and still washed, as my mother had, on Monday morning. It was a ritual I enjoyed, in fact—it was something I could have hired out but it linked me to a past and a certain stability I no longer knew.

There, among the socks, shorts, and T-shirts for the week were no less than fourteen towels, each pair representing a shower for two. Four different women had shared my bed, shower, and towels during those seven nights.

This was a man out of control.

I put the laundry back in the bag, went upstairs, packed a small carryon with enough clothes for a few days, took a subway to the Port Authority, and got on the first bus announced.

For the next six weeks, traveling by bus, occasionally hitchhiking, I wandered about the Northeast and then up into Canada. My first stops were at a Zen center, a Mennonite farm, and a charismatic evangelical house of prayer, and then, realizing I was still running away, I began to visit Catholic monasteries. Why monasteries, I don't really know; it just seemed that these were the most serious outposts of Catholicism, places where the search for meaning was center stage. I visited Benedictine, Carmelite, Augustinian, Franciscan, and Dominican monasteries.

My last stop was in Vermont. I stayed only one night at the Trappist monastery of Our Lady of New Citeaux, and while nothing extraordinary happened in the years that followed, I thought off and on of these strange, silent men, who rose in the middle of the night, owned nothing of their own—not even a toothbrush—gave up all worldly possessions, the pleasure of a woman's touch, and their very wills so that unencumbered they could pursue God. The memory would not leave me.

Then I resumed my life as before, Having It All, as feminists came to call it.

1. January

PRECISE puffs of incense ascended in the still air—tiny, vaporous angels winging their way toward the huge bronze crucifix and beyond to be lost in the darkness of the great beamed ceiling. The abbey bell resounded high in the stone tower outside, dull, stark, sure. A second time. A third. Father Columban's outstretched hands elevated the white host high above the main altar, made from a single piece of granite so massive it had to be put in place before the walls and roof were sealed.

On that day—my notes document it as the Feast of the Epiphany—the sound of the bell resonated. It was a strangely liquid sound. At first it seemed to be an echo. Then, a distant, pulsating wail, like a ship's siren sounding an alert.

At the monastery of Our Lady of New Citeaux, far from the nearest road and many miles from the water, such a sound was not possible. Surely I was imagining it. Sound did not easily penetrate these fieldstone walls so carefully laid in place by monks' holy hands over a century ago. Trappists were not foolish enough to build a place of worship only to have the noise of the world they had renounced afflict them daily in their silent vocation.

The smell of incense wafted over the low brick wall that separated the monks from visitors and suffused the tiny side chapel where I knelt. I pressed my hands even more tightly together. My throat was parched.

It must be dry in here.

The priests, gathered about the altar in a semicircle,

bowed low in the ancient ritual, the gold tassels of their white stoles touching the glistening marble floor. Their faces were calm, even passive, no shred of emotion allowed them at this mystical moment. The chalice gleamed in the narrow beam of the spotlights these wise Trappists had implanted in the ceiling, dramatically concentrating all attention on the central fact of their lives. ". . . this is the cup of my blood, the blood of the new and everlasting covenant; it will be shed for you. . . ." Father Columban intoned the sacred words without the slightest inflection, giving them even greater weight.

The bell sounded once more. And the alien sound, that haunting wail, now seemed closer, a single plaintive tone. Yes, it was a siren. I hunched my shoulders, hiking up the collar of my jacket to snuff it out. My days of chasing fire engines and ambulances were long over.

Then abruptly, as the chalice touched the altar and the priests bowed again in unison, the noise was gone.

Inaudibly, I exhaled the air my lungs had unconsciously withheld during the consecration. I rubbed one hand over the other. The knuckles were chapped. I had forgotten to put lotion on them that morning. Someone coughed behind me. The moment was slipping away, and I fought to hold on, or at least to imprint it on my mind so I could later record it in my notes.

From where I sat, I could see the crucified one only in paltry profile. He was no more than a collection of lumpy, hardened drippings of once-molten metal—an uninspiring and not particularly symmetrical work of art. But from the main body of the church—a view I could still remember exactly from my first visit here five years before—the figure, set as it was on a blood-red wooden cross, was overwhelming.

I closed my eyes and imagined myself for an instant hidden in the shadows at the rear door of the church, a place where I had spent several early-morning hours, half awake, half dozing after a restless night. From there the structure had opened up to me, enveloping me with its sheer massiveness and quiet elegance. Before me were four long rows of polished choir stalls in which monks spent a full third of their waking hours. Calling out to God in the ancient words of the Psalms, pleading in those majestic, unwavering, uncompromising verses, they daily offered their humble lives, what they considered broken, sinful selves. Clothed in white robes, the huge sleeves of which afforded no ease for anything but prayer, and whose very shape—a cross—was a constant reminder of their life's choice, the priests and lay brothers of New Citeaux bowed and knelt and sat in unselfconscious unison.

Overhead were soaring oak arches, hand-tooled at a time when machines could have speeded the work. In my vision of the nave from the door, the shimmering main aisle stretched before me like a still river, in which the imposing three-story stained-glass Virgin Mary behind the main altar was constantly reflected. On either side of the huge window were floor-to-ceiling tapestries—sixteenth-century Venetian was my guess—their rich yet muted purples, ambers, and golds beckoning the eye and soul to be lost in the epic stories of Moses and Isaiah, John the Baptist and Mary Magdalene. The sight line from my imagined vantage point was unencumbered, as sweeping as grace, as liberating as forgiveness, as spacious as God himself.

When I first walked into that abbey church, the beauty of New Citeaux possessed me as no other place ever had. I couldn't forget it. But I was not graced to be within the body of the church worshiping with the monks on that morning. I was in an alcove, the visitors' side chapel, with a handful of ordinary lay people. That would have to change. I couldn't experience this life from the bleachers. I had to get onto the playing field. I had to impress that on Father Columban when I met with him the next day.

At Communion, I received the host on my outstretched palm, drank from the chalice, and returned to my seat. I closed my eyes. For a short while I was unaware of anything; a certain blankness had overtaken me, neither a feeling of well-being nor any other sensation I could identify.

I can only describe it as a state of . . . well, rest, deep rest, meanwhile being incredibly alert—but the alertness had no goal; it was a blank slate but not one to be written upon. All about me was quiet and, behind the main altar, Father Columban and the two concelebrants sat, heads inclined forward, making their thanksgiving after Communion.

Then, I could hear myself breathing. And once aware of that, the most simple of human actions, I was at once cognizant of everything. The place, the people about me, the position of my hands on the pew, the angle of my shoulders and head. I shuddered as if I were a child forced at last to swallow the mouthful of foul-tasting medicine.

This kind of introspection was not helpful. I had to stop being so self-conscious. I had to relax, absorb. And record. I needed some coffee. I'd gotten up too early.

There was a soft rustle in the sanctuary. The three priests rose from their stone benches. I stood with them. As Father Columban raised his hand to give the final blessing I heard the siren again. It grew fainter as I walked to the door to leave, and by the time I came out into the crisp morning air, all was quiet.

In the front seat of the car I had rented at the airport, I slowly slipped off my right glove, as if someone were watching me and I had to perform this act in secret. The notebook lay there on the seat. The ballpoint pen was already in my hand. I flipped back the cover and leafed through the first dozen pages, which were filled with writing. I came to a blank page. I wrote down what I had seen and felt and then drew a line under my observations.

My notes always had two parts. In this second part I listed questions I might have about what I had written down, and any fleeting thoughts—which were not necessarily factual (and often not usable), but which might help me get beyond the surface quotes and descriptions I had dutifully set down. Part two for that morning read:

Try to remember exactly. Feel it. Experience it. Just like you always do. Don't just take notes on it.

I had to laugh at myself. I had actually written the words "Don't just take notes on it."

A few minutes later, notes completed, I came around a bend in the road that led from the rear of the monastery to the highway. The ambulance's light was still flashing. There was a local police car and a state trooper's cruiser alongside the ambulance, blocking my view of it. At first, I could see no one. Then, as I pulled forward, I saw two men in white pants and parkas just inside the ambulance, fastening the gurney to the floor.

I got out of the car and followed the tracks the vehicles had made. I could see the victim's feet, two points holding up a spotless sheet. A blanket, folded into a neat square, rested near the shins.

"There's no reason to go any farther."

The words, coming unexpectedly as they did from behind, startled me. The monk's eyes, magnified by the thick lenses of his glasses, appeared red-rimmed, no doubt from the cold. He pulled his cowl forward to shield more of his face from the wind. I could see he had a very short haircut.

"Can I help? What happened? Hurt bad?"

He stared at me as if I had asked the most profound of questions. "You can help by leaving," he said, the words butting up against one another. "These men"—he motioned toward the two emergency medical technicians closing the ambulance's back doors—"have seen to everything. It was an accident."

A state trooper and the local officer emerged from a stand of pines just beyond the ambulance, carrying a large plastic garbage bag.

When I decided I would go back to New Citeaux to do a long magazine article and perhaps a book on life in a monastery, I found that, in contrast to most of my writing projects, I wasn't talking much about this one to my friends. As for my six weeks on the road years before, I had kept that quiet too, confiding only in Dr. Sandra Hersch, my Jungian psychologist, whom I visited twice and three times a week for the next four years. She was more impressed by Joseph Campbell, but she seemed to encourage my growing interest in monasticism and the Order of Cistercians of the Strict Observance, the formal name for the monks popularly known as Trappists.

I became quite knowledgeable about Trappists and other monks. Thomas Merton, the prolific and enormously talented Trappist monk, had produced several dozen books on a staggeringly wide range of subjects—from graphic depictions of the primitive life at his abbey in Kentucky in the 1940s and 1950s to impassioned essays against war and racism, as well as lovely treatises on the lost art and practice of contemplation. I didn't stop with Merton. I read widely in the early Desert Fathers, the rise of monasticism, its art and architecture. I even subscribed to *Cistercian Studies*, the Trappist scholarly quarterly. I had more than a passing knowledge of the *Verba Seniorum*, and names like William of St. Thierry, Alberic, Guerric of Igny, and Armand DeRance were familiar to me.

I was somewhat like those folks who subscribe to *Organic Gardening* yet never turn the soil, the fellow who avidly reads *Country Living* and *Country Journal* but whose only concession to actually going rural is to wear a Ralph Lauren flannel shirt to the office on a Saturday. I was an armchair connoisseur of a way of life.

Yet, I came to realize that my days with Merton and Guerric, at Solesmes and Fontainebleau, were more than a pleasant diversion.

No, my newfound monastic obsession didn't do anything so dramatic as save my life, but it surely supplied a poultice or two. I can recall returning from an especially sybaritic week in Puerto Vallarta and taking a cab directly from the International Arrivals Building at JFK to a bookstore called The Mad Monk in Greenwich Village. There I stood, suntanned in February, out of breath, a cab double-parked on Sixth Avenue, juggling an oversized book on Cistercian architecture, two volumes of Merton's poems, which I had not yet read, and three slender volumes on the Desert Fathers of the fifth and sixth centuries. It took most of the day, looking at the magnificent pictures and hearing the wisdom of Abba Pambo and Abba Arsenius, to be able to breathe easier.

It was not the first or last time I took this "cure."

Mort Brunt was the first person I told.

Between his glass of San Pellegrino and the hearts-of-palm salad at our lunch in New York just before Christmas, I told him I wanted to write about monastic life at New Citeaux. I had expected him to resist, but before the poached chicken with dill sauce had arrived, he'd made three phone calls. Mort prided himself on moving quickly once what he considered a good idea was presented. He had trouble getting to his chocolate hazelnut soufflé because the calls were being returned. I had the impression of conversation between two spaceships. Two of the calls came from other portable telephones in other midtown restaurants.

"Mort, I don't think you understand me. This might not be so commercial. It's an interest of mine. Nothing flashy. Maybe nobody else wants to know about—"

"In the *Times* last week. I read too, Joey. You think I don't read. Big religious upsurge. They say it's bubbling right below the surface. Gallup Poll says ditto. Hunger. Spiritual hunger. Like what happened after World War Two. That guy you talk about—Martin? Martian? Motrin? what the hell's his name?—started writing about the Trappists. People went for it. Twelve hardback printings. *Seven Stories in My Mountain*? What was that title again? Monasteries had to pitch tents to keep up with the demand.

"Today?" He kept going, asking questions but seeking no answers. "Not just the born-agains and the Hasids and the Moondogs, right? Normal folks, not nuts. Say it again, Joey, say it slow, so I don't miss a word."

"Say what?"

"What you said at the Book Awards party last week."

"Was this before or after my fourth Rob Roy?"

"When the Literary Guild lady was up your nose so far

you couldn't breathe. When all those tall, thin sweethearts were on you like flypaper and you were talking about the 'hunger of our days.' "

"Mort, I was drinking too much."

"Remember? About people being sick to death of themselves and their Porsches and their fat farms and their credit cards and their friends who aren't friends. Their therapy groups and their interior decorators and their personal trainers. And the way they talk: like if you did a transcript, you'd find that zero, nothing, zip came out of their mouths. Joey, say it again."

"I'm not doing this to be on the leading edge of some trend, Mort. I want to have an honest experience, and then write an honest piece—"

"Sure, Joey, sure. Honest, right, honest. When Brando did Kowalski, he *was* Kowalski. Method acting, method writing. Who's going to play you? Nolte, he can do serious. The guy from *Accidental Tourist*—what's his name? William Hurt. Maybe Jeremy Irons? Absolutely yes! Tone down the accent. We're going for a feature on this one. No, not Irons, this is Kevin Costner. Hoffman? He can do young, he can do old. The kid—Tom Hanks. They say he wants serious. A seeker. If they can't play Othello, they want to be seekers."

"Mort, this book is about them, the monks. Not me. I can't go up there thinking about a casting call and playing as if I'm serious. It just doesn't work."

"Why not?" He was shocked. "You're the absolute best at this kind of thing."

"That is not a compliment."

He finally plowed into his soufflé, summoning the waiter with his free hand for a few fresh strawberries and whipped cream. "Don't you see it, Joey? *You* are the main character, sick to death with his life, looking for Meaning, capital *M* Meaning in life. But we need a broad in this. Classy but sexy. Page-boy haircut. No, dammit, she'll look too much like the fifties. Joey, if some sweetheart comes your way up there and wants to weigh in on the side of simple pleasures,

don't pass her by. Subplot. A little sex? Never hurt anybody. *The World, the Flesh, the Search.* Is that a title? No,
Morty, sounds like the thirties! But the girl has to win out;
you fall in love. Love has to conquer."

"Mort, I'm not going to put myself through some artifi-
cial situation just to write a book."

"And a screenplay?"

The next day, according to the public radio station I had on
during my predawn ride over to the monastery, was the
coldest of the winter in Vermont—in the twenties below
zero. Obviously because of the weather, the visitors' alcove
was empty except for myself and another man, who sat
several rows in front of me. Although the New Citeaux liturgical calendar—which I had purchased at their gift shop
the day before so that I might quickly fall into the monastic
cadence—listed the Feast of Saints Timothy and Titus, who
were martyrs, I noted the priests were vested in white, not
the red that is customary for such feasts.

". . . and especially we pray for the soul of our dearly beloved brother Trevor, a gentle soul called to His Father's
bosom . . ."

So, it was a Mass for the Dead. I didn't recognize the
name; it seemed odd for a Trappist.

The young monk reading the prayers of the faithful
paused for a moment of silent reflection. And then something happened that was so uncommon in a church full of
Trappist monks that I couldn't fail to notice. Was I imagining it or was it indeed a hum, a certain low murmuring that
came from the choir stalls? Or was it a sound of shuffling
feet?

In front of me, the other worshiper abruptly turned
around. Even in the poor light of the alcove his face bore
a look of great pain. His slitted, swollen eyes looked like
recent knife wounds and his skin had the color and consis-
tency of melted candle wax. He was wearing an olive-drab
loden coat. He stared at me for an instant.

He must have been a loved one, this Brother Trevor, to

elicit such a response from these monks so schooled in curbing their emotions. And to strike such grief in this man. He was obviously an old friend or a relative—perhaps the only one, as Trappists often outlived family and friends—and he had so gallantly come to the service. And now he was searching my face for some sign of recognition—mine, the only face to which the design of the monastery's church allowed him direct access.

After Mass, embarrassed by my inability to have in some way helped him through that moment, I hesitated in my pew to allow the man to leave. I walked the hundred yards or so up a flagstone path that led to the guesthouse, where Father Columban had said in his letter he would meet me.

"I'm here to see Father Columban," I said through the screen door to the monk who answered the bell. At first I couldn't make out his face, but as he stepped forward into the daylight to unlatch the screen I recognized the thick glasses of the monk I had encountered the day before.

He said nothing as he opened the door.

"Brother Trevor—was he . . . was he one of yours? Brother . . ."

"Brother Polycarp," he replied, but didn't answer my question. He was holding the handle of a dust mop, loosening and tightening his grip. His bottom lip began to quiver. "You may wait in the parlor to the left. I'll tell Father you're here." He slammed the heavy door behind me. He shuffled down the hallway to his office, his sandals slapping at his bare feet.

I went to the parlor on the left.

Father Columban arrived a few minutes later. I rose to greet him, extending my hand. He took my hand and put his other hand on top of it.

"Welcome back; how long has it been, Joseph? My goodness, you haven't changed a bit. I've enjoyed your postcards from all over the world. You're quite the traveler."

"Five years. Imagine. By the way, thanks for working out the details so I can do the story."

"Well, I don't think I've worked out all that much. We get so many requests for people to come in and observe us—social scientists, behavioral scientists, reporters. A closed environment is a researcher's dream, I guess. So we usually say no. But the community remembered your wonderful book on the family poisoned from that factory's waste. Batteries—they made batteries. We read it in refectory. Let's just proceed slowly and see how things go."

As he spoke, telling me of frozen waterlines that had burst during the night, flooding the monastery kitchen, I found myself studying his face. Father Columban Mellary had a remarkably clear complexion—radiant would not be an excessive description—and his eyes, unsullied by drinking or smoking, were almost glassy in their clarity. He was quite bald, with thick lips and the heavy though not flabby cheeks of his ancestors, who, he had told me, were French peasants. He was now fifty-eight years old. His was a strong, intelligent face, more European than American, and I found my mind wandering, uncharacteristically so at a time like this when a story was just beginning to be researched and I needed utmost concentration to register my first, unfettered impressions. He had been a monk for almost thirty years, yet for some reason I began to imagine what he might look like if he were not a Trappist, not dressed in a floor-length white robe, with a black scapular, some eighteen inches wide, over his shoulders and reaching almost to the floor. As he stood there I could visualize him in a patched jacket of faded denim, a pipe with a gnawed stem hanging from his mouth while his heavily veined hands picked up a box of grapes in Provence or a crate of eggs in Normandy—and all the while his fertile mind wrestling with Rimbaud or Flaubert.

Yet there was a childlike simplicity and wonder about him; when we had met five years before, he was awestruck that I was routinely invited to parties where authors he had read were present, that a beachside house in Southampton could cost three hundred thousand dollars for a summer's rental, that living together without the benefit of marriage was not only ordinary but condoned.

"And how have these years treated you, Joseph?" he asked, motioning me toward a chair. "It seems like yesterday you were here. I still remember the day."

"I'm much better, Father, thank you. Psychoanalysis helped me sort out my life. And helped build a new kitchen for my therapist. I'm not that nut who appeared on your doorstep. And I'm still one of that dying breed, the 'practicing Catholic'—not a good one, mind you, but practicing at it."

"You weren't all that nutty." He laughed. "I found you pretty serious about life's questions. That's to be complimented. Don't ever stop asking them."

I opened my notebook to the series of points I wanted to discuss.

"I'll stay for at least a month, Father, and I hope that I can have access to the monks, one on one, and that I can observe the daily life up close. For one thing, I need to be sitting in the main body of the church."

He put his hands on the table. "That's what I meant before; I haven't done that much. Ours is a life away from the world and we can't live it very well if we feel we're being observed."

"I'll be part of the wall hangings. After a short time I'll seem like a member of the community. Just give me a chance. I'm very good at this; I'm very good at documenting commitment."

"I'm sure you are, but the main body of the church is for the monks, retreatants, and guesthouse guests only, Joseph. We can't make exceptions. Our life would be chaos if each monk made up his own rules."

"But unless I can feel the life, taste it, smell it, I can't write about it. I want to live it, as much as I can."

"Yes, I understand completely, but you must understand this from our point of view."

"That story about the family and the toxic waste. I just

about moved in with them. That's why it worked. I need to do that here."

He smiled. It was the look of a man who was used to requests—for the monastery's vocation director I'm sure they must have come frequently—and used to having to say no, but saying it kindly each time.

"Father, I hope you don't think this is just another story for me. I'm fascinated with your life. I've done quite a bit of reading since you saw me. This place, the memory of this place, just wouldn't leave me."

"The services are all open to the public, Joseph. Vigils at three-thirty A.M. to Compline at seven-forty P.M. Our community life of prayer is really the backbone of our life. You can witness all that."

"Father Columban." His head jerked slightly at my tone of irritation. I lowered my voice. "Let's do it this way. Let us assume that I am a person interested in your life—more than interested. A person who wants to think about joining. A postulant. Treat me that way."

"It would be false to pretend, Joseph. We Trappists have enormous faults and shortcomings, but we are terribly bad at pretending. When you live nose-to-nose for years with the same men, pretenses don't hold up. But let us do this another way. May I propose something?"

"Fitting me for a hair shirt? Land's End has some nice ones and they have an 800 number."

"An 800 number?"

"Never mind, I was trying to be funny. Please go on."

"Why don't you live the monastic day, in tandem with us. That way you will experience what we experience, although in a slightly different way. I will set out for you the hours, the activities, and recommend some books—as I normally do for those aspiring to the life. Basically, it is *ora et labora*, prayer and work. At worst, it will be a quiet period of retreat for you. A period of reflection about one or two of those big questions you still might have."

"A monk manqué staying at the local Marriott."

"Marriott?"

"It's a hotel chain. Never mind. When was the last time you went into town?"

He scratched the top of his head. "My appendix. Let's see, I was five years ordained; it was just after Abbot Alberic died. I was thirty-four. What is that, twenty-four years ago?"

" 'Room service,' " I said with a smile. " 'Bread and water, please. Brother Joseph in room 214.' "

"Let me help you with one part of this. Brother Bruno has just reentered after a leave of absence. He has a small hermitage—really a rather comfortable small cottage from the pictures I saw—why not live there? He has a four-wheel-drive pickup truck, which the monastery might sell or use. I'll see that you have it at your disposal. He lived on a back road; not plowed too quickly."

I looked at him squarely. "This is not the way I like to work. But let me try it for a week or so. If it's not happening, I'll let you know. I'll be honest."

"As will I. We can meet once a week or so. Would that be convenient?"

"I'll be asking some very serious questions."

"Oh"—he smiled boyishly—"I think we can deal with those."

"It never works if the questions aren't real, if the emotions behind them are false. So, if it appears that I'm shedding some skin . . ."

"Yes, Joseph, go on."

"Well, I might be. I tend to get into my stories."

"Shed if you will."

"I want to understand your life, what motivates people to live it, what the monk receives in return."

"Ours is a strange way of living one's days. And difficult to grasp. You stake your entire life on the reality and the overriding importance of God. Makes no sense in the secular world, none whatsoever. And sometimes in here"—he winked—"it makes even less sense. Brood over that, my friend. Shall we talk next Wednesday after Mass? The hour flies by. Let me write out a list of books you might find interesting. I believe the gift shop has most of them."

He stood by the door.

"One other thing," I said. "Out by the back gate yesterday. There was an ambulance. The guestmaster, Brother Poly—"

"Polycarp."

"—was there. Reporter's curiosity. Sorry."

"What did Brother Polycarp say?"

"Nothing. He asked me to leave."

"Oh," he said in reply. He then reached for a book on the table near the door. When he did so, the glow from a table lamp illuminated his face from below, giving it a strange cast that unflatteringly accentuated the overhang of his bottom lip and his large earlobes, characteristics I had not noticed. For that instant, he was another man, forbidding, almost grotesque.

"*Speculum Caritatis*, The Mirror of Charity," he said in a low voice—one of deep appreciation—that brought me quickly back to who he was. "Cistercian Publications brought it out recently; it may not be in the bookstores yet, so you may not have read it. Long overdue. Sorry the pages are wrinkled; I left it by a window and it rained."

He began to hand the book to me, but then, seeing something within, pulled it back. "You won't need this," he said, removing an envelope from a place about midway in the book. "My bookmark. Start where you will."

"Usually in the middle—short attention span, Father. A problem of mine."

He smiled. "Don't worry. See you next week."

Part two of my notes, written after I had pulled off the road on my way back to check out of the motel:

Well, what could be so hard about it? Even if a drifted-away Catholic, I was still a Catholic. Shed skin? (His chuckle—somewhat dismissive.) Shed if you will. Or did he say: Shed if you must?

2. February

BEHIND the simple four-room house was a gradually rising hill studded with boulders. It was the land of my neighbor, a farmer who told me when I stopped by for directions that it was a lush, grassy cow pasture in summer. But in the days that I came to know it, the hillside was a constantly roiling, messy stew, skimmed and stirred by the prevailing northeast wind that blew melted snow about in the momentary warmth of a sunny day and then instantly froze all matter in motion as night fell. Throughout the month, the hillside was a drab, steely color, curdled and lumpy.

The monks of New Citeaux had taken the vow of poverty, but for their morning meditation they could glory in their magnificent abbey church, with those soaring arches, rich tapestries, carved choir stalls and stained glass, while I, for all my affluence, gazed out on this desolate hillside and a single tall barren oak that had cropped up, startled, among a small cluster of white birches. Was there a message in this somewhere? Was this intended by Father Columban? Had he ever been here? In winter?

In helping me establish a routine little different from that of the monks, Father Columban had emphasized the absolute necessity of capitalizing on the transparent moments afforded by awakening in what most of us call the middle of the night. "Fatigue and the lucidness of a brain yet uncluttered by the day's needs and events provide a wonderful combination for a childlike openness," he had said. And so, I arose each morning at 3:30, spending my first two and a half hours in attempts at meditation and spiritual reading before having a light breakfast and going to New Citeaux for Lauds and Mass. I tried to still and lay open my wandering, bleary mind at that hour, but inspiration and transcendence were elusive. I recalled a phrase from one of my books about "entering into the mind of God," but instead of entering God's, I seemed obsessed with wallowing in my own.

It was not that I was unused to the "lived experience" for the purpose of writing about it. But a week with the rebels in the mountains above Kabul or days at the bedside of the woman with AIDS had been interspersed with a more normal life. Except for a quick trip to New York for more and warmer clothes, I'd been here almost a month, and Columban, when I told him about my restlessness—an itchiness, I'd dubbed it—had said that if I wanted to know anything about the Trappist life, I should not try to scratch it.

Kneeling, my legs tucked under the low, slanted Zen stool Columban had lent me (a famous roshi had presented it to him during the first, now historic, Christian-Buddhist *sasheen* at New Citeaux some twenty years before), I stared into the morning blackness. As the days went along, the outline of the hill gradually appeared earlier and earlier during my meditation period, the oak's branches filigreed against a blue-black sky. It was the exact color of the Scripto ink the Dominican nuns at St. Procopius School required of their grade-school charges for penmanship lessons. These nuns who first taught me to write believed in uniformity. During my eight years with them the ink's color never varied; it was as precious and inviolable a standard of behavior as any of the edicts given to Moses on the mountain.

Uniformity. Blue-black ink. This was my level of insight as I expectantly gazed out at the windswept hillside.

Much of the rest of the day I rather enjoyed. There was wood to cut and split for the stove, which warmed the entire house; a rotted stairway to replace; and other repairs and upkeep to perform. I was surprised to find that these tasks, which were denied a New York apartment dweller,

were ones that I was actually pretty good at. I spent an inordinate amount of time preparing my meals, but then
again, without mail, phone calls, or appointments, there was
no need to hurry, no take-out food within twelve miles, and
the open maw of time to fill. Columban had said that for a
monk each act was its own prayer; over the salad spinner
and propane stove I guess I said my most affective prayers.

The periods of meditation and silent prayer were the
most difficult, and while Columban allowed that it was the
same for almost everyone entering the monastery, I found
myself frustrated with my lack of discipline and concentration. (Then again, I didn't know what I should be concentrating on. Columban had failed to give me a target or
goal.) Merely looking down at my knee in the early light
one morning reminded me of Felice in a pair of snug-fitting
corduroys, her arms clasped around her legs as she sat on
a jetty near Montauk. Running my hand over the back of
my neck—unconsciously checking to see if I needed a
haircut—recalled that young art student from Parsons with
her short-cropped hair and multisyllabic words. The warmth
from the stove evoked the heat coming up through the ra-
diator into my attic bedroom when I was a boy.

Although I struggled to clear my mind and stay in the
moment, I found myself drifting. I often found myself in
the laundry room that morning five years before, or on the
subway headed for the Port Authority, or looking at the
blank expression on the bus driver's face when, handing
him a hundred-dollar bill, I said I wanted to ride for a while
and would tell him when I wanted to get off.

When I went on the road and eventually arrived at New
Citeaux, it was not only because I had too many towels at
my feet.

It was at one of those not entirely unpredictable times
when everything on the surface of a life seems absolutely
wonderful, thus accentuating the hollowness within. When
I was again thinking clearly—some two days later and eight
hundred miles from New York City—I envisioned myself

as a sort of middle-aged mendicant, a troubled soul in search of itself, and, I guess, I was hoping that through adversity might come a beam of wisdom. I wanted to talk through this muddle called my life with the holy men and women who inhabited these spiritual crucibles, and in each place I babbled on about "meaning" and "worth." I don't know how they looked upon me, but had I been confronted with such a kook I would have called for the straitjacket. More than once I heard from one of them that my life was not as false as I had made it out to be, that my writing was its own vocation and that I was doing good, in my way. But I couldn't accept that and had to go on.

In my travels—which began once I found out that there is a monastic circuit, a network of such places, and the pilgrim could go easily from one to another—I deliberately avoided the Trappists. I thought that they still lived as they did when Merton wrote his autobiography, *The Seven Storey Mountain*, a book that was pressed into my hand in high school by the librarian, Brother Justin ("He was wild, too, like you, Joseph, but look how he turned out," he whispered to me in Saturday-morning detention hall). I knew the Trappists to be silent monks who talked not even to one another, and surely not to the pilgrim. This was the Marine Corps of Catholicism, the few and the brave. Somehow, I never expected that the Second Vatican Council would have altered their life.

On a rainy November afternoon, after a long ride down from the Canadian border with a French-speaking truck driver to whom one *monastère* was like another, I was dropped off at the porter's lodge of New Citeaux. Realizing when I saw the word "Trappist" on the sign that I was at the wrong place, I asked the man in a yellow slicker raking damp leaves from beneath the perfectly trimmed bushes how I might get to the nearest bus station. He extended his hand in welcome and I blurted out my name.

"Not the author?" he said with an immediately infectious enthusiasm. "Well, isn't that something! We read that book of yours on South Africa in refectory last year. You're quite the writer. What great ability. I'm Father Columban. They have me as the vocation director, but I take every chance I can to work outdoors."

"Oh, oh—the vocation director! No candidate here," I said rather self-consciously.

"We'll see," he said, laughing. "C'mon, I'll give you a ride up the road."

"Ride?"

"Sure, it's about time for supper. Hungry? We can find a bed for you. Somebody'll give you a ride to Falmouth in the morning."

"Yes?"

"Father Columban, Brother. He's expecting me."

Brother Polycarp stepped back from the screen door without opening it. "Then come in."

I stepped inside the guesthouse foyer and he closed the door without speaking. He motioned to the room where Columban and I met.

"I brought a thermos of coffee for the meeting, Brother. That's permissible, isn't it? Got the beans in New York."

"Father Columban will attend to everything," he said stiffly. The sandals slapped at his feet as he walked away, but the sound was muffled. Socks today.

Why this one was giving me such a hard time I don't know. Father Columban had said that some members of the community were categorically opposed to any contact with the outside world and thought that anything written about monastic life was usually so superficial and naïve as to be useless and misleading, but I expected these to be the older monks. Polycarp was no more than thirty.

"Oh, Joseph, it's wonderful coffee." Father Columban seemed genuinely pleased with this small gesture. "Dean and DeLuca? Is that something of a fancy store?"

"Nothing personal, Father, but without a good cup of coffee, what is life? Mocha java and French roast blend."

"Indeed."

This was the third or fourth meeting I had had with Father Columban, and I was very conscious about not letting another hour slip away fruitlessly. In our previous one-hour sessions, after the exchange of pleasantries, I would usually pull out my list of questions, but it was the priest who pre-emptively struck with a question. He might ask what I had read—his favorite authors ranged from Flannery O'Connor, Walker Percy, and Graham Greene to Joan Didion, Barbara Pym, and Nadine Gordimer—and we would launch on a discussion of style, content, or message. He was fascinated with New York literary gossip. He asked about the magazines I wrote for, parties I attended, the food served, the behavior of people whose names he knew, the talk of movie contracts and paperback deals. I often felt foolish going into such detail about a life of such shallowness, but Columban's expressive face and "Oh really!" brightening the still-musty air in the retreat-house parlor encouraged me to go on. Perhaps he was just being kind. But I think he loved the stories of my crowd in New York—about a huge poached salmon on a bed of radicchio, white-coated waiters serving drinks, a Fifth Avenue triplex overlooking Central Park with floor-to-ceiling windows, a cake decorated to resemble the potboiler novel that had just made number one on the best-seller list, the drunken Nobel laureate falling headfirst into the punch bowl. And, while I was aware of the time passing, I did not want to manipulate the conversation. It was not a good interviewing technique—it made the subject all the more aware of a reporter's agenda. But I found myself reluctant to specifically ask about monastic life. It was not my style. I usually observed and wrote from those observations. My questions had a tinny sound, but I had to ask them nonetheless.

"Father, I've been reading a lot about the order," I said as he brought the coffee cup to his lips. "It might be good for me to hear it from you, a quick picture: the eleventh century to the twentieth, you know, and then let's zero in on what it is today."

"And your own experience with monastic life thus far? Joseph, that part is far more interesting, but, yes, I'll give a quick summary." He leaned back in his chair and put his hands behind his head. "It was the eleventh century and a group of men—dreamers, really—led by Robert of Molesme left their monastery, distressed with the fancy meals and fine furs the monks had gotten accustomed to, and settled in an insect-infested swamp by the river Saône. They were determined to live the rule Saint Benedict had written, a rule for communities written shortly after A.D. 500 that is, after all is said and done, a practical interpretation of how the Gospels tell us to be. Interestingly enough, they were just one of hundreds of communities at the time that had gone 'back to the land' and away from the embarrassing social obligations, business dealings, and general corruption of their various monasteries. Their purity of vision and their simplicity were enormously appealing to men of the time, men tired of the rampant materialism—does this sound like today, Joseph? Amazing, isn't it? From those twenty men came a religious order that quickly spawned hundreds of houses throughout Europe.

"There wasn't a hint of any sappy piety in Cistercian writings, in their discipline or in their architecture. No foolish adornments, no easy answers. They lived in utter simplicity, in poverty, worked and prayed and shut out anything that would get in the way of direct knowledge of God. It seemed an altogether worthy way to spend a life, a constant conversion, a constant attempt to be better. Their day was divided, as is ours, between the Hours of the Divine Office, based largely on the Psalms and spread throughout the day—an Old Testament practice, really—community liturgy, individual prayer and meditation, and, of course, physical labor, so that we might support ourselves. All the while the life is to be a 'school of charity,' as we call it. If we can't love the brother next to us, whom we see, how can we say we love God, whom we cannot? It requires a constant conversion of manners—changing your ways." He looked at me and paused. "But once you give yourself over to this conversion of manners, when you change the way you look at the world, how you treat others, how you approach God, it is quite satisfying. Peaceful. Happy.

"So, where does that leave us today? We are a small order, really—so many left after the Vatican Two reforms— perhaps fifteen hundred of us in ninety monasteries for men and fifty-nine for women worldwide. In the States twelve monasteries for men, five for women—no more than a few hundred of us in this land of so many millions. But the goals are the same—to live for something beyond our individual tastes, ambitions, desires. To live for God, and to come to know him in this life as best we can. It's not a life for everyone, but some are called—and, of those, some respond. But it's important to note that we are not worshiping that crucifix out there—no, Joseph, we seek a relationship with a living God, who is part of our lives, with whom we can have a satisfying and growing and deepening relationship. Otherwise"—he smiled as he paused for effect—"this life would be foolish and ultimately impossible to sustain. So as a man approaches us and wants to live this life, while we monks are there for one another, it is ultimately that man's personal, unique, and intimate relationship with God that is the most important."

"So here comes Joseph," I said, leaning forward in my chair, "a card-carrying, somewhat observant Catholic, who knows the Mass, knows the basics of Catholic theology and—"

"And what, Joseph?" Columban interrupted, his voice, now lower, no longer that of the teacher.

"It's not working. I'm not getting it."

"Joseph, there is no 'it' to get. Rather, the life demands openness. Openness to God. First his voice must be heard. This is not something a person can *will*; there is no sure path."

"All well and good, Father, but I could be sitting there, still looking at the hillside, twenty years from now."

"Indeed." He laughed out loud, his eyes glistening with what I took to be the absurdity of such a thought. "But, at least looking for where the path might begin."

I closed my notebook.

"Perhaps that's a little too pie in the sky," Father Columban said. "Waiting. We're good at that in this life. Let me be more practical."

"Just say a postulant said those same things to you. They have problems sorting this thing out, don't they?"

"Oh, many problems. But instead of a postulant, let me treat you as you are—a man living very close to our life, living away from the world, albeit for a short period. But incidentally, Joseph, it makes no difference, postulant or man in the hermitage; each is seeking, seeking something he often can't articulate. Tell me, what is the best part of your day in the hermitage?"

"Please don't call it that. To me, it's just a comfortable cabin. Work is the best. *Labora*. Physical work."

"Your meditation?"

"I spend a lot of time at it. Not much there. Scripto ink."

"Ink?"

"A long and not very interesting story."

"Reading? The books I gave you, or others?"

"As I try to think of something I read and can remember, I draw a blank. What does that say? I just finished a wonderful Alison Lurie novel we could talk about."

"Aelred?"

"Ditto. Blank."

"I think he might have something to say to you. He's an interesting man in addition to being a spiritual giant. At the monastery of Rievaulx, Aelred let men enter who were rejected by everybody else. The worst kind, scoundrels. Rough, sinful men, like the rough, sinful world of the eleventh century. No—how do you call them?—yuppies there, Joseph. As Saint Benedict said, 'Those of ruder minds.' We are all pathetic sinners. But Aelred had a knack for seeing deeply into people. In his last days he lived alone in a little stone hut. He had terrible arthritis and the young monks used to lay their heads on his bed and just listen to him talk. He was like a loving father to them. Think of him that way. The fire is burning in the hearth and the venerable Aelred is talking. Put yourself at his bedside."

"Sorry."

"Other than work. The best moment of the day. Don't respond quickly, Joseph. Let your unconscious work."

I closed my eyes, as much to hide my irritation at the interrogation of the interrogator as at the fact that I had no answer.

"To be honest, only once, once each day am I guaranteed to feel anything approaching . . . well—"

His eyes bade me to go on.

"—what might be called—"

"When is that, Joseph?"

"Actually, it's at Communion. I say those words 'Lord, I am not worthy to receive you, but only say the word and I shall be healed.' *Healed.* That's the word that sticks with me. I want that to happen. I take that tasteless little circle of bread in my mouth and a sip of the wine and everything seems possible. I feel a surge, strong and sure and calm. It was always like that, even when I was going through the worst days of my life."

"What word?"

"I don't understand."

"What word would you have the Lord say that you might be healed?"

I reached for the thermos of coffee, but stopped and looked up at him.

" 'Joseph.' That's all I want Him to say."

"I understand. Completely."

"Do you? I don't."

"He says your name all day and all night. And mine. But we put our hands over our ears and block Him out. He loves us so desperately. Don't be concerned that a prayer isn't on your lips every waking moment. I've been a Trappist for almost thirty years now, and if five minutes out of an hour of my prayer are really focused on God, I feel blessed. All of our minds are junkyards and we keep picking them over. You must learn to relax; you're in God's presence. Always."

"That's not easy for an aggressive, assertive, driven, Type A American male. Maybe it would be better for me to come into the monastery for a while and get this thing finished. I think a shorter piece might be all I can do. Reporter-at-large piece. What the hell—excuse me—am I going to fill three or four hundred pages with? Kneeling, waiting, listening. Being open? Father, that does not translate to the written page, believe me. A week inside would do it. A few days? Maybe proximity would break through this . . ." I didn't know how to complete the thought and Columban was not one to fill in gaps.

"And what shall I tell the abbot? That wall hanging resembling a man—pay no attention to it, Reverend Father."

"You don't have to go into details. I need to know what it looks like in there, how people sustain it, what you joke about."

"Do you think there is a special God in here, another one outside the cloister? That we have some exclusive franchise?"

"Well, I must be living in the wrong zip code, because He hasn't paid me a visit out there in the hermi— cabin."

"Keep rowing, my son; let God tend to the tiller."

"I'm starting to get tired."

"Joseph, you've just begun. I think it can actually be a wonderful story. And remember the words of Jung: 'There are hardly any exceptions to the rule that a person must pay dearly for the divine gift of the creative fire.' It's about writing; it's about the inner life, it's about most worthwhile things. Next week, then?"

There was a short part one to my notes. Part two:

There had always been excitement, moment in my life: the thrill of a new project could keep me going for months, years. And each time, I managed to bring it off. Now, no moment. Staying put. By force of will, I could always create something in my life to convince myself I had a purpose. Now I was doing the opposite: premeditated lack of purpose. Why in the hell am I doing this?

The telephone rang. I jumped up from my chair at the breakfast table. Where was it? I had thought it was disconnected. I found the phone in a kitchen closet.

"Joey, is that you, Joey? You sound different. You feeling okay? Haven't heard from you. Unlisted number, Joey. Do you know what I had to do to get it? Just tell me you still love Uncle Morty."

"I'm fine, Mort; I was just—reading."

"I didn't wake you up, did I? You know me, early bird gets the paperback deal. Only agent in New York in his office by eight o'clock."

"No, I've been up for a while. It's already nine o'clock."

"Reading?"

"Well, yes. Aelred. Of Rievaulx."

"Alfred? Sounds familiar. Hum me a few bars and I'll catch the tune. You know Uncle Morty. Quick take. So, Joey, how is it so far? Beautiful, right? I could be one of those monks. Sweet music, no woman hacking at you. Yeah, I could do it in a minute. But, my father, Joey, it would kill my father. Orthodox to this day. Manischewitz and Hebrew National hot dogs. He wouldn't know a pork chop if it talked to him. Wanted me to be a rabbi, and look, I'm at a Reform temple and only at High Holy Days. So give me the details; give me a taste. I got three publishers drooling for this one, because it's you. You and God. I want to slip them a few goodies before I start talking money. Give me some goodies, Joey. The place, the people, you know—atmosphere."

"Well . . . it's good; I like it all right. I think. I'm not really inside."

"Good? You like it? All right? You think?"

"It's hard to explain, Mort. It's different. Interesting. Strange."

"You want me to sell 'interesting,' Joey? I wouldn't get

twenty thou for 'interesting.' And leave 'strange' to Stephen King. Details, Joey. I had Jeremy Irons's agent on the phone yesterday. He returned the call in only three days. Hoffman's guy, Nolte's guy—we are getting some nice nibbles on this one. Maybe a bit part for you, Joey; you got a look that could work. So give me more than 'interesting' to go back to these *machers* with."

"Mort, don't push. I've got to do this one at my own pace. And maybe it's only a piece."

"Jo-ey, now you're hurting my feelings. And don't even *think* piece. Book, Joey, book! Screenplay!"

"Mort, I need time to figure out what it all means. If it means anything."

"Sure, sure, I understand. Space. Your generation always needs their space. We wanted a pair of shoes without a hole in the bottom. Need anything up there? Anything at all."

"I'm fine. I have everything I need."

"I'm calling Zabar's right now. Sending up a CARE package. Nova and scallion cream cheese, bagels. Miriam! Call Zabar's. Gotta go. Send me an outline, okay? Cheese-cake too. Think facial expression. Think understatement. Think dialogue. Think lots and lots of money. Love and kisses from Uncle Morty."

Columban had urged me to read Aelred's *Mirror of Charity*, but I had resisted. I don't know exactly why. The few times I'd dipped into the book, I found it preachy and stiff. Merton was a beautiful writer and he had a wonderful sense of humor. Not this guy. But I thought I would take Columban at his word—and also not risk embarrassment when he asked me again about his beloved Aelred of Rievaulx. I skipped over the introduction and the long section on Aelred's life and works, dismissed such early chapters as "Nothing is more deserved than a creature's love for its Creator," and plunged into the middle of the book, intending to have a grasp of this man before my first cup of coffee.

By the time Mort called I had missed Mass and the coffee was still not made.

It was a passage in chapter 22—the chapters were short, often only two or three pages—that stopped me.

A rational creature rests only once he attains happiness; he hopes for happiness, but unhappily avoids the path by which he may arrive at it.

After a while I found my eyes racing compulsively ahead, then flashing back either to reread certain sentences to make sure that such simple words contained what I thought they did or to read them carefully a second time. Aelred went on:

You will never satisfy your desire until by a felicitous curiosity you reach what is highest and best, what nothing surpasses and nothing excels. Wherever you stand below that, however high or great or pleasant it may be adjudged, you will doubtlessly remain miserable.

And later,

Moreover the blind perversity of miserable man is lamentable enough. Although he desires happiness ardently, not only does he not do those things by which he may obtain his desire but rather, with contrary disaffection, takes steps to add to his misery.

And still later,

He is like a sick person who earnestly hopes to recover but because of the immediate pain shuns an amputation ...

Although I had first been taken with Aelred's words, when I reflected on them I started to get angry. This Columban had his nerve to drag me through breast-beating like this. We couldn't play postulant and vocation director, but he obviously wanted to give me a good swig from the bottle of Catholic guilt. Did men who joined New Citeaux buy all this?

I was about to turn the page, which, like all the pages in this section, was wrinkled and lightly stuck. My pen was already in my hand and I was ready to make a note, something to the effect that "Aelred seems to be saying that the spiritual life demands anguish, suffering, but that this will lead eventually to true pleasure. Two points: 1) Isn't this just refried old Catholic thought that life is a series of deferrals? and 2) How do young men today reconcile this when today nobody in his right mind—and with the insights of modern psychology—courts suffering, regardless of what the payout might be?"

I turned the page. And there in the margin, in a block of neat script: "C: Pain leads to triumph. Pain, a necessary path. Pain, not to be avoided, but—as hard as this may be—greeted. There is no other way, I know that now. Thank you."

I sat up straight at the kitchen table, where I had been reading.

There were five footnotes on the facing page, which left an unusually large amount of white space. And in that white space, I could see some faint lines. Was it an erasure of further notes? A rough sketch? What more had this reader before me observed or commented upon? Were these Columban's own thoughts or thoughts directed *to* him?

I felt a little heady, the result, I assured myself, of my early rising and lack of food, so I put some oatmeal on the stove and took a shower. As I shaved, it came to me. Shaving cream still everywhere except my left cheek, I brought that page of *The Mirror of Charity* to the mirror and put it alongside my face.

Now viewed in reverse, it was clear that this was a return address from the envelope Columban had removed from the book. The handwriting was the same as that in the margin. There were three lines, the first one illegible. On the second line I could make out a *4*; the number or letter next to it I could not. The last began with the letters *B-a-i-n* and ended with the numbers *0-3-5*.

I found myself taken over by a reporter's curiosity—a proclivity as natural and morally neutral as the desire to complete a crossword puzzle or to solve the riddle in a murder mystery by page 100—and consumed, strangely, with an overpowering jealousy. I wanted to interview this person for my story. Equally, I wanted to know what kind of person would so bare his soul to Columban; what kind of relationship did they have?

Putting the rest of the third line together was simple, and by noon I had reached the town of Bainbridge, Vermont, some forty-five miles distant from where I was staying, outside Falmouth. Bainbridge was no more than an imposing fieldstone library, bearing Rodney N. Bainbridge's name, which was open three afternoons and one morning a week; a Congregational church whose weathered sides looked more whitewashed than painted; and a post office.

The postmistress, a young but extremely homely woman in a remarkably fashionable shirtwaist dress, frowned at me as I stood before her.

"Yes?"

"Stamps."

"What *kind* of stamps?" The skin around her nose seemed to collapse and, in extremis, the skin from her cheeks wrinkled in waves, trying to fill the gap. "We have all denominations from one cent to five dollars. We have commemorative stamps, standard-issue stamps, blocks of stamps, rolls of stamps, sheets of stamps."

"For letters."

"Under one ounce?"

"Huh? Yes. Ten, please."

She handed over my stamps after I paid her and there I stood dumbly.

"I have four bags of bulk mail to sort, if that's all."

"I . . . I got a letter from Bainbridge," I said. Why was

I so nervous? This was not like me, the professional snoop. "Couldn't read the return address. Like to reply."

"Mister, I have seven hundred forty-six residents here, full time and some of those summer folks, from Boston, mostly. Over two hundred boxes and the rest pick up their mail or Lucy delivers it." She screwed up her nose again, this time as if she'd smelled something awful. "Can't be expected to know everything." She sniffed, and went back to her mail.

To my right were the post office boxes. They were in banks of ten, those at the top larger. I stopped at the row for the 40s. The box at the top had a few letters, the rest of the 40s were empty. I put my face closer to the window for P.O. Box 40. It was dark inside the box and the tinted glass designed to make this kind of viewing difficult was serving its purpose.

A flash of light at the back of Box 40 almost blinded me. It was nothing more than a fluorescent light.

"You there—get away from these boxes," her muffled voice came through the wall of metal and glass. "Against federal law. Now move on, or I'll call the police." She slammed a flier for the Ames Department Store sale on top of the letters in Box 40.

But I had already seen the address.

After driving back out to the main road and asking at a convenience store—another reporter's tactic so as not to stir up suspicion in a small town once on the trail of a story—I drove a few miles north of Bainbridge. I could see a water tower, shaped like a huge white rubber syringe, a strange counterpart to the weather-beaten red silos that dotted the countryside. Old Bridge Road was only a spur off the highway and it ended at a set of 1950s-modern buildings—low slung, beige brick, uniform windows.

The receptionist called the administrator.

"I know it's a little foolish," I said, "but I have a letter from someone who lives here. Without going into the whys of this, I'd like to see him."

The administrator was an older man, slightly hunched over, who looked at me over the top of his half-lens reading glasses. In a low, quiet voice, he parried, "This must be very important to you, to come all this way with such scanty information." It was obvious from both his tone and his evasiveness that he was a therapist of some kind. "But it's against our policy to have random visitors. I'm sure you understand. Perhaps if you can give me a few more details?"

All I had was New Citeaux.

"I see." He took off the glasses and put them in his pocket. "Your relationship to New Citeaux? You say you are 'affiliated with New Citeaux.' Are you in religious life?"

"I'm—I'm looking at it," I blurted out.

"Martha, I'll be in my office," he said, and although he didn't directly ask me to accompany him, it was implied that I could.

He closed the door behind me and motioned to a chair at his desk. "I'm Catholic," he said as he sat down and then added, puzzlingly, given the fact that his skin was florid and he was at least fifty pounds overweight, "and a healthy one, dammit."

He didn't seem to know what to say next, and as I was there on the thinnest of pretexts, I remained silent. He rotated in his chair until his shoulder was toward me and he could see out the window, which was behind his desk. It was a sunny February day, and on the path that started near his window and cut diagonally across a flat piece of land and ended at an imposing old stone building with an amazing cluster of chimneys, I could see a half-dozen people walking our way. They were wearing identical deep-blue parkas.

"Are you Catholic?" he asked.

"I am."

"How Catholic?"

"That depends on when you ask. Right now, I'm very Catholic."

"Thinking of religious life? At New Citeaux?"

"I'm more the type that looks in the microscope than gets in the petri dish."

We reporters are constantly posing questions we have no right to ask. And, amazingly, most people answer us. Some have nothing to hide and want the truth—at least as they see it—to be told. There are others who hope that their words will somehow exact a certain revenge when they appear in print. The man before me was in another category, one I could not assess. He seemed as if he wanted to tell me something but did not have the words to express himself.

He smiled. He had found a way.

"Would you please go to the door and open it," he said. "Stand just outside the sill of the office. Make sure nobody is in the hallway."

I did as I was told.

"Now, if I have to swear to this, I will say that you left the office before I went to my file cabinet. Then I went to the cabinet, unlocked it, and retrieved a file. The file was not a patient's file, and in fact does not even list the patient's name, only a code number, which keys into another file, in another part of the building. This file simply gives information on the person or persons who are his or her next of kin or legal guardians."

He put the file on the edge of the desk nearest me.

"After our visit, I had wanted to check something in this particular file. But, before doing so, I needed to go to the bathroom. As you see, I have a bathroom adjoining. I went to the bathroom, and when I returned, the file was in place and you had apparently continued down the hallway and left the premises. Be aware that under threat of legal action, you are not allowed to copy any material, even so much as the name and address that appear on the first page of this file."

Gertrude and Stanley Trumbell lived in an aluminum-sided house some one hundred feet off a state highway, one in a line of simple homes that had been built on this strip of carefully apportioned lots with minimum frontage.

Stanley worked third shift in a local factory making disposable diapers and had just gotten up when I arrived. He was a small man, muscular and shy. His wife, a once-pretty woman with a baby-doll face, had eyes whose sadness seemed to sap the energy from the rest of her features. The Trumbells were perfect interviews, the kind of people a reporter wants to talk to after a tragedy occurs. They were unsuspicious, open, eager to have someone hear their story. Even though I represented no newspaper or magazine and really had no business being there, I did not have to convince them that they should talk to me. They were the kind of people who felt honored to have a stranger take an interest in their lives.

"He was the most popular kid in high school," his mother said, pointing at the mantel and the picture of a strapping young man, with close-cropped sandy hair, in a football uniform. "Played every sport, was good at everything. Girls were mad for him. But since he was an altar boy he always wanted to be a priest. He never made a fuss about it, but I would peek into his room and he'd be reading the lives of the saints. Damien the leper, Father Marquette and the Indians, the Maryknollers who went to China. He knew them all. When he said his night prayers, he always wanted to kneel on something hard or uneven so he could offer it up as a penance. It's kinda funny he should be like that, isn't it, Stan? We never pushed that kind of religion. We had enough of it when we were kids, you know, denying yourself anything you ever liked. But with him, we were pretty much in the middle. We went to church as a family—I couldn't have any other kids after him; he was such a big baby—but we never forced anything on him. Up there"—she pointed to a crucifix above the Formica dining-room table where we sat—"that's the only sign that we're a Catholic home at all." It was one of those crucifixes that held holy water, oils, and a small,

folded cloth, the basics for administering the last rites
should an emergency arise.

"We told him to wait, didn't we, Stan? Until he finished
college and worked a couple years. Or maybe to go to our
diocesan seminary. They were dying to get him, priests'
shortage and all. But, no, all he could talk about was New
Citeaux. And that Father Col . . ."

"Columban?"

"Right."

"Did he see Father Columban often?" I asked.

"What was it, Stan? Once a month? More than that? I
forget. When he started to get sick, we told him not to go
over there. Just to let it rest for a while. He had his whole
life to figure it out, plenty of time."

"When did it start?" I asked. "Was there anything special?"

"We've been around and around with that one, haven't
we, Stan?" she said. "Mr. Rudnik out there at the home
asked us the same question. Didn't seem like anything, but
then when we looked back, we should have seen it coming
more. He just never left his room. Reading, reading, reading. Prayers. Just about the only thing he did was go out to
New Citeaux. Then, about September, he didn't even do
that. Wasn't eating much either. Must've lost fifty pounds."

"Did you ever meet Father Columban?"

"Sure, sure, we did," she said. "Nice enough fellow. You
wouldn't even think he was a monk, seemed so regular.
Know him, do you?"

"I know him some," I replied. "What did he say?"

"He agreed. Bobby had to go slow."

The Trumbells insisted I take a half dozen of the toll-
house cookies Gertrude had put out on the table. They were
seeing me to the door when I asked if I might visit their
son.

"Be great if you could. Seemed to lose most of his
friends."

I finally, cautiously, asked, "What name should I ask
for?"

"Bobby. Big Bobby Trumbell, of course," his father said, with not a little pride in his voice.

"Have you spent a little time in that stone hut with Aelred? What is our friend whispering to you from his bed these days? Joseph? You seem so pensive today. Are *you* well?"

I could not—or did not want to—fix on Columban's words as we sat in the guesthouse parlor. Instead, I found myself making a mental inventory of the room's furnishings: the elegant eighteenth-century mahogany paneling, heavy damask curtains, porcelain lamps, the antique French refectory table, an enormous and flawless Persian rug. These were generous gifts from New Citeaux's wealthiest benefactor, the owner of a chain of clothing stores, who, in the fashion of William Randolph Hearst, had the interior of a Loire Valley château's sitting room removed in its entirety and transplanted here. It was common knowledge that he had done so in order that he might have the proper ambience when, stepping out of his helicopter, he entered the monastery for his forty-five-minute semiannual visit with the abbot.

"Joseph?"

"I'm ... I'm sorry, Father. Yes, I have read some Aelred. But you know what was going through my mind? The fine line between the pursuit of holiness in your way of life and ... and ..."

"The unreasonableness of it? How extreme in a certain way? Did something of Aelred's evoke something?"

"I guess maybe it came to me this morning as I was sitting on the Zen bench, staring into the darkness, freezing my butt off and trying to think about nothing."

"Yes? And ... ?"

I couldn't tell Columban about my bit of sleuthing, my trip to Bainbridge and then to the Trumbells'. And what did it really have to do with my story? Nothing, I knew that. I just wanted to have one of those "Ah, ha!" facts to jolt him with, in hopes that he would be impressed with my reportorial technique, in hopes that he would see that I was a man different from the pack and that he should give me access to the monastery and its inhabitants. But finally, I had been able to gain control of myself. I had not returned to Bainbridge Hospital to see the son of Gertrude and Stanley Trumbell. Why drag this poor soul and these good people into my story? A story that might never be written anyhow.

"Man is part of the world, Joseph," Columban began. "Yet man constantly pursues a relationship with Him who is greater than the world. That is the tension." It surprised me because he was not one to volunteer his thoughts on any but a direct question. "Even before man knew there was such a thing as God, he wanted a kinship with that *something* out there," he continued, choosing his words carefully. "To rational minds, that might seem irrational. But, Joseph, there are many ways to live a life, all of them worthy in the eyes of God. Tax collectors and sailmakers. One needn't pursue such a life as we fools do here at a place like New Citeaux. But if one does—and I'm sure dear Aelred has already told you—no mediocrity is allowed. Not that we are not ordinary, sinful men, for we are. Greatly in need of God's help. We acknowledge that every day. And so the postulant must ask himself: Why am I putting myself through this? Why does this fascinate me so? Is it that I hear God's voice, low though it may be? Or my own pride saying I can take on a great challenge and master it?

"Yet, Joseph, look at the yachtsman, the mountain climber or the hunter, or this new thing, jogging," he said. "People go to any extreme, any amount of physical hardship. And never feel better than when they are just about killing themselves. Talk about wretched excess. So, why not for a worthy cause? For Christ?"

"A jog is a jog and a story a story," I countered, a certain resignation in my voice. "You folks are after a lifetime of excesses, aren't you?"

"The days in the desert will continue to be difficult if you choose to try and taste in some small way what this life is about. God is difficult. He beckons and then he hides. You will think you see him; you'll reach out"—Columban's hand hovered above the table, his palm open—"and he will disappear."

His eyes, always clear, glistened with a transcendent vision of what his words meant. "But don't force it upon yourself. You don't need to wear sackcloth and ashes and spurn everything about the world that has been your home for so many years."

"You asked if I remembered anything from Aelred," I said. "It's along that tack. Something like: A person doesn't leave his personal Egypt without a lot of baggage, doesn't break with the world without running into a lot of opposition. The monastic calling is an exodus, a conversion, a pilgrimage to a promised land. Okay so far. The problem is that, alluring as it is, it's distant and mysterious. I can vouch for that. But Aelred seemed to say that if a man was really serious, it could be measured. By the genuineness of his renunciation of the world."

"And?"

"Haven't I done that? I've renounced the world. At least on a trial basis. And you tell me, 'Well, don't renounce it with *that* tone of voice.' "

"Nuance, Joseph; every thoughtful life is sculpted not by jackhammers but by deft movements with tiny tools."

"Well, here I am. I've left my paradise on the Hudson behind, peach sorbet, veal cordon bleu, piña coladas, the whole nine yards. My harem of lovelies." My voice was growing louder with each item on this stupid list. "Why don't I see this thing? In fact, why the hell am I even here, why are we having this conversation about a spiritual pursuit that I'm not making, that I don't have any interest in making?"

Columban looked at his watch and rose from his chair. "Was it Freud or Jung via Freud? Karen Horney? What is it that was said about the violent reaction of the conscious? When something deep within us is touched? Was that it? Re-action. It might even be called an over-"—he hesitated for effect—"reaction."

I stared at him stonily. "Please don't use seat-of-the-pants psychology on me, Father. I pay one hundred and seventy-five dollars for a fifty-minute hour and pay it happily to have *professional* help. And besides, it's not very kind of you."

"My apologies, Joseph; I didn't mean it like that." His was a tone of contrition I had not heard before. He buttoned his collarless black wool jacket. "I should be more direct; it's a great failing of mine—a bad habit that in years and years of this life I have yet to break. A sort of intellectual ping-pong I use. Horrible. How long have you been here?"

"I came right after the first of the year. Epiphany."

"Don't be impatient. Things are moving along. Slowly, as they should. I think you are getting a splendid taste of the monastic life. You're so much like a novice: loving the physical work, the esprit de corps, doing the tangible in the midst of a life of intangibles. But the real gold is in those quiet, sometimes torturously empty moments of contemplation where you have simply put yourself, naked, needy, in the presence of God. Continue as you are doing, Joseph, and you will find yourself with questions and thoughts about a monastery and the monks that you never could have had with an intellectual discussion or even a close observation of our life. There is plenty of time for God to do his work with you. Continue to work on bending your will to his. Ah, we are so willful, and we thank him for the brain cells he gives us by being that much more stubborn. Along with your reading of Aelred, can you work on that? Giving over your will to his? A conversion of manners, Joseph, that is what we are talking about—and in those areas of your life where it seems the greatest sacrifice."

"Let me see. Give up wine with dinner. No more novels. Get up at the absolute first ring of the alarm clock. Fasting. Lent's almost here, after all. How am I doing?"

"Fine."

"Don't sound so encouraging and enthusiastic."

"What do you think about all those things you've just mentioned?" He stood over me now, peering down.

"Window dressing. And?"

"Pay no attention to such things, Joseph. They only divert you. If you ask him, God will give you some wonderful—and usually simple—opportunities. And don't reach for them." He grinned. We both knew this was getting far too serious. "People get hernias that way."

"I've got a new Bike jockstrap."

"Perhaps we should put your will on the back burner for a while. Work on something else."

"Like?"

"Your arrogance, Joseph."

I returned to the cabin, and within the next forty-eight hours had chain-sawed my way through four cords of wood; spent so much time on the Zen bench I thought I had rheumatism in my knees; ate no solid food, subsisting mainly on fruit juices and bouillon; covered the entire Gospels of Luke and John; and wore, without my customary undershirt, the coarsest wool shirt I owned.

The rash I developed covered my chest and back with angry red bumps the size of dimes and my armpits were like raw meat. Of course, Columban, don't read anything into this. Nothing forced here. Arrogance? Me?

Exhaustion and lack of proper nutrition—age-old pathways to both sanctity and insanity—finally had their way with me by the third day. Arrogance. I couldn't get the word out of my mind, and in the morning during my meditation period that part of my makeup passed vividly before me.

For years, it had passed as a certain type of secular discernment, an urban guerrilla's martial art, sophistication—taste, if you will. My arrogance was a tough but smooth covering around the core of unworthiness I felt was the real me. It had been, now that I was putting the pieces together, the stuff of my dreams for years. Just the night before, I was subjected to the last variation on this theme. As the dream opened, I was poised to lead some sort of parade in New York—not on Fifth Avenue but on fashionable Park

Avenue. I had a fine suit to wear, sequined, tailored. Like the matador's *traje de luces*. But when the parade was about to begin, I discovered it was only half a suit. My backside was in tattered, filthy underwear. I wondered how I could keep in constant motion—twirling around?—so that my audience would see only the best, and dressed, side of me. I decided I had to stare them down, keep eye contact. The parade began. I was a nightmare of motion. Twirling frantically, leaping in the air. Eye contact. Leap. Eye contact. Twirl. I awoke sweating from exhaustion.

And while New York offered so many opportunities for my arrogance, I found it had not taken me long in my new setting at Falmouth, Vermont, to begin to work a new crowd, limited as they were. Okay, Columban, laboratory experiment coming up. I'll do it. I'll live this experience for the sake of the understanding you say I need to write this story. This is one of those opportunities you said would present themselves. My own conversion of manners within my own community. Just the way you monks do it up at New Citeaux.

Then we'll see.

My companions at New Citeaux, those civilians whom I had seen regularly attending morning Mass, were quite a group. As I knelt and stood and sat with them each day, I couldn't help noticing them and, as a reporter is wont to do, creating scenarios about their lives.

There was the pale-faced young man saved from jaundice by skin that would not even turn yellow to show it had once had life. He wore glasses and a look of pain—the good little boy who never missed daily Mass, a prisoner to religion's mandates. He was a librarian, I was sure, and probably lived with an invalid mother. Life and faith itself were burdens to this frail creature who never took off his coat, even in summer.

And the woman, perhaps forty years old, an ex-nun, I was told by the chatty monk who ran the gift shop. When she came to Mass, she sat directly in front of me, in the first pew, as close as she could get to the monks without violating their enclosure. Her head was always tilted to the side, her face uplifted to the altar or higher, to the stained-glass Virgin Mother. There was an overwhelming sense of unfulfilled longing about her.

But what struck me most was her pelvis, her buttocks specifically. She was surely no object of lust for me; but it was hard not to stare at her loose-fitting slacks and how her buttocks puckered inward, as if she'd just touched them against a hot stove. Her back swayed in a gentle curve, an anatomical necessity, or else she would have had trouble standing, with her center of gravity shifted so far forward.

Her novitiate, in one of those perfervid pre–Vatican II convents, must have been brutal. She had bought it all, the requirements of the great love affair with her Christ. She had been permanently deformed by some novice mistress who knew only that at the confluence of a woman's legs and torso was a gate never to be unlatched, even under the threat of death, a biological necessity so that waste might be eliminated from a Temple of the Holy Spirit, an area to be dealt with only in rough, swiping motions fore and aft.

There was another woman, middle-aged, in an ill-fitting bright red wig, who never sat down; and a younger girl whose face, no matter where she sat, seemed always in the shadows. There was a gray pall about her and massive black circles under her sorrowful eyes. Sprinkled about was a collection of widowers, old men who often dozed off, but, oddly enough, no elderly widows, the staple of most Catholic churches. And of course, a changing mix of day-trippers: visiting nuns, Boy Scout troops earning a Spirituality Merit Badge, tourists with their Instamatics, and well-tanned skiers who leaned over the shoulder-high wall to peer at the monks in their stalls as if they were performing sea lions.

Listing them, as I had, made me feel small and horrible. I knew nothing about them, nothing about their life's journey, their demons, their upbringing, but judged them harshly according to no more than what presented itself on the surface. It was the unspoken rule of guest-chapel regulars never to speak, except to wish one another "The peace of Christ" at the appropriate liturgical moment. I wished peace each morning, but I did not mean it. I had pronounced judgment.

The following day provided an opportunity to try my experiment at a conversion of manners. As Columban had promised, it was a straightforward, clear choice. The occasion—as proclaimed by a neatly printed notice on the guest-chapel door—was the solemn profession of one Polycarp Bennett, the Brother Polycarp who was treating me so badly. As my background reading pointed out, solemn profession was the most precious day in a Trappist's life, the day he commits himself until death to the order and to the monastery by lying prostrate while making his vows.

As I turned off Route 47 by the sign marking the monastery entrance and began the climb on the asphalt road that wound through dense, overhanging pines, I made a firm purpose of amendment. I would stage a two-pronged assault on my arrogance. I would pray that Polycarp's life as a Trappist be a holy and fulfilling one; and I would sit in the midst of my companions whom I had so easily denigrated by my typecasting. I would love them throughout the service and think nothing but good thoughts about their individual sanctity, their heroic struggle to know the same God as mine. Yes, and for Bobby Trumbell, Big Bobby, whom I would never meet—at least not in a mental hospital, where I was too likely to regard him as little more than another squiggly creature under my microscope.

The parking circle outside the abbey church was full, and in my walk from far down the icy road, I slipped, tearing a new pair of jeans on a pickup truck's rusty back bumper and taking a nice hunk of flesh out of my knee on the way down. I struggled to get up. I came face-to-face with bumper stickers on the next car: GOD AND I, GOD IS MY CO-PILOT, TRY JESUS: WHY NOT? I (followed by that infernal heart-shaped symbol for "love") FATIMA.

It was people like this car owner who gave Christianity a bad name. And me a perfect reason to be arrogant.

I limped to the door of the visitors' alcove. One of the older monks informed me with a shy grin that the guest chapels were filled, but that I should feel free to worship in the main body of the church, open to outsiders on this special day for Brother Polycarp.

It was just as well; my firm purpose of amendment was fading in inverse proportion to the increasingly throbbing pain in my knee. I walked through the wooden gate ominously marked CLOISTER—ENTRY FORBIDDEN.

But then . . . something happened. In an instant. A wondrous feeling of calm came over me. I realized I was once again within the church to which I'd been struggling so hard to gain entry. I gave up my arrogance—if only in my mind—and look what had opened up. Father Columban, do you hear?

I crept along the aisle behind the choir stalls and made my way to the second set of stalls, at one time filled by a hundred lay brothers and today with Polycarp's friends and family. I couldn't see any of my companions whom I'd vowed to love, so I took a seat at the back of the church in my favorite place, beneath the rose window, beside the great doors.

The next two hours sailed by, music, incense, words of unequivocal commitment, chant, all mingling into that special kind of exotic mystical pageantry that only the Church can afford. The abbot, Hilary Demarest, an aristocratic, silver-haired man, whose forebears were some of the first Catholics in Boston and whose family now owned a good portion of Back Bay real estate, presided regally over his flock in his high, fine miter, firmly holding on to his shepherd's crook, the symbol of his power as well as his duty. Polycarp, his head shaved, leaving just a thin crown of a tonsure—although this was no longer required of postconciliar monks—was a beam of pure light. Young enough to make his sacrifice a great gift to God, old enough to fully understand the weight of the vows. I had never heard the *schola* in finer voice, as he led the community through the ancient rite, in Latin:

> *"Veni, Creator Spiritus*
> *Mentes tuorum visita. . . ."*

And in English with those words of supplication of Psalm 67:

> *"Confirm, O God, what you have done for us,*
> *In your holy Temple*
> *Which is in Jerusalem . . ."*

I looked up at the crucifix. For how long it lasted I do not know, but something happened that morning. When this period—it may have been a second or many minutes—was over, I found myself feeling as if I were just waking up. I could not remember what had gone before. Then I blinked, realizing where I was.

> *"Holy God, we praise thy name,*
> *Lord of all, we bow before thee. . . ."*

The words of the majestic hymn swelled up from the community and congregation, filling the abbey church with a sound I was sure was reminiscent of the glorious days of blind and blissful theological certainty when New Citeaux was home to two hundred men, more than three times the present number. The monk at the keyboard, situated at the middle of the choir, opened up the full organ, all the reeds and mixtures, for the second verse.

I bowed my head. My breath was gentle and rhythmic; even my knee felt whole. Voices were rich, sonorous echoes, wave upon wave of praise for this first force, the strong Lord of all. Yes, with moments of transcendence like this, a man could spend a lifetime loving and wrestling with God. I found myself saying that over and over so I would not forget to write it down, but I had difficulty concentrating.

I raised my head. Off to my right, the doors to the cloister silently swung open. The procession of celebrants moved slowly toward me down the main aisle, in their midst one who had just committed himself to their life. For life.

Polycarp passed in front of us. He smiled broadly at me and looked to be no more than a boy of sixteen. His face was a groom's, the bride invisible on his arm. He was not wearing his glasses.

I followed him with my eyes as he left the church. The sun was brilliant on the untouched snow within the garth formed by the cloister. Pinpoints of light sparkled on the sculpted pines, on the bare azalea and rhododendron bushes, on the statue of the Blessed Virgin with her outstretched, welcoming arms. Long, silvery fingers of light radiated into the darkened church.

Beam after beam, dreamily, transported me. At first I was lifted out of the church and into the graveyard, which was visible through two sets of cloister arches, to the simple wooden crosses marking the places where monks were laid to rest. Where Polycarp would someday be buried, without a casket, with no more than the clothes he wore this day, nothing more to shield him from the Vermont clay that would quickly dispose of the earthly shell he had willingly renounced.

Then, on a ray of light atomized into fiery orange and red particles and suffused through a vaporous cloud of incense, I was swept back into the church, over carved gargoyles at the backs of choir stalls, between the silver pipes of the organ, now triumphantly proclaiming the final verse of Ignaz Fränzl's homage, past the long, even rows of choir monks, their heads precisely and uniformly inclined toward hymnals before them.

And past a head of shimmering hair.

It was a dazzling, unreal white in the sun's light,

strangely luminous and smooth. A statue? What was it doing there, so close to me? A vision? I blinked again.

There was a splash of incongruous color within the hair: a band of the Virgin Mary's special shade of eternal blue. This face, though beautiful, was punctuated by a contrasting field of—of all things—freckles. Then below, a set of fine, even shoulders, draped in a still-richer color. My eyes refused to obey; I struggled to focus.

Then my field of vision was entirely blurred, awash in a sea of gray herringbone.

I could no longer see the woman. Instead, standing no more than five feet in front of me was the man I had first seen in the guest chapel the month before. His topcoat was a good one, but worn, the lapels shiny from where his hands had traced along to find buttons and their holes. He was asking me a question, but I couldn't understand him. My dazed look must have encouraged him to repeat himself.

"Know him—anything about him?" he said in a raspy voice. I could smell that he had already had more than altar wine to drink. "Haskins was the name—Trevor Haskins. He was quite a fan of this place. *Dominus Dei*, right?"

I knew that much Latin, but the tone was wrong, this mocking reference to New Citeaux as the house of God. The monk-organist began the postlude, and worshipers and choir monks began to file out. I looked more closely at this man who had so abruptly broken into that extraordinary moment of oblivion.

For so large and puffy a face his nose was small. It was laced with tiny, abused veins that cried out in their swollen state from all the undigested alcohol that had coursed through them for too many years.

"Trevor?" I said. "No, sorry, I didn't know him."

"My name's Octavius Kiernan. Private investigator. I specialize in homicides."

"Oh, really?" I said vaguely.

"You're the writer, aren't you?" he said, leaning closer to me. "Cover of the magazine a few years back, if I'm not mistaken. I never forget a face. Well, mister, you're sitting on the best damned story of your career. Right here." He looked up to the rafters as if he expected to see someone there. Then he turned abruptly and walked toward the altar.

Something remarkable happened today. I think. I can't sort it out yet. I need to be calm about it. And not be confused by too many voices. Homicides?

3. March

I HAD thought that after the wonderful, peaceful morning of Brother Polycarp's solemn profession my somewhat contrived near-monastic life would be better. But the afterglow of that morning did not last even to the setting of the day's sun. What followed were lonely, fitful nights (what was I doing here?) and worse mornings, gazing out at that barren hillside. I had trouble concentrating on the simplest of tasks. I shattered a sliding glass door when I tried to walk through it. I lost my keys. One night, taking off my socks, I found I had been wearing one blue, one gray.

On my way over to New Citeaux one morning early in the month, I decided I would see Father Columban and tell him that I was going back to New York immediately. The story was not working out. Why force it? I could pack and be on my way before noon.

About a mile from the monastery entrance, I found myself slowing down, my foot lifting from the accelerator. I was on the shoulder of the highway. No cars in sight. It was dawn, about five-thirty. As I sat there, staring stonily ahead into a swirling snowstorm, a word formed on my lips. *Help.* I sat there for a moment in a sort of stupor, then drove on, thinking nothing about it. I had called out to God for help many times in my life—from help in freshman algebra, which remains a mystery to me, to help in getting me out of this place, this conversation. Help me with an idea, help me with these next ten push-ups, help my application be approved.

But this was different. A generic, unspecific, categorical help.

I drove on to the monastery and took my seat. The Mass began, and it was not a particularly wonderful Mass—Father Charles, the magpie monk who was Brother Polycarp's relief in the guesthouse, was presiding, a pompous blowhard, with his shaved head (an ugly, misshapen, lumpy, sickly pink head at that), turning the simple Trappist Mass into bad theater with his basso profundo intonations and exaggerated moves. The readings floated by, the consecration was spoken. I was already back at the cabin, packing my clothes.

"Lord"—I followed the words that the monks on the altar were saying in unison—"I am not worthy to receive you, but only say the word and I shall be healed." I repeated the words to myself, without feeling, without intent. "Lord, I am not worthy to receive you." I paused. "But only say the word." I paused again. "And I shall be healed."

I stood by the low wall that separated the visitors' alcove from the sanctuary and extended my hand. I stared at the host placed there. I turned it so the small cross at its center was straight before me. I put it into my mouth. I lifted the simple pewter chalice and took a drink of the wine. I returned to my seat.

I could feel the wine—a sweet but good Tokay—making its way down my throat, my esophagus, and finally entering my stomach.

Healed.

The word, now unspoken by me, began to resonate.

Healed.

Perhaps it was because I was not able to see Columban soon after—a devastating influenza epidemic had leveled the community and our appointments were necessarily canceled—and therefore had no opportunity to talk about and otherwise dissect the experience that it took root in me. During morning meditation my mind meandered less and less back to my life in New York. I stopped making lists of things I absolutely had to do at the cabin or chores that would take me into Falmouth that day. More important, I stopped watching myself as I knelt there on the Zen bench. Up to that time, I realized I had been operating like some constantly running camera, recording every change of breathing, any facial twitch on The Subject, putting more attention into critiquing his sincerity, posture, and intensity than in allowing him to simply be there.

Healed. I kept thinking of that word.

In the days that followed, there were a few times when I reached what I can describe no better than as moments of blankness, stasis, where the tree, the dawning outline of the hillside, and the strange rippled terrain blurred. There was a kind of suspension, a light-headedness. I was hardly lost in the cosmos, and certainly had not even approached the "mind of God," but I was aware that something different from anything I had experienced before in my life was occurring.

Strangely, I found that I had great difficulty recalling in detail what I had experienced and equally great difficulty committing it to paper. I was amazed by my inability. After all, this was my business, my craft. But all I had to show was a single word, which I wrote down on three occasions. *Healed.*

Whatever they were, I grasped at those moments of quiet neutrality when they chose to come, held on to them almost greedily, hoping they would last. But they never did. An hour later, what had seemed so real seemed again like a dream. And while it struck me that I was a man adrift from everything he'd ever known, I convinced myself that such a thought no longer held the terror it did during my early days in the cabin. I rationalized that at worst I could go back to New York, certainly having become better for the time away.

I recalled Father Columban's oft-repeated advice that he gave to all novices, postulants, and those interested in considering the Trappist life. "Look only to him, with eyes open and breathing calm. Wait upon him. Go slow. Be patient. Let the oars make sure, steady strokes, unhurried. Keep rowing."

Even Brother Polycarp's usual rudeness didn't bother me. I offered him some of the hazelnut coffee I had found in a Falmouth delicatessen and brewed at home that morning. His answer was to stare at me, before turning to walk away. I smiled and went to the parlor to await Father Columban.

He had brought some croissants that Father Antoine, on leave from Bellefontaine in France, had fashioned. "Ah, the simple pleasures," he said through a full mouth.

I couldn't wait to begin.

"Something happened, Father," I said. "I think 'it' happened."

"It?"

"I had a moment."

"A moment of what?"

What came out of my mouth surprised even me. "Where I felt . . ."—I struggled for the word—"at one with . . ."

"With?"

"With God, Father Columban."

I explained in some detail Brother Polycarp's profession, the bad week leading up to that moment when I felt healed and then the twelve days following. "I realize this is pretty new, but I have never felt something so real in all my life. It has stayed with me. I have a sense, in some small way, of what you meant by a love affair with God. Is this a typical or predictable novice experience?"

Father Columban ran his hand over his bald pate. "Did I use that phrase? 'Love affair?' I must have gotten a bit carried away, my friend." He closed his eyes in a lazy smile.

"If not those words, something like them. I want to go a little further now, Father. I think I can."

"For the story, of course."

"Yes and no. Yes, that might be what comes of this. But no, it may be more than that."

"Like?"

I mimicked his lazy smile as my own eyes closed. "I'm leaving that up to God."

"Wise."

My eyes opened wide and suddenly. "But in my gut I feel this thing so strongly. I can see what sustains a man in this life. Once you taste that, you know what you're looking for. I mean, I've had the experience, but this is—"

"Joseph?"

"Yes?"

"Do you know what this means?"

"What, Father?" I asked softly.

"Absolutely nothing." The voice was flat, uninflected.

"Thanks for the affirmation."

"Let me qualify that: little if anything. Yes, as with a man and a woman falling in love, there can be a first blush. But quickly that is gone. Falling in love, *feeling* love, are good things, but they are emotions, Joseph, and a life with God is not ruled by emotions. If it is, it is a foolish, fickle game."

"I think it's more than that."

"Yes?"

"Since that day I have done a few things. For one, I called New York and told a friend he could have my apartment for the next month or two. I'm going to stay for a while. If it only works out that this is an article I'm writing, I'll write it here. If it's more—well, I'm here. Another thing: I've gone out and bought a gardening book and packs of seeds. I'm going to plant a garden out by my place. If I'm gone by harvest time, I'm sure all that stuff won't go to waste. Father, don't you realize? An enormous change has come over me."

He rose from his seat. We were only halfway through our hour.

"Joseph, I hope you'll excuse me today. A podiatrist is here for the morning and this monk before you has the worst bunions in the Western world."

"But, Father, what—"

"Should you do?" He paused, as if in profound thought. "Just as before. Continue the monastic day and please stay with Aelred. If you care to go a bit deeper into this, try to further reduce your contacts with the outside world as much as possible. I'll be most interested in our next talk. Let's delay it a week. So I'll see you two weeks from today."

It began that same day. At first it was a free-floating anxiety (when all else failed, the malady of preference of my crowd in New York) where I found I couldn't sit, stand, kneel, or lie down for more than a few minutes in the same position. By nightfall I was sure—and almost relieved—that I had the flu. The achiness and fever left me only to be replaced by stabbing chest pains and a recurring teariness. At times the pain was so intense I had to wrap my arms around my chest and squeeze as hard as I could to breathe. I pounded on my rib cage, took hot baths and cold showers, anything I could think of to break the spell. Nothing worked. One evening it was so bad, I drove to the Falmouth Family Health Center. My blood pressure was slightly elevated, but the EKG was absolutely normal. The solicitous young resident asked if anything particularly stressful was happening in my life.

I said no. He prescribed Valium. Five milligrams. Light dose.

As for my tears, they were not by-products of the pain but merely its soppy handmaiden. I awoke with moist eyes, prepared meals, meditated, read, prayed, worked with them. I had only to think that my eyes were dry and normal and they would immediately mist over.

As I thought back to my last talk with Columban, I was alternately embarrassed by what I had said and haunted by how little he had said in return. How much deeper into this desert was I willing to go? So deep that I wouldn't be able to find my way out? There were no easy rescues in the middle of a wasteland, no roads. If you walked in, you must have the strength to walk out.

Healed? Love affair? Who in the hell was I kidding?

And what of Columban himself? Who was this man, really? Could he rescue me if I ventured beyond the point of no return? Would he know that I had reached it? Before I stepped out of the boat, as Peter had done, would he stop me? He had hardly extended a hand as I was floundering that day.

I continued to read Aelred, as Columban had advised, seeking some comfort. But the venerable abbot of Rievaulx evangelically and repetitiously extolled the hardship and suffering of the journey into darkness and the unknown. If there was even a lumen of light in his words, it was when he pointed out that no one stays in the desert. It is a place to pass through. So easy for a dead and sainted man to say as he goaded me on.

"You look terrible, Joseph. Have you seen a doctor?"

"I don't need a doctor; I need a psychiatrist."

"Tell me about it, Joseph. Honestly. You felt you'd rounded a corner."

Father Columban moved his chair back from the fine refectory table on which rested my copy of Aelred's *Mirror of Charity* alongside the soggy untouched pancakes he'd brought me from the retreat-house kitchen. He folded his hands, index fingers extended, and rested the tips against his mouth. It was a markedly serious look on a man who smiled much of the time.

"I have never felt worse—physically, mentally or spiritually," I began. "These have been the worst two weeks of my life. Maybe I have the flu, but that's the least of it. My body is so tense I can't sleep and my stomach is upset all the time. It's amazing I can get up to make a cup of coffee. Coffee—what a joke! My beverage of necessity is herb tea." I involuntarily sprang up from my chair and virtually shouted, "God, is it hot in here!"

"Perhaps we should walk a bit today," he said.

"Walk?"

"Well, yes, Joseph, we have twelve hundred acres. Let's see some of it."

We started down the hill, monk and man, an altogether normal sight at New Citeaux, as lay people came to seek guidance for lives in the world from those who had renounced it. It was a brilliantly sunny day, the air clean and cold.

"When I think of God, when I attempt to pray or to meditate, I realize what a cruel joke this whole business has been," I began, the words tumbling angrily out of my mouth. "Parallel monk. The lived experience. My ass!"

"When did this all begin?"

"What 'this' are you referring to?"

"Your search."

"Thirty years ago? At birth? When I looked in the mirror one morning and saw myself for the first time? Hell, I don't know! When I rationalize what's going on, I tell myself, 'You're in a sophomore slump. The first flush is past, the infatuation is over. Reality is setting in.' It often happens with a story, once you see how much work it's really going to be. Shit! I've got plenty of excuses and pat answers, more than I need. Columban, I'm dried out, dead inside. Nothing. The nights are pure hell. The days I can barely cope with. Is this what the hopeful young Trappist goes through? They can book you on cruel and unusual punishment for this."

We walked a few yards in silence.

"The seeds? How are they?"

"Lettuce, celery, kohlrabi, Chinese cabbage, leeks—all the early stuff has sprouted in this window box I made. To the seed! I hate every last one of the little fertile bastards. They mock me. Green, the most sickeningly healthy green you've ever seen. Why, Columban, why couldn't I just be one of those guys who got married, had a couple of kids, and watched sports on television all weekend? Paunchy and happy—that's what I want."

"He's a funny fellow," he said in a voice I'd not heard before, as if God were no less a mystery to him. "Jesus told the tax collector to go on extracting from already poor and oppressed Jews every cent the law allowed. But no more.

And from the rich young man, he wanted everything. Charles de Foucauld had to live in the desert and I had to leave a budding little academic career at Duke some considered quite promising. And you? Who knows? Listen. Wait upon him."

"Patient! Be patient! I'm going nuts, don't you understand? I'm not de Foucauld or Dorothy Day or Bernanos's country priest; I'm not John of the Cross. I'm not you. I'm a simple, vain, weak, venal man. And I'm lonely. At least in Egypt I had company. Try to live alone with your demons. You'd be wacky, too."

"Don't torture yourself. It's just a story that you are trying to do, Joseph, something you're trying honestly to experience so you can tell others about it. God asks no more of you than you can give. Thousands of lives that people live, all satisfactory—"

"Don't patronize me."

"I pray for you, Joseph, and I know it's hard. But I have such a strong feeling you're making progress. Pain and tension like this are not suffered in vain. My experience with so many young men proves it so. The breakthrough will come. Or it won't. Keep reading the Scriptures. And Aelred."

"Don't give me that Zen gibberish. It's coming. It's not coming. Give me Western rationalism anytime."

His emotionless face, which I was watching in profile as we walked along, turned toward me. He smiled, at once warm and shy, the look of the old and kindly pastor, deeply concerned yet confessing his inability to satisfactorily answer another man's question, acknowledging the inequality of the situation: one man, the spiritual director, metaphysically whole and self-fulfilled; the other, the wounded and confused supplicant.

"I try to convince myself I'm not afraid, but I am, Columban."

"God is aware of that. But you're special to him. He loves you intensely. That's why he's asking for still more,

Joseph. Like the rich young man. I feel he wants more from you."

The long quiet that followed at first seemed a peaceful respite. A wind was up on this sunny day at the end of winter, whistling through the stately pines that lined the road on the windward side. A few hundred yards in front of us one of the old Ford pickups sputtered and backfired as it negotiated the final, steep hill that led to the church. (The monastery had three Fords, none with less than two hundred thousand miles. Their accumulated age was a pride to Brother Amadeus, careful keeper of the cars. On Saint Joseph's feast day, the nineteenth of this month, the day he designated as their collective birthday, they would be one hundred fifteen years old.)

"How do you know that?"

"After a while at this you sense it."

"I'm just doing this for a story, remember. Are you sure?"

"As sure as I can be."

"Then I want to tell you something; please don't interrupt, okay?"

He nodded.

"I don't understand exactly what's going on. But something is. I asked for this, in a way. And now I'm in the middle of something that scares the hell out of me. In ways I can explain and ways I can't just yet.

"First, I have to get this out, so you can hear it and I can too. When I told my agent about New Citeaux and you and this quote, unquote interest of mine, he said 'Great.' To him it was commercial; he loved it. A spiritual revolution was going on, he said, and I'd be first on the bandwagon. I could method-act it; who has to be real about anything today?

"As for me, I figured I couldn't lose. After a few months up here I could slip back into my Jean-Paul Germain blazer and dazzle them this summer in the Hamptons. 'Oh, Joseph, what a character you are; what a smashing idea.' 'Bread and water, was it, or a brioche and Perrier?' There would be enough material for all season. My arrogance would be sweetly flavored by a sprinkling of humility. Unbeatable combination, no? But I got caught. I can't play it both ways anymore."

"Joseph." The barely audible sound of my name stopped me. "What do you want of yourself?" Father Columban asked.

"You know what it is? Now, don't laugh out loud." I stopped and dug my hands into my jacket pockets. "I've never been a hero. Simple as that. I want to be a hero. I tried once. I was going to join the Maryknolls. I read all their literature, attended the Sunday-afternoon sessions, saw the slides, was ready to go over to convert China. But I didn't. Something wouldn't let me give myself to that. It wasn't whether I had a vocation or not. It never got to that. I just chickened out. No guts.

"Then I went through college at the end of the silent fifties. Nobody stood for anything but white bucks and Snowflake Frolics and getting a job as a sales trainee with Sears. It was such a pathetic time. I couldn't assimilate fast enough. Stand for something? What a joke! Me, the kid with dirty fingernails and parents who didn't know a predicate from a pirogi. When I got that rare letter from home, I burned it, scared to death somebody would read it and find out where I came from. I wanted to be stamped out cookie-cutter-perfect. The right haircut, starched khakis, trench coat with a Black Watch plaid lining. Sameness was next to godliness. An art form. I was an angry young man. I read Salinger and wore a duck hunter's hat and smoked Camels and felt misunderstood. I knew I wanted to live for something great, to be tested, but I wasn't willing to stand up for anything. I put on my happy face and cleaned under my fingernails and tried to get dates with the girls from Grosse Pointe and Winnetka. 'Oh, my father? In the steel business,' I would say.

"Then the sixties. What a time to be counted! Civil rights. Vietnam. Did I march, picket, get arrested? I was too busy. *Writing* about involvement, so I never had to involve myself. In my personal life, I was even worse. In the seventies and eighties I lived with a woman who loved me and wanted to marry me and I smiled and said, 'Let's wait a bit.' Then we broke up just as America was coming apart. There was no morality anymore and I loved it. AIDS didn't even slow me down; it took me only ten, maybe fifteen minutes longer and a couple of questions before I got what I wanted.

"You know why these are sick times, Columban? Because people like me set the stage for it. I never believed in anything strong or long enough to really make a sacrifice for it."

By now we had turned around and were headed up the hill. I was watching Columban's face for any expression of recognition or approval—or disapproval—but he merely walked along, his face telling me nothing, his arms behind his back.

"Look at that man we sent to the White House. Twice. He was perfect. Our high priest, our Moses for the Me Generation. An icon. The patron saint of the yuppies. Swagger. Skinny wife. Rich friends. I got mine, buddy, you work for yours. Told the poor how much he cared about them as he was sticking it in their butt. Give us a Pied Piper, and legions of us rats with our tailored clothes and tax shelters and nutrition counselors will march merrily along until we go right off the cliff. But what about the rats behind us; will they see? Not a chance.

"It's wonderful, these days we're living in. The Lite Decade, the *Times* called it. L-i-t-e. Even the spelling doesn't waste any letters. Seven hundred pages of *Moby-Dick* reduced to a minute on a cassette. Drink three 'lite' beers with the calories of two. Who needs soul-searching? Commitment? Really! What a starchy, heavy old word! Nibble your way along; the great smorgasbord. 'I'll have a little of this, a little of—' "

"I think the article idea was a wonderful subterfuge to get closer to God," he cut me off. "He appreciates such creativity, Joseph. And He hears the groaning of your heart."

"What do you mean?"

"Isaiah and Saul didn't think they had it in them. But God saw within these men the makings of something beyond anything they might have imagined of themselves."

By now we had reached the low front steps of the guesthouse. Columban paused, one foot on the huge, flat rock that formed the porch. I felt he was hesitating because of the seriousness of what he had to say and also to give him time to study my face, to see if I was prepared to hear it.

"I think there is something within you, asking if you should not devote the rest of your life to God as a Trappist monk, Joseph."

I felt a certain numbness in my forehead. "Are you nuts, Father?"

"Perhaps."

He said no more and proceeded into the guesthouse. Bewildered, I followed. He disappeared into the rest room.

I collected our dishes from the parlor and took them into the small pantry off the retreatants' dining room. There was milk left in the pitcher, so I opened the door to the kitchen to take it to the refrigerator there. On the door was one of the signs that demarcated the Trappists' world, signs that were posted at all points where incursions might occur: MONASTIC ENCLOSURE. ENTRY FORBIDDEN.

Reaching into the refrigerator, I realized I was not alone. I turned slowly. It was Brother Polycarp.

His face was frozen in a disapproving scowl, his magnified, unblinking eyes fixed on me in their rage. "This is part of the cloister," he said coldly. "Do you know what that means?"

"I was just putting away the milk from our breakfast. I'll make sure everything is in its place."

"Are you on retreat? Retreatants eat at seven-forty, eleven-forty and five-forty; the times are well posted."

"You know I'm not on retreat, Brother."

"Then leave."

"I'm—I'm sorry—"

The door opened and Father Columban stepped into the kitchen. It was clear from the look on his face that he knew immediately what had happened.

"I'll take care of these things, Joseph; I didn't mean to hold you up," he said breezily, as if all three of us were fast friends.

Although as guestmaster Brother Polycarp was the prince of this tiny fiefdom within the monastery, he said nothing in the presence of a priest, who held a status from which he was still one large step removed. He stood stiffly in front of the open refrigerator.

"Apologies if there's been any inconvenience, Brother," Father Columban said, this time in a tone that was more proper than overtly friendly.

Brother Polycarp slammed the refrigerator door with uncharacteristic Trappist bile.

"Please tell your entourage, Father, to have the grace to leave the rest of us alone. Every one of them thinks he's the first person to walk up the road. And the last."

Father Columban and Brother Polycarp stared at each other for what seemed an interminable time. What made it all the more uncomfortable—at least for me—was that neither showed the slightest emotion. It was as if they could stand like that for hours, separated by a low butcher-block worktable. Their Trappist formation had unwittingly prepared them well for such moments of human confrontation: each certainly had feelings, but seemed willing to sublimate his personal emotion to allow the moment to find its own equilibrium.

The late winter sun beating down on the green slate roof had begun to melt snow, which dripped off the eaves in a maddening, predictable rhythm.

"It's my fault, I know the rules," I said, finally, almost in desperation.

"We must respect the wishes of others," Father Columban said as if reading from some outdated and boring religious tract. "It's a cardinal rule of monastic life, most necessary to our mutual salvation. Not to mention sanity."

Brother Polycarp said nothing in return and left.

"He really has a thing about me," I said in a whisper. "Despises me, doesn't he?"

" 'Despises'?" Columban turned toward me at the sound of a foreign word he seemingly could not understand. "Don't flatter yourself. He's merely preserving the integrity of the cloister."

"He doesn't have to do it with a club."

"Give Polycarp some distance, Joseph; he's a very complicated young man. One last thing. I think I spoke prematurely."

"About?"

"Our life. Your seeking it. I want to withdraw that. If you feel you should go back to New York, please do that. Please."

I stared at him. I found my teeth tapping together in anger. "I'm going to play this out."

"It can hurt."

"Like this fellow," I said, holding up *Mirror of Charity*.

"Aelred?" he said in a puzzled tone.

"No, this guy," I said, flipping the pages to the page I had so often turned to. "Here's how he puts it: 'Pain leads to triumph. Pain, a necessary path. Pain, not to be avoided, but—as hard as this may be—greeted. There is no other way, I know that now. Thank you.' " I slammed the book closed.

Father Columban lowered his eyes. I saw his shoulders heave as he took a deep breath.

"Imagine saying thank you for *that*!"

"One person's interpretation," Father Columban said quietly.

"One Bobby Trumbell and that interpretation didn't settle too well, did it?"

"Do you know him?"

"*Of* him."

"How did you—?"

"Reporter at work, Father."

"So, this is no more than a story, Joseph," Father Columban said, a trace of irritation seeping through the filter of his control. "But you may do as you will."

"I know that."

"And?"

"I'm still going to see this through. I wouldn't go back to New York now if you bound and gagged me."

The article is dismissed as no more than an excuse. Then it is thrown in my face. Does Columban know more about this man than the man knows of himself? (Not too hard to do!)

To get through the days that followed, I plunged even harder into my outdoor work, felling a tree or two a day, adding to a woodpile of some eight cords—already enough for two or three years. I put maximum effort into all my household chores, dusting, cleaning, gleaning the bleak countryside for dried flowers and then endlessly arranging and rearranging the bouquets. I painted my bedroom, which didn't need to be painted. And the paint dried to an assaulting yellow. I repainted. I scoured my cookbooks for the most elegant recipes, ones that took inordinate amounts of time and provided me with meals that proclaimed—and this was my tortured logic—that I still had respect and concern for my well-being.

Eggs Florentine, cream of asparagus soup, beef bourguignon, stuffed trout, cheese truffles, curried lamb; béchamel and béarnaise sauces—and never the shortcut blender versions. From the time my workday ended until almost bedtime, I was a blur of culinary activity.

On the last Friday of the month, at lunch, I reached to the back of the refrigerator for lemon yogurt, with which to make an exotic fruit dressing. I bumped a covered casserole and sent it smashing to the floor. There, on my spotless linoleum, was the Rorschach of my life: clots of reddish rice congealed onto five pieces of chicken, the exact number I had made four days before. I looked closer and deeper into the refrigerator. The dim light, obscured by a maze of pots, bowls, foil-covered dishes stacked one upon another, flickered distantly. Osso buco, stuffed manicotti, duck with wild rice, moussaka.

I dropped to my knees in the middle of arroz con pollo and sobbed.

I couldn't go on like this. I didn't have that much faith. I had to find out.

"Did you think I'd come back?" I asked.

"I was hoping that you'd just forget about the whole business. And then—happened last Sunday at Mass—I thought, Well, he's got to follow up on this thing."

" '*Got* to'?"

"One way or another. As a Catholic. Or a reporter. Never knew a reporter worth his salt who didn't follow his nose. Never knew anybody with what we call this 'true faith' of ours who didn't pick off the last scab just to see what was underneath. Comes with the territory."

"Tell me about Bobby."

"Oh, don't call him that. Hates it. Robert, if you please." Charles Rudnik turned to look out the window as he had in our first meeting. "No, I can't do that. I'm his primary therapist. And someday I want him to walk out of here and go out to live a normal life. Which I think he'll do. You ask him. That much I can do. And if he wants to tell you, he can. It all depends on how he's doing on any particular day."

The young man—as best as I could estimate, in his late twenties—was dressed in a loose-fitting sweatshirt, a pair of neatly pressed jeans and polished loafers. He was freshly shaven and smelled of cologne. Robert Trumbell was well over six feet tall and had the body of a wide receiver—he had been an All-State—large hands, long legs, narrow hips. He was much better attired and had performed a more exacting toilet than his keeper, a short, stubby orderly in battered sneakers and a bleach-stained uniform who, on the approach of the director, wandered out of the sun-drenched room.

His face was not like those of the other patients around him, which made him even more distinctive than his clothes. His companions dozed in chairs or stared out the windows, but Robert was seated at a table, alert, erect, attentive. He had the fierce, sure look of a prophet: glowing, unblinking eyes and a way of holding his head cocked slightly to the side as if he were listening for the next challenge or command so that he might immediately respond or march.

"A friend from New Citeaux," the director said. Robert's eyes brightened. He sat up even more erect in the molded plastic chair.

"Father Columban and I are very, very close," he said, obviously cherishing even the sound of the priest's name. "We have a relationship that is very special. He isn't angry, is he? Please explain that I've been so busy here. I'm like a Mother Teresa to these poor people. If I were to leave, they'd be lost."

"I—"

"I'm keeping up with my reading," he continued, interrupting. "I want to reapply for admittance to New Citeaux, but—well, Father said I . . . I have so many loose ends to take care of. I want to leave it all behind. The peace of the cloister; that's what I want."

"Mr. Toomey," he said authoritatively to the orderly, who had returned and was now sitting listlessly in the corner watching a television set whose volume had been turned so low as to be barely audible. "You can see the gentleman to the door. You will excuse me, won't you? Time for *lectio divina*."

"Robert?"

He stopped immediately and looked straight at me. "I do run at the mouth. Sorry. Yes?"

"I visited your parents, Robert. They said I could come and see you."

"They're the best, but I wish they understood what this is about."

"If I could, I want to ask you about something you wrote in a book Father Columban lent you. Aelred of Rievaulx. It had to do with suffering. Suffering so you could find yourself. Robert?"

The expression on his face had changed gradually, as if he had swallowed some mind-altering medication that entered his bloodstream slowly so as not to assault his system with its power. When he spoke, his face had a strange sense of sadness about it, a sadness so deep and yet so faint that I felt he was not sure if it was proper to speak of it with a perfect stranger.

"Everybody wants to find themselves," he said. "I'm no different. It's hard to say," he added, shaking his head.

"I know."

"One thing I'm sure of."

"And that is?"

"It's worth anything. Any suffering. Any length of time in waiting. Look up there. He died on the Cross for us. Can we do any less for him?"

Robert Trumbell pointed to something on the wall behind me. I turned. It was an electric clock, its plug—pulled from a scorched socket—dangling beneath. The outstretched, unmoving hands had stopped at 3:45.

I pulled over a few times on my way home and opened my notebook. I found I had nothing to say. By the time I returned to the hermitage I was perspiring profusely, exhausted. I took a shower and, contrary to my normal sleeping patterns, slept for the rest of the afternoon. I awoke with a start and looked over at the clock radio.

6:05.

If 3:45—A.M. or P.M.—could symbolize Christ on the Cross to Robert Trumbell, 6:05 P.M. represented a daily crucifixion for anyone living alone, especially a person like me who had just awakened and could not hold out to himself the promise of turning in for the night in a few hours. Especially me, in the state I was in after the afternoon's visit.

In New York I called these the "hungry hours," and I had developed filling them into a fine art. Drinking, sometimes with a companion, but never letting that be a prerequisite. Interviews for whatever work was in progress. Phone calls to just about anyone. A publishing party, a lecture, a movie, whether marginally good or excellent—virtually anything was better than being home and alone.

I flipped through my address book. I had not taken it out in months.

I hesitated at three names: Millicent, my last New York lady, a successful and well-known Off Broadway producer; my sister in Cleveland; and my best friends, a married couple in Brooklyn.

What would I say? And they?

Perhaps I could call some of the bunch I had run around with these past few years, the cream of New York literati, the mordant wits, masters and mistresses of the bon mot, able to be funny or intelligent in three or four languages, to quote Wittgenstein or Sontag, talk of Djuna Barnes or Trollope or "films" or various fusions—in music, politics, sex. Multimedia people. I had ample listings for most letters of the alphabet. G—Gaston, Jill. G—Goldsmith, Jack. G—Guillemie, Françoise.

They would love to hear from me; I had been such a wonderful and willing playmate for all the New York games. And what could I say to them today? My life now would make no sense to them. A pursuit? Yes, that they could understand. Struggle? Of course. But this was not training for the marathon or a journey through psychoanalysis. No, good friends, I'm not just talking about I. Or I and the trainer or I and Doctor Q in his office just off Park Avenue. I'm talking about I and Thou.

How could I say: "Remember me, the good-time Joseph—handsome, horny Joseph? Well, I came up here to do this story about Trappist monks and you'll never guess what happened. Are you sitting down? I know, you know me as that guy in the West Side bars under those suspended jungles of ferns, on the beach at Amagansett with Bain de Soleil simmering on my evenly tanned body. Yes, yes, it's really me but I've been told I should think real seriously about giving it all up, giving you up, dear playmates, and becoming a Trappist monk. What a twist, huh? But, you see, there is a slight problem: I visited this young man today in a loony bin. He thought the same thing. We walked up the same road and look where he landed. Long story. Talk to you again soon when I'm a bit more lucid."

I got to the blank page of Z and closed the address book.

It was now 6:17. Although the temperature inside the cabin was no more than 65, I was sweating again.

Transplant the seedlings. Yes, the broccoli, romaine, and the bok choy were ready. That took exactly thirty-one minutes. It was 6:48.

I needed something in town. Yes, I was sure of it—something I had thought of that morning at Mass. I couldn't remember exactly what it was, but I knew I needed it badly enough to travel the fourteen miles into the town of Falmouth. It was something I would need before the stores opened the next morning. Yes, of course, I would remember what it was by the time I got there.

Falmouth proper is no more than a main street lined with the usual assortment of hardware, food, package and drug stores, two gas stations and a fading but still-imposing old guesthouse, the Hotel Evergreen. Outside the town, to the west, was the Big Barn. It was shaped vaguely like a barn, but there any rustic or rural similarity ended. Made of orange-and-lime-colored prefabricated aluminum, it was certainly larger than ten barns and had a huge plastic farm boy waving to passersby with an arm as thick as a silo. The farm boy was surrounded by a barbed-wire fence. Falmouth High School pranksters had been known to climb into his palm for a ride. And to leave behind long pink objects.

The Big Barn was prominently advertised as a "discount house," but its prices were actually higher than those in the stores in town, which closed promptly at 5:30. I found a parking space near the entrance.

Pushing an empty cart, I rambled from the home-improvement section to hardware, on to housewares, men's clothing, through the record and book department, and for some reason, through children's and women's apparel. The food section, the stove and chain-saw departments, tools, sporting goods. The clock at the back of the store showed 7:30.

I made the rounds again.

I must have been walking even faster on this second pass in great urgency to find an item I still could not remember when I rounded a corner in the drug department. I looked up at the clock. The large hand had not perceptibly moved.

I crashed headlong into a towering display of a new underarm deodorant for women. A pyramid of cans fell all about me, clattering to the tile floor. Even the cardboard display itself, which had been suddenly unbalanced, sagged, teetered, then came down with hundreds more cans.

I grabbed an armful of the light-blue cans, vainly trying to restack them, only to have my frantic effort collapse.

"Handy little devil, aren't you?"

She was backlighted at that moment not with the sun's rays diffused with incense and streaming through a Gothic arch but with fiercely garish overhead lights. But I would have recognized that blond head anywhere. And that particular color of ribbon in her hair. And those freckles.

"I—I—"

Her blue eyes, squeezed almost closed by an enormous grin, waited for my stammering to either stop or lead to some more coherent communication.

"Should we be a good little boy and girl and clean it up, like I was taught—and I bet you were too? Or get the hell out of here and have a beer?"

I looked around me. No one else was visible in the aisles. "Beer," I whispered.

The bar not far down the road was smoky, the jukebox magnificent. The best of the fifties: both "Earth Angel" and "Hey Senorita" by the Penguins, Sam Cooke singing "Summertime," Bo Diddley, Buddy Holly, and that wonderfully sensuous theme song from the movie *Picnic*. It was the music of those febrile high school years when my hormones had finally arrived, working overtime, and *Maryknoll* magazines accumulated in the back of my closet, unread.

Margery Fowler insisted on buying the first round.

In the ghastly light shining down from a rotating Budweiser sign, she drank her Molson from the bottle. Her nail polish matched her lipstick, and the dusting of freckles on her nose converted me in an instant to an appreciation of what I had always considered a facial flaw. She smelled wonderful, a lemony fragrance rounded off with a musky sandalwood.

She had read de Foucauld, some Aelred, but none of me.

She matched my seventeen years of Catholic education and then bested me with a master's degree from Georgetown.

"Oh, there's something to be said for it," she said, referring to our vaunted Catholic faith. "That is, if you end up as Theresa of Ávila or Augustine. But the rest of us? Phooey."

" 'Phooey'? What is that, Aramaic? Farsi? Not my best languages."

"Don't be a wiseass or I'll have one of these good old Vermont boys pound the bejesus out of you." She motioned down the bar to the mountains of flannel-covered flesh that were now turned our way.

"Yes, phooey, of course. But there's something to it, no? I mean, what else is there? I do my books. You, your—?"

"Health food store right now, but I was awfully mainstream before. And, looking back over this life of mine, I never had worse years than when the nuns were telling me to keep my eyes on the altar and my knees together."

"Obeying about neither now, I assume."

I was now finishing my third beer and I could feel the sensation low in my groin that I had all but forgotten about over the past few months. I shifted uneasily on the stool, embarrassed by my blatant come-on. Instead of answering me, she brushed her hand over a bristly haircut I had hastily gotten one day in town, almost jubilant that I had paid six dollars and not the usual New York sixty. She drew her hand back quickly as if she'd been pricked. "I know it's a bit hard to obtain certain services up here, old man, but let me recommend a barber, could I?" she said, laughing.

I looked over the edge—and there was Robert Trumbell looking back at me. Well-intentioned, pathetic, cursed with both a quest and a weakness not under his control.

4. April

"Irons! Irons, Joey!"

"Mort?"

"No, it's Genghis Khan. Of course it's me; did you hear what I told you?"

"Irons."

"Jeremy Irons' agent—on the phone twice yesterday, once over the weekend," Mort was saying. "From London, from Madrid, from a frigging yacht off Morocco this guy's been calling me. From a bathroom on the frigging yacht, no less. Could hear the water running. Just going into the shower. Joey, send me an outline, a treatment, your notes, send me a piece of your brain, fax, disc, anything. Send me something so I can go back to him. Please. Jo-ey. These people don't like to be kept waiting."

"Mort."

"A Brit, Joey. Can you just see it, hear it? Light accent, nothing heavy. When you write dialogue, think Irons, Joey. Are any of them Trappists Brits?"

"Mort."

"Mort, snort; c'mon, Joey, don't use that tone of voice with me. We go way back. I know you like my own son. Better. I talk to you more than I talk to him. Give me an idea of time—a treatment in a couple weeks, screenplay by midsummer? A Brit! The piece should come out in the winter, get the public saliva up. Christmas. Everybody's thinking about this stuff at Christmas. Maybe the magazine will do a two-parter. The book can follow, spring list? Movie in a year with a paperback tie-in.

GOD!—Excuse me, Joey. This package we can get big bucks for. B-I-G. And *now*! We're riding the crest, but the wave breaks and it's over. I like the sound of that. Maybe a book title? Joey, you hearing me?"

"I understand, Mort, but this is working out a little differently. My life—"

"Life, schmife. Material, Joey, think of the beautiful material you got going here. Your life you're not going to lose. But the moment, that we can lose. You're happy?"

"I'm doing better, Mort."

"Well, don't get so happy that you stop writing. You hear me, Joey?"

"You're screaming. You shouldn't have to pay AT and T—you don't need a phone."

"What a comedian. Now, what can I give them when I call back; give me a scene, fax me a scene."

"They barely have electricity up here, Mort. The fax era has not dawned in Falmouth, Vermont. Anyway, I wouldn't know what to write. It's confusing right now, but sometimes I think I'm beginning to sort out what—"

" 'Confusing'! I can't get bupkus for 'confusing.' I can't sell 'confusing' even to the gothics or the pulp westerns paperback houses. Sort out!"

"But that's what I'm trying to do, Mort; things like this take time. Be patient. Please. I won't let you down. Have I ever? Maybe I should send you a CARE package from Falmouth? Maple syrup? Budweiser? Cranberry juice? A smooch to you, too."

The first patches of green came to the hillside behind the cabin, and the filigreed branches of the line of trees, which formed a windbreak for the rolling fields beyond, filled with the tiny dots of buds. I had never really seen spring before, before my spring at Falmouth.

How the low spots thaw first and glisten with moisture, then suddenly turn surrealistically emerald after a single day's sun. Then, like a blush spreading over a cheek, the color suffuses the dull brown terrain, pausing longer at tall stands of lank, dead goldenrod and clumps of witchgrass but inexorably having its way. Life triumphing over death, warmth over the frozen crust of winter, the tiny, unseen seed battling its way through the tangle of matted waste, seeking light and air and freedom to grow. The world exploded in its yearly festival of life, but for me it was the first spring ever.

And as for me as a person, something that had been dormant for too long was also being overcome; new life was taking root. The trip to Bainbridge had shaken me, but it was over now. I had seen close up the utter fragility of a man in the midst of spiritual pursuit. But I was not he. No, I was a man with common sense, balance, intuition—and yet a strange and new (and frightening, when I thought about it) openness. I had no clearer vision of my life. Yet there was—fleeting but recurrent—this tranquillity, this confidence. Why else would spring come just now?

On top of everything else, physically I had never felt better. The way I was eating was pure textbook—a totally meatless (Trappist) diet—and I had acquired a ravenous taste, an absolute need, for fresh fruit and vegetable juices. Carrot, celery, apple, orange, pear, even kumquat, and cabbage and beet. It became part of my daily routine, after Mass and in lieu of breakfast, or after I'd said the hour of None before starting my afternoon's work, to drive south to the small hamlet of Vernon to have a huge glass of the daily special. I looked forward to that tumbler of pure, vitamin-laden liquid. It seemed to invigorate me, refresh me, quiet me, strengthen me on the path to—well, wherever.

That the squeezer, strainer, and pourer of these healthy drinks was Margery Fowler was to me a pleasant bonus, but certainly not the reason I traveled twenty-six miles round-trip, six days a week. Nature's Bountiful Harvest health food store was closed on Sundays.

She was beautiful, but then I'd known beautiful women in my life. If I had been totally honest with myself then, I would have admitted that what made her even more attractive in the midst of a store teeming with red-cheeked, white-toothed, robust, healthily trim women was that she never failed to wear makeup. This included blush, eyeliner, and an eye shadow of an exotic, luminescent teal blue. She was perhaps five feet eight inches tall—let me guess—130 pounds well distributed on her shapely frame. She had a nose that plastic surgeons on the East Side of Manhattan would have loved to use for their brochures ("This, my dear, can be you in six weeks for just twenty thousand dollars"), full lips, and a way of crinkling her cheeks when she smiled that squeezed her crystalline blue eyes into a look of almost childish ecstasy.

When business was slow and the weather good, I would take my daily megadose of natural vitamins out to a bench behind the store where Margery could have a cigarette without drawing disapproving glances from her clientele of health-food zealots.

Our backgrounds were amazingly similar: Catholic schools, the early rumblings of a religious vocation, a failed marriage for her, the years with Felice for me. The seventies and eighties had allowed us to uncork our bottled-up sexuality, but we both had done serious, though too often interrupted, spiritual reading. Sex, booze, junior varsity drugs and Thomas Merton. Great experiences, horrible aftermaths. Diversions, plenty of diversions, running away from ourselves. We checked off item after item, sitting on that bench, howling at our distinct distaste for temperateness.

Both of us had ended up in Vermont—me from New York City and she from Great Neck on Long Island, where she had had what sounded like a very lucrative import-export business—in an attempt, consciously or unconsciously, to find out about a life that was, if not meaningful with a capital *M*, one that at least made a modicum of sense. Margery had become involved in town affairs and had even joined the local volunteer fire department. She joked about it as her "delayed vocation."

"I traded one cloister for another," I said one lushly

warm morning halfway through my third glass of carrot juice. "Yeah, really," I protested as she rolled her eyes. "Or maybe I left one tribe to study another. The literary crowd in New York migrates to the right parties and out to Long Island as sure as the Masai follow the lion. And the cloister part—amen, Sister Margery, it be! After you spend a day alone at the computer, you'll do anything to get out. Gay Talese always said that after a day of writing he'd willingly go to a supermarket opening. But with the Trappists that I'm writing about, all the exits are sealed. Maybe that's why their life is so fascinating to me. How the hell do they do it? I sure couldn't."

"Catholicism, your magic spell—"

"No clichés, please, Miss Fowler; my editors don't permit it."

"Hey, I'm not some Presbyterian; I have the same indelible sign on my immortal soul as you do, Buster."

"Now, to continue our work on the salvation of those immortal souls; if we were only the good Catholics we know we should be, we could be like some modern-day version of Héloïse and Abélard," I said, draining my glass. "How did they say it: 'stirring each other's spiritual passions so that each might find the face of God.' "

"Did you make that up?" she said.

"Honest, no."

"Give me a break."

I saw no reason to mention this part of my monastic day to Father Columban or to tell Margery too much about New Citeaux. Neither had any bearing on the other. After all, Margery was a passing acquaintance, the owner of a store I frequented. I told her in barest—and selective—outline what I was doing at New Citeaux and made those authorial sputterings that the knowing person usually takes to be creative angst. She never pressed for details.

After our fight over the Robert Trumbell visit, Father Columban received me with pronounced coolness, but then his own monastic training overcame what I sensed was a painful memory.

"Joseph," he said at the beginning of our next session, "if a person holds on to hurt, he will live a life in pain. Christ died on the Cross. He didn't *live* on the Cross. Let's put this behind us and go on."

He seemed genuinely pleased with my new optimism and enthusiasm, and noted that I had, as every novice must do, "weathered the storm of the first romance." He smiled as I waxed ecstatic about the miracle of spring, about my magnificently sturdy two-inch-high tomato, pepper, and eggplant seedlings. I even presented him with the first leaves of black-seeded Simpson, a lettuce that I had carefully nurtured to early maturity in the cold frame I had built.

"Best of all, Columban—" I paused, momentarily overcome by the memory of the cool rush of that morning's celery-sauerkraut-beet drink Margery had concocted. "—is that my meditation is coming alive. I think it is, anyhow. I feel I can concentrate on God. Simple, but amazing to me. Nothing special, no fireworks, no fluttering wings of the Holy Ghost, just that deep, real, uncanny but *sure*—that's the word, *sure*—feeling that he's present. Right there in the room. Columban, I'm not playing games with my mind, am I?"

"No, Joseph, you are not," he said softly, closing his eyes. "It is only the monk's utter belief in the personal presence of God within these walls, a God who has somehow revealed himself—in a road sign, in prayer, with a drink of water, in a written or spoken word—that gives any meaning to this life. If it were not so, we would be the greatest fools of all. A barely furnished cell, hour after hour spent in prayer, humble food three times a day, and more sparsely now in Lent—ah, who could take all that? Realistically, who would want to?"

His eyes still closed, he nodded in a slow, steady arc, affirming his own thoughts. It was at times like these that I began to sense that I was communing with a person other than Columban Mellary, OCSO, that the man across the antique refectory table served as but a medium between God and men who wanted so badly to know him. To see a man who had surely known the Divine Lover intimately was at once the greatest encouragement and the most convincing advertisement I could imagine.

My eyes were trained on a spot of sun at the base of the door as Columban, quoting from Aelred, continued on the sublimeness of God's presence in contemplation. Suddenly the spot disappeared. Someone was outside the door. I looked up at Columban and then to the door and he read my thoughts.

He opened the door slowly. It was Brother Polycarp. His arm was raised as if he were just about to knock.

"A call for you, Father," Brother Polycarp announced, pushing open the door as if to expose some illicit act in progress. "I didn't know if I should disturb you." The sleeves of Polycarp's white tunic were rolled up past his elbows and his apron was covered with baking flour.

"Who is it, please, Brother?"

"He said to tell you it was Steven," Brother Polycarp replied stiffly, "just Steven. Don't people have last names anymore? He sounded most ardent."

Father Columban's face was at once and cleanly swept of transcendence. "Tell him I'll call him back," he snapped. "Later—later in the week." He stared stonily out the window. "I'm not to be disturbed. This isn't a parish house."

"Yes, Father," Brother Polycarp said all too sweetly, obviously pleased that he, the humble guestmaster, had ruffled the unshakable composure of the vocation director of New Citeaux.

We sat in an uncomfortable silence for a few minutes, the only sound the ticking of the Louis XIV clock on the mantel, a museum-quality piece that here in the monastery was open to public view and touch. When he turned to me, he had regained his equanimity, as if a toggle that had been tripped by Polycarp had been eased back into place.

"Ours is a difficult life, to be sure," he continued calmly.

"But the bodily mortifications we endure, much more discreetly and humanely done now than before the Council reforms—"

" 'I hold the very opposite and make bold to declare that bodily mortifications for the proper reason and discreetly done, so far from—' " I said, catching the pace of his sentence.

" '—so far from hindering God-sent consolation rather demands it,' " he continued. "Very good, Joseph, Aelred sticks with you, no?"

The look on my face gave me away.

"What is it, Joseph?" Father Columban asked.

"Nothing, no, nothing; mind wandering."

"It's not good to be dishonest. Or to hold back. Whatever you have to say has a place here. Put it on the table, we can discuss it, see what it means."

"Old stuff."

"We change slowly. We have to go back over the same ground again and again."

"For some it doesn't work out, does it?" I said. "I say this not really as a criticism, Columban."

"Joseph, you are quite poor at duplicity," he replied. He sat impassively, waiting for me to fill the silence.

"You know, the fanatics walking around with rosaries around their necks, that kind of thing."

"Joseph." It was at once a final statement and an invitation. "You are playing games with yourself. And with me. What is it?"

"Robert. Robert Trumbell. Why didn't it work out for him? What's the difference between what he was after and what I'm after? Why am I sitting here today, while he's in there?"

Columban looked at me blankly. Then he blinked as if he were not sure what he had heard. His face seemed ready to harden into a stern look of annoyance, even anger. But then it softened.

"How is that dear boy?" he said in a low voice.

"As best I can tell, okay; seems like a good enough place

for a state hospital. Considering his folks don't have money for this sort of thing."

"The staff?"

"A pretty decent director who is also his therapist; the everyday folks don't look the best, but when you make what they do, what can you expect?"

"You know quite a bit, Joseph. You never did fully explain how you came to meet Robert. It was left at 'reporter at work,' before we got rather angry at each other."

"It's not important now. I just did."

"Joseph."

"Yes?"

"How, Joseph, and I would add, *why*?"

I tried to hold Columban off with my stare, but he was much better in such a standoff. "The book you gave me. Aelred's. I wanted to see who was thinking the same way I was. Simple."

"But there was no name in that book."

"The envelope you took out. It left an imprint. I was able to—well, piece the address together."

Columban rose from the table. His lips were pursed; it was obvious he was trying to control himself. He turned his back to me and stood before the ornately carved mantel. He appeared ready to rest his head upon it. Instead, he spun around. "So this is the way you want to play this game, my friend," he said, almost shouting at me. "Your sleuthing around, Joseph. Fine reporting. Never miss a trick, do you?"

"I didn't mean it like that, Father."

"And here I was, about to ask our abbot for permission for you to enter for a month's observorship. 'Fine young man, very accomplished writer. Possibly with a monastic vocation,' I planned to say. I would have looked a bit foolish, don't you think, Joseph? You'd be no more than a literary mole, after your story, and to hell with the reality of the Trappist life."

"It's out of my system now, Father."

"Sounds like you took a laxative."

"You can think what you want, but it's over. I want that side of me to die. My agent loves it, but it doesn't make me very proud. I want you to ask the abbot on my behalf."

"Agent? Abbot? Which master do you want to serve, Joseph? Give me a very good reason, Joseph."

"I don't have one. Except that I can't turn back now. Don't abandon me, Columban. Please."

"Don't be dramatic."

"It's hard to kill the instincts, Father, but, believe me, I'm trying. I want to come into the monastery in order to see if—"

"Go ahead," he said.

"All right—if this is more than a story. If it is the life I should live. I'm a wounded man, Columban; I can't claim that I'm not, but I want to be made whole."

He looked at me as though he were seeing me for the first time. His voice was low, so low I found myself leaning toward him to hear better. "The vast majority of the men who enter Trappist life are wounded, so you are not alone. And more so today, coming from the fractured world they are forced to live in. We do provide a place where a person can become whole. But it demands that you not *seek* this wholeness, for that would be just another act of selfishness. No, the wholeness comes through a total self-less-ness." He pronounced each syllable distinctly. "Living a life for others. And God. But, ultimately, if the person lives our life honestly, his own life will be far richer and fuller than he could have imagined."

My mouth was dry with a stale taste.

"Yes, Joseph, you are wounded, you are sick. It is the sickness of self-involvement, self-interest. The sickness of deceit. Of yourself. Of me, I feel, at times. If you are still fooling me, that is not a major issue. If you are deluding yourself, you alone will continue to suffer. Not because of a sin or purgatory or hell, but because you will hate yourself bitterly for such dishonesty. A man cannot suddenly begin to live life honestly if he is a continual liar."

"I realize that. And I want to come in."

"So be it." There was a finality in his voice, as if it were not so much a wish that had been granted as a sentence that had been imposed.

It has happened. I'm going in. No longer do I have to press my nose to the window. I will know it, experience it for what it is. Firsthand. Everything I have gone through has been worth it. Finally, finally, I have a chance to live the life.

On the last Sunday of the month I felt that with a slip of a mere mortal's tongue, something profound, something prophetic, had been said to me.

I was at Mass with the regular supplicants—among them the pallid boy, the woman with concave buttocks, the one with the garish red wig, plus some recent additions: two sad-eyed older men, perhaps recently widowed, obviously looking for whatever consolation they could find. And the man who had introduced himself to me as Octavius Kiernan. At Communion, as I extended my hands to accept the host, Father Athanasius, whose fifty-seven years as a Trappist had been celebrated the week before, looked me directly in the eyes and said, "The body of Christ, *Brother*."

Brother. Just as he would have said to a member of the community.

I returned to my pew, my body tingling, almost dizzy with elation. I had read of those moments when, after years of struggling, praying, searching, the answer came in the most unexpected way. Father Columban had said it could be a single word. And it was. I felt humbled by this word. *Brother*. Was I mouthing the word when I heard it again?

"Brother?"

The Mass was over and there sitting beside me was Kiernan. There was a dank, stale smell about his clothes, as if he had been caught in a downpour. He was in midsentence by the time his words began to register.

". . . investigation moving along. Amazing stuff I'm generating. Pictures are coming in. More on the way. My people all over working on this. Did you know him at all?"

"Know . . . ?"

"Haskins, Trevor Haskins—young man in his late twenties. Medium height. Glasses. Brown hair. Usually in need of a trim." He pulled some color snapshots from a brown envelope, along with a more formal black-and-white, obviously a graduation photo. "He was quite a fan of this place. Did you know him?"

I had difficulty focusing my eyes: my mind was elsewhere, although the photo was inches from my nose. "Don't think so. Should I have?"

He looked at me, plumbing the depths of my eyes, as a man might do looking into a pool into which he had dropped something. "*Pax Intrantibus.* Peace to all who enter; isn't that the motto of this place?"

"They used that at Gethsemane in Merton's time. Do they use it here, too?"

"You don't know much about Trevor, do you? Just stick around and you'll find out more than you want to know."

"Yes, sure. Thank you," I said as I nodded and slipped on my windbreaker. Kiernan followed me to my pickup. He silently walked beside me, and although I looked over at him a few times, he said nothing. He opened the door for me and then, when I was inside the cab, closed it. When I started the engine, he walked away.

As I reached down for the emergency-brake release, I saw that on the passenger seat there was a folded piece of paper with my name on the outside.

I was puzzled by the contents.

By the time I returned to what I now proudly called my hermitage, the first "Brother" was again foremost in my mind, the second all but forgotten. I stood before the sliding glass door and looked out at the hillside, now so brilliantly green. The holsteins on the horizon feasted on their first living food after a long winter of brown silage. I knew their pleasure, their feeling of rejuvenation, their relief.

I bowed my head, and thanked God for the blessing of

the word that had been directed to me, a word so important and needed. I found myself beginning to kneel, right there, when I heard a foreign sound, so dissonant and jarring I immediately bolted upright.

I hadn't heard the doorbell for months. The local deliveryman knew to enter unannounced through the basement door, which opened out onto the gravel driveway, where I parked my pickup truck.

I opened the door slowly.

"You called, sir."

"Well, I—"

"One quart of orange juice, freshly squeezed. Coffee beans ground this morning, half mocha java, half French roast—wasn't that a combo I once heard from your lips? Danish, unbelievably good for this godforsaken part of the world. A wonderful pâté, even if it is vegetarian. Assorted cheeses; the Brie is sinfully good and runny. A few Granny Smiths, chilled, of course. It pays to know the owner. The keys to the kingdom, so to speak."

"Margery." Was it a question, a statement of fact, a greeting? Was there panic, friendliness, coolness, surprise, in my voice?

"Sunday special. For preferred customers only. Straight to your taste buds from Nature's Bountiful Harvest. Have you eaten yet? Are you hungry?"

Margery Fowler was wearing a Kelly-green turtleneck, an oversized Pendleton plaid shirt that picked up the exact shade of green, and jeans that even in the afterglow of a profound religious experience seemed tighter and more formfitting than those she wore at the health food store.

Her makeup was perfect and freshly done. Her lips glistened with a faint red gloss.

"Are you busy, did I disturb something?"

"I'm starving," I blurted out. "Come in, come in!"

For the next eight hours, our mouths had little rest. Moving from danish, pâté and the cheeses—and the smoked eel she had held back as a surprise—we took on Aquinas, Jacques Maritain, and Scholasticism. After a tossed salad with my fresh arugula and Bibb lettuce and a bottle of Frascati, we moved on to Simone Weil, Bonhoeffer, J. F. Powers, Latin conjugations, and those worn tales of a Catholic education: nuns with steel-edged rulers gouging the skin off young knuckles, absolution denied in the confessional after admitting to experiencing the first French kiss. Thomas à Kempis, Augustine, liberation theology, Leonardo Boff, Küng, Rahner, and some cold chicken breast with tarragon, ratatouille, and rhubarb crisp she had intended to take to her own home rounded out the afternoon.

She was on her way to a doctorate in international relations at Georgetown, she told me, when she took a year off to work in Southeast Asia. As a favor to a group of Franciscan nuns who ran an orphanage in northern Thailand, Margery helped them find an American outlet for their beautiful silk batiks, and soon the word was out on the religious grapevine about her abilities. She found exquisite handicraft items and pressing human needs from Thailand to Singapore, and when she came back to the States, frustrated by the way the good nuns had been treated by some less-than-altruistic buyers, she took over. From Children's Hands proved to be an extremely lucrative store in Great Neck, and Margery Fowler being Margery—the Good Catholic Girl Educated by the Madams of the Sacred Heart—she designated 20 percent of her profits for groups that worked with poor Asian children. "Why not?" she said. "I was marking up one hundred percent; the ladies of the North Shore could well afford to feed children other than their spoiled little Jasons and Amandas."

It grew dark outside, and I put the screen on the wood stove so we could watch the fire as we sipped Romana Sambuca—which we vowed would be the very last thing we would ingest that night. My jaw was tired, not only from eating and drinking and talking but from constantly smiling at Margery.

"Ah, Margery, one of those nice days in a lifetime of agony and struggle, eh?" I sighed, stretching out my legs toward the fire.

"Matter of fact, it is," she said.

She took off the woolen shirt. Her skin's pent-up heat released a pleasant smell of body oil. Patchouli? Or was it sandalwood? She lay back on the couch, her hands behind her head, eyes closed. She had just come back from the bathroom, having applied another flawless coat of lip gloss. I loved the way she followed and filled out her lip line, right up into the dark recesses at the corners of her mouth.

"Now that we're mature, sophisticated, seasoned single people," I said, "having been through our wars and so little peace, we could posit a question: How many days in a lifetime have you had like this—"

She raised her hand.

"Now let me finish. Days like this and then find out that the other person had some glaring, horrible fault? Something you couldn't get by, ever?"

Her eyes opened a slit.

" 'ey, José, wha' you, nuts or sometheen?"

"Come on, you understand. Catholic neurosis. Catholics can't believe it when something goes right. Something so effortless and easy, spontaneous and—God forgive me—fun. We're supposed to suffer, and when we don't suffer we better look hard at what we're doing. It can't be right, as they used to say, 'in the eyes of God.' "

"Such an optimist you are."

"Genes, Catholic genes."

"Bullshit; learned behavior. That can be unlearned. It took me six years and many thousands of my hard-earned dollars paid to a very bald, very rich Manhasset shrink."

"Four years and exactly forty-six thousand on lower Fifth Avenue for me, so there!" I retorted.

She closed her eyes and sank still deeper into the couch. With her long legs extended, she was lying almost flat.

How often I had done this very thing in my days of rage in New York. First, I was my charming, engaging self, bringing my companion of the moment to a point of trust and closeness so that I might, as the quaint old expression goes, have my way with her.

Then, after I had, I'd continue my train of thought, safely distancing myself, pushing away that someone I had just lured so successfully. Yes, it was manipulative and cruel, but I was so confused and hungry for intimacy that I took it like a box off a shelf, devoured the contents, tossed the container away and moved down the aisle. I seemed to abhor stability. Permanence meant deprivation; I was missing something even better. I imagine I was also terrified my game would be discovered and I wanted to be out of town before it was.

But there would be no move on Margery. I was preparing to enter a Trappist monastery. And besides, low in my groin all was calm. To me it was a sign of both God's grace and the sure knowledge that this was a woman in whom I had no sexual interest. The fire was dying down and the licorice-flavored liqueur was warming my chest cavity and making my head light, but that piece of flesh knew that this would not be one of its times to plunder.

"Okay, my dear, twenty questions to prove that we have nothing whatsoever in common," I said.

"Badger on, if you must, José. You Catholic boys! Wacky, the whole bunch of you. Never met a mentally healthy one."

I rubbed my chin. "No easy questions like: 'Do you hang up your towels in the bathroom and pick up your underwear in the morning?' I'm going for the heavies. Then it's your turn."

"You invented this silliness. No questions here. This, dear boy, is a one-way street."

"First, a thing I cannot stand. When riding a bicycle, do you wear a helmet?"

"One of those foolish-looking mixing bowls? Safer, I know, but hell no."

"Ah," I said, exhaling slowly. "You have children someplace?"

"None."

"Gay?"

"Don't think so, but then I've never been asked to indulge."

"Don't shave under your arms?"

She peered down her sleeve.

"Forgive the five o'clock shadow, but I didn't think I'd be inspected today. Of course I shave. What do you want, some feminist gorilla, where every follicle is a political statement?"

"Cats?"

"Good in their place. Buy them the cheapest cat food and never use 'Mitzi doesn't feel good today' as an excuse when you don't want to go out yourself."

"Professional sports, watching of?"

"Once, twice a year for baseball, always at the park. Eat seventeen hot dogs, drink as many beers as you can without wrecking your liver or distending your kidneys. Yell and scream for whoever's losing."

"Watching on television?"

"Must admit I like those clingy, ultrasexy uniforms on the baseball boys but, basically, no. They do too many poor commercials, wear their hair too long to fit with any dignity under a baseball cap and all the announcers have toupees or poorly capped teeth."

"Margery, you stole the crib sheet. How do you know all this? An automatic 'F' for cheating and trying to brown up to the teacher."

"Bless me, Father, for I have sinned. But not in the last five minutes." Her eyes crinkled in that irresistible childish grin.

"Well, my dear, this is where I blow you out of the water. The absolute killer question, guaranteed to show that we have nothing in common and can therefore go plodding and moaning along in our respective lives, keeping this precious day safely encased in the Lucite cube of our memory."

"Just so I won't have to waste any time once proven guilty and banished," she said, putting on her shirt. She flicked on the front-porch light and opened the door. There was a gentle evening breeze up and it blew strands of hair around in front of her mouth.

"This is the all-or-nothing question."

"Oh, Lord, a veiled proposition."

I smiled. "Did I, as Attila the Hun, use that one before? Sounds vaguely familiar; I'll have to check my files. But don't think you can throw me off with SoHo singles-bar talk."

"Proceed." She pulled out her car keys. It was a blue Saab.

"Greatest years of the Cleveland Indians—the idols of my youth—is the topic," I said gravely. "Two-part, seven-answer question. Are you ready? First. They went how many years without a pennant to win it in what year when they had a player-manager at shortstop whose name was what? Then, sweet Margery Morningstar, in what year did they set the American League record for games won, how many did they win, and then name the not one, not two, but three twenty-game winners of that golden season?"

The light had left her eyes. Hers was a look of sudden sadness of which I had not thought her capable, an amazingly profound grief. She fingered the ring in her palm and picked out the ignition key. She turned and looked over her shoulder at me.

I thought she was going to cry.

"Twenty years. 1948. Lou Boudreau. 1954. One hundred eleven. And there were four twenty-game winners, not in '54 when they won the pennant, but in '52: Bob 'Fireball' Feller; 'Burly' Early Wynn; Mike 'The Big Bear' Garcia; and Bob Lemon, no nickname. After all that muscle on the mound, the Indians went on to lose in four straight to the Giants in the '54 series. Amazing but true. Garcia died recently," she said, starting down the stairs. "Nice obit in the *Times*. Ran a cleaning business with his wife. Gerda. What a sweet name, Gerda."

At the bottom of the stairs, she looked up at me. "Joseph, you are quite strange."

5. May

I BEGAN to meditate with a new intensity, spending three half-hour periods a day on the Zen bench, gazing out at a flourishing hillside and, in the midst of the stand of birches, that tall oak, now thickening with leaves. I devoted more time to spiritual reading, delving deeper into Aelred, even stumbling through his *Speculum Caritatis* in the original to test what was left of four years of high school Latin. I began daily *lectio divina*, the ancient practice of "praying" the Scriptures instead of merely reading them. With the advent of warmer weather, there was also an enormous amount of work to do in the garden: tilling the soil, transplanting seedlings, planting early crops like beets, Swiss chard, radishes, spinach, and potatoes that could withstand May's light frost, and building another cold frame, demanded by the abundance of plants I had started from seed.

My day was now structured exactly like that of the Trappists at New Citeaux, a balance of private prayer and meditation, community prayer and manual labor. As Saint Benedict had mandated, *ora et labora*—and no diversions, no late-evening trips into town. Oddly enough, I found that the life of the would-be contemplative was one lived at a whirlwind pace, with literally no time to think. There was no need of thinking, I assured myself. I had done enough of that in my old life, playing mind games, positing this A and that B, hoping to come up with a new and exciting C. Now, the clock was both my liberator and my master. I obeyed without questioning.

I had sublet my New York apartment to a writer friend

with an open-ended verbal lease. He was trying to finish a novel he'd been working on for the past five years. His wife had just filed for divorce; he'd just come back from drying out. I told him to pay me what he could—knowing it would be nothing.

At last, freedom. I've put a lot behind me and for once I am a man willing to be led by something other than my own whims and desires. Father Athanasius called me brother and since that day my spiritual life has taken me to places I, like the armchair tourist, had read of but never visited.

It was slow and murky, but I was beginning to see what Father Columban was talking about. The spiritual life was indeed a kind of love affair, and God was not this distant entity I had prayed to before, escaped from, and rationalized to for much of my life. No, there was far more to him than that, far more real and tangible. Receiving the Eucharist became a daily experience I hungered for, and from which I came away fully fed. As the host dissolved in my mouth, I felt an intimacy with this great power so overwhelming that I wanted to reach out immediately to the poor, beleaguered regulars scattered around me in the visitors' chapel and tell them what it was like when the Lord finally touched you. And that the journey was worth the pain.

I felt stronger, tested, ready to take on, if only on a trial basis, the awesome challenge of the "school of the Lord's service"—Saint Benedict's succinct description of life within a monastery.

"I have loved you with an everlasting love." The words of the hymn—words that had always struck me as so much soppy, wishful thinking—now made complete sense when I heard them at the abbey Mass on the second Sunday of the month. Sitting there in chapel, the sacramental wine coursing its hot, sweet way through my chest, I felt I had a premonition of what the great spiritual writers and Columban

Mellary were talking about. Nothing I could recall matched that sublime feeling. Surely, I had never felt this way with a woman, before, during, or after sex. It was, I concluded, a foretaste of the monastic life Father Columban talked about, which in turn was a foretaste of the eternal joy that man might share with God.

Pascal had said it best—in one of the few quotations of *Bartlett's* I could always recall: "There is in every person the infinite abyss that can only be filled by an infinite and immutable object, that is to say, only by God himself."

Yet, in these days of activity and euphoria, the question did not escape me: Was I still doing a story, or was I researching a way to possibly live my life? There was yet no firm answer, I had to admit, so I usually pushed it to the back of my mind, jotted down my continuing dilemma in a notebook, and went on about my day. After all, I reasoned, I had been here before. Journalists like me, of the lived-experience school, always walked a thin line. Prisoners found themselves identifying with their captors—look at Patty Hearst or the hostages held in Lebanon. Given enough time with bloodthirsty Shining Path guerrillas in Peru or with a ruthless death squad in El Salvador, not a few journalists found themselves understanding them, liking them, even thinking about joining their cause. Once I was removed from my current situation and had time to think about it coolly, with my notebooks and my memory as my guides, I would be able to decide—I always could for a story. I knew this was different, but—

Margery also came into my mind from time to time. I played back the Sunday we'd spent together. And, in doing so, I recalled quite objectively that while I had enormously enjoyed being with her, at no time had there been any hint of arousal. No stirring, no tingling, nothing but the pleasure of good company, which could just as easily have been an eighty-year-old woman. My old, sensual side, which had possessed me for most of my adult life, was finally reined in—and far surpassed by the depth of my newfound relationship with God.

Still, my decision not to make any more trips to Nature's Bountiful Harvest was a necessary choice and the right one. I couldn't be a fool about this.

While he had seemed to be, if not wildly enthusiastic, at least understanding of my April (and, I realize, spring-enhanced) bliss, Columban held me off as the month progressed. I thought the explanations of my inner feelings, deeper understanding of the presence of God and a sense of calm were quite rational. His retorts often made me feel as if I were a babbling maniac.

"Emotion does not rule the inner life, Joseph," he said rather categorically, interrupting as I was speaking one morning. "It is faith, regardless of the seasons of the soul. One of our little mottoes that we keep before our eyes all the time is 'Faith, Not Feeling.' There's talk of tattooing it on our foreheads."

This ravishment would be tempered, I was sure, just as the first flush of new love always subsided. But it was a necessary sign in my own spiritual development—wherever it would take me. After all, even in the secular world, how could you propose to a woman for whom you didn't have such a feeling? I confronted Father Columban with this question. He declined to answer.

For some reason, Father Columban was more interested in trying to discern what I saw in the leafing out of the oak tree behind the hermitage. I was not very good at remembering dreams—even when I was in psychoanalysis—but I was a bit of a shaman, constantly looking for signs and symbols, portents to guide me through life. In this case, it was that oak tree on the hill behind the house. As its bare branches blurred and cleared before my eyes in meditation each morning, I hoped that somehow, some way, there would be a message there for me.

Those buds swelled and opened into small leaves and then grew thicker, into what appeared to be a scraggly beard. Then a single, short line, which later proved to be the nosepiece for a set of small, round sunglasses. A messy head full of curly hair was added overnight. I thought it was Jesus, but Father Columban reminded me there were no eyeglasses then.

"I can almost see it, Joseph," he said.

"Why not come over for lunch—I won't tell on you."

"I would love that, one of your gourmet meals, but I must say no. If I gave in to all the temptations, I'd be outside the monastery all the time. Sunglasses, beard, that hair. Yes," he breathed, closing his eyes.

"Saint Peter, Saint Paul? Moses? No, his beard was longer than this," I said.

"Catholic?" He smiled.

"For some reason I think not. A Jew, I would say."

"Slender, stocky? Short or tall?"

"Thin and short."

"A religious? Someone you know?"

"I seem to know of him, but no, I've never met him. And no, not a religious or a saint or some figure from history. Contemporary, I'm sure of that."

"I was just entering religious life and this young man was so powerful, his songs so right," Columban said, turning his head to the side and tapping his teeth as he tried to resurrect the name. "A singer. Folksinger. Bob . . . Bob . . ."

He was right.

"Dylan."

"Exactly."

"And what does it mean?"

He closed his eyes again and tilted his head back so far that the hood of his cowl seemed to engulf him as he thought, a sort of spiritual shield against the earth's rays so that the Divine might come through unfiltered. "Dylan, Dylan." The words were whispered as a password might be, through a crack in a door, so that it might be fully opened. "Dylan. What comes to mind?"

"All right, the sixties," I began. "The world discovering folk music, pot, and unfettered sex. Assassinations, burning cities, Vietnam, college kids going bonkers, acid trips, the Pill. Me, college student and the young writer, getting it all down. And doing absolutely nothing about anything. But Dylan? Dylan? Troubled. Never sold out. The acclaim accorded him probably never matched how important he was. His albums rarely made the charts, but many of his songs are classics. What does all that prove?"

"Deeper, Joseph, deeper," he whispered.

"Lived in Greenwich Village—I did for a while—Woodstock, a couple of marriages, some kids. Aha! A convert, wasn't he, Columban? Didn't he become a Christian a while back? 'Everybody's Got to Pay Somebody'—great song from that album after he came over to our side." I took a sip of coffee, sure I had it. "Our lives paralleled in a way. Trying to stick to some sort of vision. Pretty bumpy road for both of us. Apparently I'd . . ."

"Go on, Joseph." The tone of his voice had changed.

My pause wasn't long. "Not that he was any model of virtue, because he wasn't. He was vain—arrogant—did too many drugs and roadies; the list of excesses goes on. But the man was after something. Columban, he explained a generation to itself. Their pain was his pain, their struggle to be just and good and true to themselves was his struggle."

Father Columban's head moved slowly forward, out of the cowl's shadow. He came face-to-face with me. His stare was so intense as to be frightening, the way it seemed fixed not at all on me but on an object beyond the back of my head.

"And you? Is that what you want to do?"

"Me?" My voice had gone up an octave. "I . . . I . . ."

"Perhaps you hark back to Augustine or to, more recently, dear Father Louis—Thomas Merton. What if the talents God has given you could be employed to write about the struggles of the soul of your generation, the Promethean battle to live a decent life in this self-involved, heathen time? Couldn't you do that? Faith? What has happened to good old-fashioned faith in God? There's inspiration in your heart, Joseph, isn't there? And your thoughts could be tempered in the cloister. 'Where silence reigns, prayer is eloquent.' The wild uninhabited valley of the river Anio where Benedict sought his God, at Clairvaux for Bernard, those caves for the Desert Fathers. Could they think or pray in the crammed cities? Jesus Himself, for forty days and forty nights.

"Yes, Joseph, by living composed and quiet, in community, you could inform a new generation about contemplation, about the beauty and balance of a life built around the Rule of Saint Benedict. Isn't that what you've experienced in your days in the hermitage? You could bring cool water to people dying of thirst. And it would be no intellectual exercise, would it? Nothing trivial; the pursuit of God is not like that."

He placed his palms down on the table and rested, his eyes still upon me, but now beckoning more than demanding. I could feel the pulse in my neck, in my thumbs; a quiver ran down the side of my leg.

"To be honest, right now I'm just trying to live a life. Not live it through my writing. I thought I wanted to leave my writing behind. Columban, you're giving me spiritual whiplash."

"But, Dylan," he breathed. "Dylan. Had he written those songs but never sung them, published them, who would have known?"

"Well, I guess," I said with an expectancy that even as it escaped from me reeked of disingenuousness, "maybe I could do that. Tell the world about what was happening in the monastery, what was happening within me—"

"Then the vision in the tree is a false god, Joseph!" Columban said, his voice suddenly cold. "A road sign for a fool like you to guide the way. The wrong way."

"Columban." I had no other defense but the sound of his name.

The chilliness in his voice now turned to derision. "You used the words 'I thought I wanted.' Good God, Joseph, you can't build a life on such flimsiness. Again, Joseph, you have opted for a stage on which to present your little play of life. You can have that if you wish, but God is not with you, nor is he in your audience. He stands out by the stage door, in the darkness, far from the bright lights, waiting. Waiting with no drama, in utter simplicity."

"Dammit, Columban, you urged me on, encouraged me. You coax me to crawl and then you step on my fingers."

"Me? Encourage? No, Joseph, the vocation director of a Trappist monastery can do no such thing. Direct, perhaps, channel, *test*, but never encourage. So let me direct you— back to something else you said. About your writing life. How you were great at getting the facts down, but never did anything about them." He was rising out of his seat. "Do something about it," he said. "That's all. Or you will die as you have lived—"

I awaited his judgment.

"—a middling writer." He paused. "If you want to understand the Trappist life, be prepared to give yourself up so as to be nothing more than an anonymous monk, lost to the sight of the world, never to be heard from again. Only then can you know this life. Or, you can go on, chronicling your every breath and movement and observation—and you will drown in a sea of petty perceptions." He adjusted his huge belt buckle to the side and straightened his black scapular. "May God's grace be with you, Joseph—you are in my prayers constantly."

The encouragement, the seeming progress, then the deflation. A testament to my utter shallowness. Can I keep at this? Should I? Who is fooling whom? Of course I'm going on with it. I must do whatever it takes to keep my mind both clear and open. Meanwhile, I've got to give myself over—honestly—to the mercy of God.

If I had been assiduous both in my work and in my prayer life before that meeting, after it I realized I could do much more. I didn't know I had such capacity for so much of both the *labora* and the *ora* that Saint Benedict had found necessary for a balanced life. My garden, which was largely planted early in the month, except for tomatoes, peppers, and eggplant, covered almost an eighth of an acre. It required only a few hours a day, so when I heard at the farmers' exchange that my neighbor, a fine old Yankee grandly named W. Percival Standish, had suffered a mild heart attack and had had a pacemaker implanted, I gladly offered to help him so that his spring planting of corn and alfalfa would not be delayed any further.

I drove a tractor for Mr. Standish—a skill I learned, to my astonishment, quickly—every morning or afternoon, never missed my three meditation periods, read Aelred and prayed the Scriptures, started to study Greek, and was a faithful attendee at Lauds, conventual Mass, and evening Compline at the monastery. One area, besides my sleep, suffered. There seemed to be no time for shopping or the preparation of food. I ate spinach, lettuce, and kohlrabi from the garden, mostly by the handful, flavored only with a quick sprinkling of salt. My jeans began to hang on my hips. When I weighed myself near the end of the month, I was thirteen pounds below my normal weight.

Of course I tried to put Columban's words out of my mind—so that I might put myself completely in the hands of God—but I couldn't. Columban's words pounded in my ears; they haunted me. And spurred me on.

The look on his face, the tone of his voice, the prayer he offered as he left the room that day—as if I were dying of cancer—drove home the ignominy of secular mediocrity. What could be worse than to be a "middling" writer when the opportunity was at hand to live the life of a monk for even a short while, a monk who, even if the least of the brethren at New Citeaux, would surely have lived his life for a heroic ideal? Was it not better to die failing at some great quest than to have lived in the pursuit of fleeting journalistic fame?

Columban Mellary was no longer the gently chiding spiritual director; he was my Grand Inquisitor. Although I tried not to let the choices that he had delineated possess me, day after day they did.

I was proud of one accomplishment that I could not tell

him about. The note that had been left on the seat of my pickup that morning I talked with Kiernan had been followed by another, which was even more enticing. The second note confirmed to me that the writer was Brother Polycarp; the distinctive green ink and the broad stroke of a thick pen that were characteristic of the notes and schedules posted in the guesthouse betrayed him. Out of his obvious dislike for me and suspicion of my motives, Brother Polycarp was offering the seduction of diversion, the seduction of evidence, of fact. He was singing the siren's song and he knew that I would be tempted to follow this melody to its source.

I placed both notes in my wallet, wanting the temptation to be with me each day, a sort of reporter's hair shirt, a constant irritant. But each day I said no to them.

It was an unusually warm May for Vermont and my broccoli and cauliflower leaped from the rich soil. Rows of beans and spinach glistened in the morning dew. Six types of corn, of varying maturity, assuring a steady crop from July through September, sprouted almost to the seed. I had an admirable range of lettuces, and some wonderful bok choy was almost ready to harvest. I could have put my favorite Bleecker Street Italian greengrocer to shame. I continued working for Mr. Standish, whose offers of pay I refused. I told him that what I needed was his prayers. And a steady supply of cow manure. Only nightfall forced me indoors and, soon thereafter, to bed. I was totally exhausted and hoped for my few hours of sleep to be deep and untroubled. I was successful one night out of two.

Near the end of the month, on a particularly balmy evening—temperatures had hovered in the mid-seventies all day—I was burying rotted manure and mounding my cantaloupe and watermelon hills when I sensed I wasn't alone. I looked up.

On the far side of the garden, through the blur of sweat streaming into my eyes, I could see someone near the old

fencing where I'd planted my snow peas. I had no handker-
chief, so I used my sleeve to clear my vision.

I was exhausted, as usual, but so exhausted as to be op-
timistic that this would be one of the peaceful nights for
sleep. And so my first reaction was irritation when I saw
that it was Margery. She plucked a few pods off the vine,
seemingly unaware that she was in my yard, in my presence, after we had not seen each other in nearly a month.
I leaned on the handle of my shovel and waited. I said
nothing and neither did she.

She bit down on a succulent pale-green pea pod and
started toward me.

I had never seen her walk before, not at this distance
anyhow. She negotiated my raised beds and neat rows of
vegetables with the grace and perfect posture that well-bred
and well-schooled women possess. Each footfall on the
bumpy pathways did not disturb her upper body; she
seemed destined to follow a preordained course to me, regardless of what lay between us.

The wind was from the south that evening, unnaturally
warm. Her fine blond hair blew in strands onto her face.
The peas eaten, she refastened a bone barrette to keep the
hair out of her mouth. She was wearing tailored cream-
colored slacks, a gauzy Indian shirt and a single strand of
something green—beads or stones I couldn't tell—and a serene smile. As if she had something wonderful to tell me.

In the quickly fading ocher light of sundown, as she
came closer, I could make out her lips, glistening from a
fresh application of gloss.

And her bare nipples beneath her shirt.

I wore battered sneakers, shorts hastily cut from a pair of
jeans I'd torn on a barbed-wire fence, and a tar-stained
T-shirt (I'd promised myself each washing would be its
last). I hadn't shaved in four days.

"The Lord be with you, holy man," she said briskly.
"Nice peas there."

"And with your spirit, queen of the juices."

"More trivia today to fend off the world?"

I rubbed my grizzly chin. "I can play rough."

"Try me."

"Emil Bossard."

She stopped short some five yards from me and looked sadly at her hands. Then, with a devilish smile, said reverentially: "The American League's greatest grounds keeper. With Jack Grainy doing play by play on WERE radio, brought to you by 'POC, The Standard Beer,' a significant number of which—they say—old Jack used to get down his gullet in nine innings. Thank God we both adored the Cleveland Indians. Bill Veeck, Satchel Paige, and the midget nobody could pitch to."

"Smartie. Say, I'd offer you something, but I haven't been to the store in a couple weeks. Planting time, this neighbor of mine needed some help; I've just been going at a hell's pace and—"

"My, my, what a good Catholic boy you are, José. Guilt always and excuses. I don't have any POC for old times' sake, but I do have some Molson's Golden Ale, which you seemed to favor that night after you played bulldozer in the deodorant aisle."

"Not cold Molson's, of course?"

"Thirty-eight degrees. Two six-packs. All that's needed is an opener. Thank God they never went to twist-off caps. Some things are sacred, no? My religiosity amazes even me."

I ran my tongue along my lips, coated with a fine layer of Vermont dust. I tried to swallow but I had no saliva. My mouth had gone dry.

"Follow me."

I insisted I shower and shave, having a beer meanwhile, and when I came out of the bathroom, the fatigue was gone. Margery had brought along some records, a marvelous mix: the Mamas and Papas' greatest hits; Patti Austin's first album, before she went disco; "Dream Weaver," by a British rocker, Gary Wright, who made that one tremendous album and was never heard from again; Lionel Richie, Linda Ronstadt, and, for a kicker, Billie Holiday. She had rifled through my virtually bare refrigerator and depleted cupboards and had miraculously concocted a tangy horse-radish dip, and found an unopened box of crackers and a can of smoked oysters. A mound of New Citeaux's fine incense, which I often used for my Zen sittings, was smoldering in a saucer.

"Do this professionally?" I said as I ran the towel through my wet hair.

"Don't be a wiseass," she said, pouring a beer into a glass she'd frosted for me. "So, why did you run away?"

"Get right to it, don't you?"

"Think journalists have a corner on getting to it? C'mon, I'm waiting."

"Just got busy—spring planting, the story. I wasn't running from anything. Why should I?"

She held her glass in the air and looked over the rim at me. She took a healthy swig. "For a graduate of Saint Procopius grade school, you lie just like a goddamned Protestant. Didn't those Vincentian nuns teach you anything?"

"Okay, kiddo, you read my bio. Now what do want from me?"

"I think you're cute."

"And so are you and I'm sure Héloïse and Abélard didn't exactly hate looking at each other."

"You can be holy and human, too. I'll bet your name-sake, good old Saint Joseph, nuzzled up to Mary every once in a while."

"I'm not so good on doctrine; I wouldn't know."

I felt dizzy from the beer; I was already started on the third and I had barely eaten that day.

"What's the story, José, I mean what kind of guy—?"

Her words floated by. My stomach was starting to sour. Why had I asked her in? What was I doing? Especially now. Why had I put myself in such a situation? Could a couple of beers and the presence of a woman still—? I didn't want to ask myself the rest of the question.

That boyish, winning smile, the weapon and mask I'd used so effectively in so many situations, left my face.

"If I can be dead serious for a while, I'll tell you. And you have to be serious, too. And then, Margery, I've got to get to bed."

She nodded. She leaned back on the couch. Her nipples pressed against the nubby cotton fabric.

"I told you the basics the first night. You have before you a guy who's had these spiritual groanings all his life and usually swallowed Tums or Alka-Seltzer, or Chivas Regal on the rocks and thought he had a cure. Down deep I always felt I should be about something bigger than this writing of mine and all my life I've been running away from it. Marriage—if not on paper, almost as real—to Felice, my brilliant career, screwing around. Various cures, various games to keep myself amused. I'm tired of running from the Hound of Heaven. I came up here to do this story, but—well, it's gotten to be more than that. A lot more."

She closed her eyes. "Exactly *how* much more?"

"I want to take a look at Trappist life."

"Like visiting the aquarium, that kind of look?"

"Margery."

"Joseph. Well, drop the other shoe, Buster."

"Okay. At first, I was doing a story about the Trappists—I really wanted to taste and feel what their life was about, but I had a shield in front of me: the reporter's pad. But something got out of control, went off the tracks. I'm beginning to wonder if I'm not just writing a story anymore."

"Fill in some blanks for me," she said without inflection.

"Margery, you've got to understand that how I am toward you has nothing to do with *you*. It's me. As a matter of fact, you are an excellent-looking woman, very hip on the Catholicism we can both laugh and cry over—obviously a fine person. I can still taste the pâté, for God's sake. But if I continued this in its logical manner, you'd be just the latest in a long line. It would be great fun, terrific pleasure, and then you and I would be right back where we started. I've jumped from one thing to another, filling my life with what felt good for the moment. I've got to find out what's right for me. Does this make sense to you?"

She said something so softly I had to ask her to repeat it.

"God wants what you want," she said in a whisper.

"Nice and neat. See, that's the problem! Exactly the problem." I found I was shouting. "Like all those fake swamis in their Rolls-Royces, est nonsense, Robert Schuller, Norman Vincent Peale, some no-fault school of quote relevant unquote belief system. Belief system! The intentional life asks for more. You know that. It requires real discipline. You don't just lie back on your couch and think: Let's see, what do I want today? God, you listening? Soon as I decide I'll let you know.

"I'm reading our mutual friend Aelred of Rievaulx," I continued, "and just this morning he says something like: you've got to be stripped like Christ, laid bare. Clean house; everything comfortable and familiar has to go. Or else you'll cling to the old stuff like some drowning rat. When you try to live and breathe asceticism, you find it's absolutely incompatible with the life of mediocrity you lived before. I know from mediocrity, but more on that later. Point is—I'm beginning to get a taste of something. Life. A life that is so sweet and full you wonder why you messed around with anything else. That's what it's about! Look, I'm unsure about it too, but I've got to give it a chance. I don't know what I want, but—"

"What you want is change. Stability terrifies you. Even as you seek stability, *that* is the change!" Her voice had gone up even higher in pitch and mine followed.

"Where did you get that from, the latest pop-psychology book? The best-seller list? I expected better of you."

"Through the magic of information retrieval at my friendly local library I know a bit about you, Buster. Want facts to back up my analysis?"

"Spare me."

"José, I'm sorry. I didn't drive over here to be belligerent." She slid over to the end of the couch until our knees touched. "I just saw something in you I liked, something I rarely find in a man. So, I'm not shy; I'm interested. But when you get that tone of voice like the clouds are going to open or you go on with this stupidity about putting yourself away in some cloister with a bunch of monks being the only way, it just sounds, well . . . like a kid talking. Foolishly."

I could feel the skin on my face heating up.

" 'ey, José?" she said softly.

"I'm right here, listening to myself being dissected and laughed at— What?"

"What's driving you so wild? Why are you after this thing with clenched fists and this fierce face? You're already doing a lot of good in the world. Your books are great! These aren't sleazy romance novels you're writing. C'mon. Even in grade school, they didn't say it had to be like this. Or did I get the wrong order of nuns?"

"I wouldn't—"

"Don't be defensive, please, just tell me honestly."

"It's simple. I don't have any of the answers, but for the first time, I'm finally asking real questions. Do you know how important that is?"

"Then why is your body screaming? You look like hell, even after a shave. You've got bags under your eyes, you—"

"It's the price you pay. Seeking the face of God is not a leisure-time activity."

"Forget God's face. Look at mine."

I was sitting in a chair at the end of the couch. Margery got up and leaned over me. Then she kissed me. So lightly I'm sure my pursed, angry lips neither yielded nor acknowledged. She drew back and, searching my eyes, ran her fingers over my chin, then up into my hair. She kissed me a second time, lightly but longer.

I took her hand and, for an embarrassing moment, did nothing more. Her eyes never left mine. She had made her offer clear and was waiting for my response.

I drew her down into my lap.

She curled up comfortably, putting both arms around my neck. She rested her head on my shoulder. The sweet, fresh scent of her hair rose gently into my nostrils. She rubbed her lips gently across my cheek.

She smelled so wonderful this close, that intoxicating amalgam of soap and shampoo and one of those fine lemony oils she sold at the health food store. The skin of her forearms was silken beneath my cracked, callused palms. My hands, moving toward her shoulders, seemed to have little hooks on them, catching on the nubs of her cotton shirt.

I touched her neck tentatively, almost expecting her to recoil. I kissed her neck, nudging aside her shirt and slowly traced her collarbone. Then, her mouth, her nose, her forehead. The kisses were as tender as those rendered to me, not with heated lust, but with passion nonetheless—a rare, finely honed, muted, restrained surge of the purest passion.

From deep within me, the orphaned animal, the motherless child, the abandoned, lonely one, cried out with such a painful wail I'm sure I let out a sound.

I was an old man, too long without being touched.

I was de Foucauld in the desert, tasting cool water; Bonhoeffer in jail feeling the transcendent presence; Merton before the giant statues at Polunnaruwa; Wesley at Aldersgate; Saint Theresa at prayer; Aelred in his cell, finally *knowing*.

I cradled her breast in my hand, restraint leaving me, hungry now, and coaxed it toward my face, toward eyes filling with tears, toward my mouth, choking with its first sob.

How long I cried in her arms, I can't recall. Margery held me close, stroking my head. The Madonna and her bleeding Son.

"It's all right, José. I'm here. I'm here. I'm with you."

I was swallowed up by the sweet smell of this good woman, enveloped in her firm embrace; flooded out of prison by my own tears.

I felt as though my body were being stretched on a rack.

My feet were bound tightly, my shoulders being wrenched away. Or was the pull greatest from the middle of my body? Perhaps both head and feet were anchored, one by conscience, the other by the solidness of the earth the hermit had tilled and tended so faithfully.

My throat finally cleared so I could speak. "I'm such a pathetic . . . so needy."

She lifted my head from her breast so I would have to face her. "I know what you need."

It was the voice of that substitute in the sixth grade at St. Procopius, the first secular teacher I'd ever had in a classroom. She said I could come back in when I wasn't picked for stickball, and we could play a game together, just she and I.

The voice of a friend.

I slept through Lauds and Mass—not to mention a sunrise meditation period, not stirring except to find another way of holding Margery. Or pressing more of her body to mine: back, side, front. I wanted to touch all of her at once. She made an amazing omelet out of a few eggs, desiccated onion, wrinkled green pepper, and a blend of spices. For the occasion, I even broke out the espresso maker I'd brought from New York and we drank frothy mugsful of cappuccino, thanks to the creamy, unpasteurized milk Mr. Standish insisted I take each day I worked for him.

We talked nonstop, except to eat; played records, danced. When I saw the red Ford Bronco of the rural mail lady, Margery and I, arms locked around each other's waist, walked down the winding, rocky drive to the road. It was almost as if we feared the other might disappear if physical contact was lost for even an instant.

A form letter was there from *The New York Times*, taking me to task for canceling my subscription and alluding to what I was missing. My Troy Bilt hiller-furrower had been shipped and would be here in time for mounding my potato plants. A postcard from Greece carried a signature I couldn't quite make out. And then there was a letter I took to be some form of advertising, with a Falmouth post office box as a return address.

Somehow assured I wouldn't evaporate, Margery let go of me and walked ahead, picking bearded irises that had come to blossom along the drive. I opened the last letter.

I was reading it when Margery, with a practiced curtsy, presented me with the bouquet. I forced a smile, which she immediately saw was bogus. She asked if anything was wrong and I said no.

"Don't be afraid, José; everything's going to be fine. I know the feeling. After a wonderful time, too good a time, it's only Catholic to think it's going to go away. If it felt that good, it had to be wrong. We're mature adults. It's just fine, don't tax that overworked conscience of yours."

Fine. Yes, everything would be fine. I repeated that to myself.

I folded the letter from the abbot of New Citeaux— telling me that I had been accepted for a month's observorship in August—and shoved it into a back pocket.

6. June

With such things did I find rest . . . but all was labor lost
and lamentation and grief and pain . . . there I lay, filthy
and bewildered, prisoner in chains, stuck fast in the
clinging mire of sin, in thrall to the burden of long habit.
So when I came to myself . . . I was horrified at my con-
dition. I was disgusted with myself.

—AELRED OF RIEVAULX

FOR two people who had first encountered each other in
church, between them having been graced with thirty-five
years of solid Catholic education, and to whom the spiritual
dimension of life was, at a minimum, a topic still worthy of
consideration, Margery Fowler and I each had a remarkably
heathen past. Early one evening as we lay on the couch,
scantily clothed, drinking brandy Alexanders, we confessed
our worst excesses to each other. And then took strange
comfort that my aged friend and mentor Aelred had walked
on the wild side as well.

"If I could have just kept going, it would have been fabulous," Margery said, gazing out at the hillside, brilliantly
illuminated by a full moon. "I was having a great time; it
was fun being that bad. But, dammit, then I'd wake up to
some face I couldn't call by name. Or look in the mirror at
an unrecognizable, bloodshot hag." She shuddered with the
memory.

"We both should have had at least a taste of it when we
were young, like everybody else," I said. "Not in our thir-

ties. I can't imagine that Protestants and Jews went as nuts as Catholics in the Me and post-Me generations."

"Sure, they did. But what do they know from mortal sin?" Her tone of mock indignation was on key. "AIDS? Nothing by comparison. The fires of hell, peeling flesh, the agonizing screams from the netherworld. Forever! Joseph, back then, it was not the pursuit of goodness, it was avoiding rank terror. Who wanted a one-way, nonstop ticket to hell? How old were you before your virginity was offered up on the padded altar of somebody's backseat? I was a ripe old twenty-five."

"Well, I wasn't that nerdy!"

"Well, excuse me, sorry I was the latest of the late bloomers in the sexual revolution. But let the record show that the dew on this blossom was still damp and much in demand when a certain Mister Honey Bee—Catholic, of course—buzzed in for the first taste of the nectar."

"Get my notebook; can I use that?"

"Is that the kind of stuff you write?"

"Why is it that Catholics are always last for the best stuff? You know, even when I saved all my candy during Lent, I still couldn't touch it on Easter Sunday. I wanted to give a little more, be a little bit better, show God I really cared. I waited until Monday, ate everything and puked my guts out."

"Joseph, you outdo me. I was a Sunday-afternoon girl— late Sunday afternoon."

Insights from a newfound fellow traveler. Strangely, Margery confirms what I'm after. I'm not the only one who thinks this way. It's a kind of reality testing. Very important when reality seems so far away. I'm lucky I met her just now. Very lucky.

Why, during those weeks, didn't I tell Father Columban about Margery or say any more to her about New Citeaux? After I had been so honest at the start of that teary evening, I had clammed up about the monastery and she never brought it up. Underneath it all, we each knew that to talk about the monastery and what had been my growing interest in monastic life was to open up a subject that, like the fox in the henhouse, had no place. Yet, I persisted in this stupid charade, lying even to my notebooks—notebooks whose very existence and continuing entries proclaimed my duplicity. In moments of clarity—and they were few—I asked myself why I had said nothing to the man who had become my spiritual guide or to the woman with whom I was falling in love when they would eventually have to find out about each other?

The answer was obvious; I knew that. I was having an affair with each of them, yet only one of them could exist in my life. One of them would have to be put aside if I embraced the other fully.

Perhaps even more than I owed Margery an explanation, I needed to tell Father Columban what was happening. But I couldn't bring myself to say anything about her in our weekly conferences. My carefully rebuilt life began to go to hell and I was frankly ashamed of myself. Spiritual discipline had evaporated: there was little time for meditation, less for private reading; I attended Mass only when Margery didn't stay overnight. My most extended Scripture reading occurred when she and I read the Song of Songs aloud, alternating chapters, savoring the juicy lines. I read Aelred late at night, sporadically, when alone and tired. Like a needle stuck in a groove, I seemed to read the same page over and over, unable to move on.

My horticultural life suffered parallel damage. Bales of spoiled hay, which I'd gotten from a pile next to the monastery garage and had used for mulch, turned out to have been sprayed with a broad-spectrum herbicide for some sort of agricultural test. Dozens of eggplant, tomato, and pepper plants slowly withered and died before I discovered the deadly mantle with which I had cloaked them. Gypsy moths descended and literally ate Bob Dylan's face out of the oak tree on the hill. Temporal metaphors for a spiritual life laid waste.

Dying plants and bare branches—so much for new life. Poisoned straw, pestilence and a Manhattanville graduate, magna cum laude ... grim reapers all.

Mort called, following up on a CARE package he'd sent from Zabar's, the contents of which provided Margery and me with a wonderful weekend of indulgence.

"What about that Saint André—triple crème, Joey!—is that stuff beautiful or not?" was his opening question. When Mort started a conversation with food, I knew I was a source of enormous frustration and irritation to him. And that business would quickly follow.

"And those bialys—crisp, onion smeared all over." I waited. "The Nova was salty, but the smoked whitefish! The whitefish, Joey! Beautiful. Even if I wasn't Jewish, I'd be Jewish for fish like that." It would not be long now. "Speaking of religion"—it was coming—"how is my favorite holy man up there? Need more stuff? I can send you a package every week. Express mail. The bagels will still be warm. Joey? Joey, are you listening to Uncle Morty down here? You're making it hard on me, Joey—"

I told him to hold on, the time wasn't yet right. What I meant by that I have no idea. I didn't say that I wasn't being honest with Margery or Father Columban or even with Mort. I was playing it both ways.

"Irons, Joey, Irons—"

"Irons, Mort? You need somebody to replace your French laundry?"

"Don't make jokes, my boy—make tracks. Make book."

But my greatest deception by far was with Father Columban. What could I say to him? Could I tell him that I *wanted* to drift along in this pleasant haze of good sex and fabulous companionship? Could I confess that August first, the day I had been given to begin my month at New Citeaux, was no longer a day I looked forward to but one I dreaded?

I was happy in the real world for the first time in a long while, and, like a selfish child, I was afraid to share it with anyone, anyone but Margery, fearing it would be snatched from me.

When I finally suggested on the last Wednesday of the month that we go to Mass together, Margery was less than enthusiastic. I thought it simply the reaction of what we used to call a "fallen away" Catholic, one burned by the years of indoctrination.

"It's a great place—Catholicism at its best. I'll show you around the grounds, gorgeous setting," I said.

"If this is a bummer, I'm going to become a Unitarian. Willing to have that on your conscience?"

"Shake, Manhattanville. Stand by."

I didn't know how I would feel having her there in the pew where I had spent so much time churning over and assessing the fragments of my life. But, as the monks chanted the Psalms at Lauds and then began the Mass in honor of Saint Lutgard, a venerated Cistercian nun, I found myself extraordinarily happy. I was certainly distracted, but, I thought, what of it? Margery was right: I had spent too much of my life with a solitary, white-knuckled approach to religion. And here I was, worshiping my Lord with a kindred spirit, a woman who shared my beliefs and who understood what the Grand Pursuit was all about. Her frequent soft touches and sighs of accord at certain lines in the readings and Gospel let me know she wanted to communicate her thoughts with me. But more often, I sensed, she was alone in her own world, working out her own life, her own relationship with our elusive God.

I watched her during Mass, sneaking sidelong glances as one might do in a car when bringing home the intended to meet the parents. We were at that crucial juncture in a relationship: to see if what we had developed in private could travel.

Many of the abbey regulars were there that morning, and so was Octavius Kiernan, whom I had not seen for a few months. I had not remembered him as an especially fastidious man, but now he looked totally unkempt. The narrow portion of his tie, poorly knotted and terribly stained, hung over his belt. The collar of his once-white shirt was long past mere yellowness. And his trench coat looked as though it could have lived one of its many lives as a cleaning rag. He was sitting a row ahead of me and to the right, out of my sight line with the altar, and I thought it mere coincidence that the few times I glanced at him he was looking at me.

At the end of Mass, I could tell Margery was eager to leave, so I didn't linger once Father Ambrose and the two concelebrants left the altar.

"They look so pathetic," she said as we walked along the circular drive in front of the abbey church.

"It's not such a bad life, the hours are a bit rough, the diet is heavy on the starches, but—"

"I'll leave the holy monks for later consideration. The lay people in there. Religion takes such a toll."

"I guess it's all they have and thank God for that, don't you think? We knew these pious ones in grade school. The ones who wore those woolly little scapulars so they could play hair shirt? It's not all that weird. Hey, the first time I saw you was right here."

"A visitor, only as a visitor. Heard about their stained glass. I'm not exactly what you would call a regular Mass goer these days. On sabbatical."

"Sins forgiven. Three Hail Marys. C'mon back."

"They'd do better to chuck the whole thing. That skinny woman in the first pew; did she have polio or something? Her body is so contorted. She ought to go out and find some guy to snuggle with. Get the tension out. God would approve, I'm sure of it. I trust the Old Boy has a sense of balance."

"You're a better confessor than I am. Just the right penance. I'll be back."

"Too many people put everything into religion and forget their basic human needs."

"Are we getting personal here?"

"No, José, I wasn't even thinking about you then."

The mild morning wind coming from the south kicked up, blowing strands of hair across Margery's face. She slowly brushed them aside while looking at me. How I loved that gentle sweep of her hand, so sensual in its ineffectualness as the wind whipped filigrees of hair over her skin. She in turn was studying my face, and seemed less trustful of her instincts now that she had taken a step into my world and had seen some of my acquaintances.

"The Church fosters their sickness," she said. "This place, too."

"Sickness? Come on."

"Dependency, neurosis, that terrible Catholic sadness. I couldn't imagine anybody in there with a smile on their face."

"Hey, I like this place. I need it; stop beating it up." My tone was light, jocular.

"You're another case. I'm not sure about you." She smiled finally and, grabbing my arms, pulled me close to her.

"Now for the grand tour—at least those places where women are allowed," I said.

"Spare me. God forbid their pious eyes should fall upon a mere female."

"Excuse me, sir." The voice was from behind me.

I turned and was no more than a few feet away from those mournful, bloodshot eyes. In the bright sunlight, the color of his shirt collar was close to khaki.

"I need to talk to you," he said. He smelled of alcohol.

My first impulse was to get rid of Octavius Kiernan, but as that thought came into my mind, I quickly pushed it aside. I couldn't treat a fellow traveler so poorly. I probably looked as bad in my worst days at New Citeaux. And there was another reason, probably stronger. I didn't want to feed Margery's fantasies about the deficiencies of the community of worshipers at New Citeaux.

"I'm showing this lady around—maybe some other morning?" I said with forced cheeriness.

"It's about a friend of yours, the Good Shepherd up here." He nodded toward the monastery buildings.

"The Good Shepherd?"

"The famous vocation director, Columban Mellary. One of his little boys, aren't ya? *Ovis errans in eremo?* A lost sheep wandering in the wilderness?"

"We've really got to get going. This isn't the—"

"Just ask him about Trevor Haskins. Remember, showed you his picture? Got more," he said, waving a large manila envelope before me. "Close-ups. Even better. Ask Mellary about Trevor; knows everything about him, he does." He smiled and his eyes frosted over with a sort of rheumy glaze.

"Let's talk some other time."

He didn't move as we started up the flagstone path toward the retreat house. "Who is he?" Margery whispered. "What's his story?"

"Told me he was some sort of detective, private investigator. Maybe today he's a neurosurgeon. I don't know. He's just a garden-variety boozer who comes up here once in a while. But he never looked this rough—must really be hitting the juice. Conspiracy everywhere with this guy. I think dear Mr. Kiernan must have read *The Name of the Rose* and he thinks somebody's put poison on the book."

Margery put her arm in mine as we walked out onto the sprawling guesthouse lawn, where I could show her a panoramic view of the valley below. We rounded the first corner of the octagon-shaped building, and there, his white tunic immaculately illuminated by the morning sun, stood a monk. It was Father Columban. Margery slipped her arm from mine. Was it the instinct of a Catholic girl before a priest or could she, as I could, read the monk's face? Devoid of any emotion except for the slightest touch of impatience, it was the look I had come to know he reserved for moments of utmost irritation.

"Father Columban, what a surprise! I'd like you to meet a friend of mine, Margery Fowler. Margery, this is Father Columban Mellary, who—"

"Miss Fowler, a pleasure." His voice held no tone, no warmth.

"And mine, Father."

He stood there impassively, almost goading either of us to say the next words.

"I was just showing Margery around the grounds," I stumbled on, my words running together. "Nothing in the cloister of course," I added with obsequiousness I didn't know I was capable of.

"Our appointment today, Joseph?" he said, his arms folded in front of him.

"Appointment? Today?"

"Or perhaps another day would be more . . . more convenient for you?"

"No, no," I stammered, "I must have forgotten. Margery?"

"I'm running late, Joseph; if we could begin?" The word "we" held room for two people, not three.

"I'll walk around, José. Pleased to meet you, Father."

"A pleasure, Miss—Fowler."

I mumbled an "Excuse me" to Margery and followed him into the parlor. Father Columban closed the door. He looked older that day, tired. His normally ruddy skin had taken on an ashen dusting. He sat looking out the window, his chin in hand, a priest within a confessional waiting for the penitent to begin. He wouldn't look directly at me. In profile, something strange was happening to his forehead. The skin rose in tiny ripples as if a great mental storm was building just beneath the surface. The rest of his face remained passive and slack.

"Are you pleased with yourself?" he finally said, still looking out the window.

"With what?"

"This poor excuse for a practical joke. You were reading Aelred, not Freud, Joseph. I think it's all quite sick."

"I didn't have a meeting with you; now I remember. It's tomorrow—yes, tomorrow."

"You're right."

"Father, I don't understand, this isn't like you."

"Now, you listen to me." He wheeled about to confront me. "Kill the father, is that the idea? Murder him? Put your penis in this woman and you think you can dispose of him? Nifty, just nifty of you to be so considerate, Joseph. I saw you in church with her, Joseph. Good God, you couldn't keep your hands to yourself. It was as though you were in a barroom someplace."

"May I speak?" I said, at no more than half the volume he was using.

He neither denied my request nor gave his assent.

"Margery . . . I've come to . . . to like her . . . quite a bit, Columban. She's a very deep and spiritual woman."

"Did you get the abbot's letter?"

The words were flat and harsh.

"I did."

"And?"

"I don't know."

"How many have there been?"

"How many what?"

"Women in your life."

"Columban, this is unfair of you."

"And do they always miraculously appear just when you've begun to take life seriously?"

"Please!"

"Answer me!"

"Dozens of women."

"The challenge met, the newness fades, and you're off to the next."

"This is different."

"How many times have you uttered, that, that—bullshit! José! How precious!" Father Columban's eyes were blazing, his palms pressed hard together. "Or maybe this works better for your plot line. Man struggles between God and woman. The ultimate choice. Hollywood will love it. Get your notebook out!"

The black scapular of his habit heaved as if he were a

fish just plucked from the water. I thought he was going to hit me.

I had nothing to say to him, so I avoided his burning eyes, staring instead at the fine grain in the ancient refectory table, the dull, exquisitely distressed surface across which so many words of fact, agony and encouragement had passed during the past months.

"But . . ." He hesitated, exhaling audibly. "There is a lesson in all this." The words seemed directed more to himself than to me. "Yes," he said with ultimate conviction.

I waited for him to continue. I felt his eyes on me. When I could stare at the table no longer, I looked up. His face was blank now, his eyes calmed to the point of a drugged glassiness, his forehead once more smooth. His eyes concentrated not on my own, but at a point beyond the back of my head.

"Even with this, I have not changed my mind about you," he said softly, "nor have I lost faith in you. This is a temptation, but it is also a signal moment in your life, a turning point, an opportunity, and I have berated you instead of giving homage to the power of the Almighty."

My mouth opened, but nothing came out.

"Venerable Aelred would not have treated you so. Please forgive me."

"It's all right. I understand," I said, not knowing where the words came from.

"Joseph, we talked about the stages of spirituality, about what is required of a person who truly wants to live a life for God alone. One thing is necessary if you are to continue on your journey for now. Only one. The world constantly ensnares you like a fly caught in the spider's web. You struggle to be free of such entanglements, but the flesh is weak and too tired to resist. The web is seductive, silken, and deceptively strong. If it would not be a woman, it would be something else. You are not alone in this; most of us have been through such trials.

"You are a seed, my Joseph, and the seed must go into

the ground. And it must die. *Die.* Before it bears fruit one hundredfold. Only in losing your life will you gain it."

He leaned across the table toward me, his breath now even and regular. He whispered, barely loud enough for me to hear. "Your *will*. This is the test from God. He wants you to give up your will. That is the seed which must die. It is time for you and him to be alone so that he might speak to your heart—to see what this earthly life of yours might be. I will step back now, Joseph. It is necessary."

The knock at the door, although appropriately light and monastic, startled me.

Brother Polycarp's voice on the other side strained for a deferential tone but fell significantly short. "A call, Father. I didn't get the name of this one."

A few minutes later I left the room. I instinctively reached out to the wall in the narrow hallway for support. In parting, Father Columban had put his hands on my limp shoulders, kissed me gently on both cheeks, but said nothing more.

In a daze I walked down the path toward the circular drive. Realizing where I was and whom I'd come with, I looked about for Margery, but couldn't see her. As I approached the pickup, I was surprised to see her inside, the windows rolled up. She was crying hysterically.

"Oh my God, tell him to go away!" she sobbed as she rolled down the window a crack.

"It's okay, honey, please. I'm sorry he was so awful to you."

"Him!" she sobbed even more pathetically, her index finger pointing out the windshield.

It was Kiernan. He stood motionless on the freshly mown grass, before the statue of Our Lady, his hands crossed in front of his jacket, holding the manila envelope.

I felt the heat of blood rushing to the back of my neck as I walked toward him.

"Lookit, buddy, what are you up to? Just what the hell is going on here?"

"Perhaps you want to see Trevor? The picture I promised?"

"I don't want to see him or you. Now get the hell out of here before I kick your ass."

"Close-up; there's a real nice one in here." He reached into the envelope.

"Didn't you hear me, you old creep? Get out of here!"

"Oh, I must show you. Your lady friend was quite taken with it."

I reached to grab him. His defense was an eight-by-ten glossy photograph, which he flashed in front of my face.

"You probably don't know how he died, do you?"

I glanced at the picture, and instinctively turned away, as if I had been slapped.

"No, I don't suppose anyone would have told you, now would they? Not good for dear Father Columban's reputation, is it?"

He moved closer, his sour breath enveloping me.

"Do you know what a cincture is? Of course you do—probably were a good little altar boy who knew all those wonderful old prayers they don't have time for anymore. Remember, when you were helping Father get dressed before Mass? *Cingo, cingere, cinxi, cinctum.* 'To bind or gird.' *Cingulum* would be the proper Latin word for it. The cincture, just a little knotted cord placed over the alb to symbolically protect the holy loins against the ravages of the Evil One. *Protege me Domine Deus aestu.*"

He was smiling now and talking slower, knowing he had me.

"Dear, poor Trevor put one end around his neck and the other around a stout pine branch. How he even got up that tree, who knows? Maybe on the wings of love? Was never much of an athlete, that's for sure. Then, as they say, he 'jumped or fell.' But with this stout *cingulum* around his neck, it's hard to call it an accident, isn't it?

"But I must compliment the ecclesiastical supplier. A Boston outfit, my investigation shows. They put out a fine product. Hardly stretched. Trevor didn't weigh all that much, but, still, that's quality, wouldn't you say?

"I've got a real close-up of his face; a bit bloated. Oddly enough, nobody saw him up there for a full day. Want to see it? Some people say it looks like he's smiling. A frozen smile, to be sure. It was January. Remember? You stopped. Ah, friend, you are just the latest in a long line."

The trip to Margery's home was made in silence, neither of us able to speak about what had happened.

When I walked in the door of my cabin, the phone was ringing. I stared at it. I was afraid to pick it up. Finally, its insistence won out.

"They're after me," the voice said. "I can't hide anymore."

"Who is this?"

"Genghis Khan, Joey, Genghis Khan."

"Mort."

"Joey, Jeremy Irons' agent! Storms into my office yesterday. Says I'm holding out on him. That I want to give the part to some American pretty boy like Tom Cruise. No, I tell him, no. Give up Irons, with that priestly, pained Jesus face? Never. Just having a little trouble with my writer. Or Nolte, he says. Give me time, I say. Irons is our man. It's developing. It'll be better. Give it time. He doesn't have time, he says. Irons doesn't have time. They want a script, a treatment, six lines on paper, anything, Joey. Don't do this to Uncle Morty."

His words seemed on some kind of time delay. I could hear their sound, but their meaning lagged.

"Joey? You there?"

"It's been a bad day, Mort."

"Bad day? It's only ten o'clock!"

"It's hard to explain."

"C'mon, tell Uncle Mort about it. Haven't I been there for you? All along? Good times and bad? When you were hot and when you couldn't catch flies?"

"There's more going on up here than I expected."

"That's great! Material, Joey."

"Mort, you don't understand—" I hesitated. Mort Brunt
was neither the most understanding nor the most profound
individual in my life. But he was on the other end of this
call.

"Joey, I'm sorry. I'll be quiet. Just tell me. Joey?"

"I'm here, Mort. I'm trying to put it into words that
make some kind of sense."

"Don't worry about sense, get it out."

"Well, for openers, this kid hanged himself up here—"

How long did I talk to Mort? Ten minutes? An hour? What
did he say in response to my tale? I can't remember. All I
recall is that I needed a drink. I poured myself a tumbler of
scotch on the rocks. And then promptly knocked the glass
off the table, soaking my pants. I was changing my pants,
emptying the pockets, when the wallet fell from my shaking hand. It hit the floor, and credit cards, receipts, driver's
license, and various pieces of paper tumbled out. The two
pieces of paper, one within the other, lay off to the side,
seemingly drawing attention to themselves. Or at least it appeared that way to me. I unfolded the small sheets and read
the first.

*You should know more about those who have walked up
the road before you. May I suggest P.V. at (802)
546-3321? He has much to tell you. A friend.*

The second note was shorter:

P.V. A seeker, like you. Interesting. Talk to him. A friend.

Polycarp, Polycarp; why was he doing this to me? I
poured myself another scotch and got this one down without spilling it on myself. I went to the phone.

"Office of attorney Peter Vanik. May I help you? Hello?
Hello?"

I hung up.

7. July

"WHY? Why, Joseph, why?"

"Listen, I didn't know that crazy bastard would be around. Forget about him, would you, for God's sake. He's an aberration with a fried brain, that's all."

"There's more to it. And that is poor imagery, author of the year! Even your metaphors go to hell. You love hanging out with the whole neurotic bunch. Jee-zus! Why me? How could you have the nerve, the duplicity, to engage in a reasonably serious relationship. . . . You're really going to do it! After all we've been through, you're going up there to . . . Shit! A frigging monastery . . ."

"Complete a sentence so I know what you're talking about, Margery. Those men are just as normal as you and me; they're working out a different destiny, that's all."

"A different destiny! Give me a break."

"You can stop screaming at me anytime it's convenient."

"My screaming is a perfectly natural reaction, you pietistic jackass, especially when you talk in that sappy tone you get into when the monastery is even mentioned. Bernard and Aelred would have choked before sounding like that. That much about them even I—decidedly a lower-caste Catholic, unlike you—would know. And, just for the record: if you cared about me one little bit, you'd be screaming too."

Our relationship in the days after Margery met an unyielding Father Columban and encountered a tortured Octavius Kiernan had been rocky, but on this night, on the eve of Margery's trip to New York, it was even worse. I could barely recognize this raging woman, stalking around my kitchen, opening cupboards and slamming them, kicking my slippers across the floor, puffing on a string of cigarettes.

Why that particular day? Because I'd gotten out of bed at sunrise and gone into the living room to meditate? Or because when Margery tried to kiss me over breakfast, I'd turned her away with some feeble words like "I don't feel like it right now"? Or did it really get started at lunch? I said a prayer over her fine asparagus quiche and she said my voice sounded like that of "a man who just gargled with Lourdes water."

If she was angry with me about New Citeaux and what it could mean about our future, I was equally—and certainly not as justifiably—furious because she was leaving me, going back to her old life for a while. What right did I have to hold on to her as I was preparing to enter New Citeaux for my month's observership? None, I knew that. But Margery Fowler represented more than a lovely and convenient link to the real world I was about to leave behind. She was a woman I loved as I had loved no other in my life. I loved being with her, holding her, talking to her, watching her mouth twitch as she fell asleep. I loved her wit, her turn of mind, the shape of her body, the sturdiness of her soul. I had never felt so at home, so secure, so delighted with a woman before, and here we were, doing our best to hurt each other. I knew it was primarily my fault. Subconsciously, I must have wanted to inflict pain, hurt her so deeply that I would drive her away. And deny myself the safe haven I so badly wanted—the haven in which I knew I must not take refuge.

"I thought you, Ms. Fowler, of all people might understand some of the complexities about a life with God. But why should I have imagined that?" My tone of voice was demeaning. "Girls like you know that an American Express card and a phone call from Daddy can solve anything. Complexity, go away. No time for you today."

She glared at me. "You don't want God," she said

evenly. "You don't want people. You sure as hell don't want a woman in your life. You're a user, a consumer. You just want to indulge your fantasies on your own terms, with your timetable, and move on when you even sense that you'll really have to give of yourself. Remember the line from the song in *Midnight Cowboy*? You're the kind of guy who wants to go where the weather suits his clothes. You'll put in a month up there and you'll be looking for change, mark my words."

"I'm just trying to see if I have—"

"A vocation?" Her control wore thinner. "Aren't you a little old to still be toying around with that?"

By now it was obvious she was more sad than angry, but I still struck back. "Even faced with your hostile world-class theatrics honed by those bit parts in class plays, I'm going ahead with it. I'm well aware that I'm sometimes full of shit, devious, selfish, but at least I'm trying to make something out of the tatters of my life. Not squeezing oranges."

"Don't play this little boy lost, the religious naïf, with me, jackass! And remember this when you get bored and horny and you're ready to put this monastic dalliance behind you: if you go up to that monastery next month, don't come down looking for me. Uh-uh. These knees aren't parting for the likes of you, be sure of that!"

"Margery, don't be coarse; it doesn't suit you. And why do you have to keep yelling? You can make a rational point with—"

It must have been that tone of voice again that infuriated her. Especially after I had stooped to such a pathetically low level. She grabbed my arm, digging her fingernails into my flesh. "I'd burn myself before letting you ever touch me again."

"I'm sure one of your Manhasset pansies can accommodate you this weekend, my dear. He'll take off his Top-Siders, toss his wrinkled one-hundred-percent natural-fiber L.L. Bean polo shirt on the chair and flash a set of even white teeth. He might even say, 'Boola, boola.' "

She swung, missed, and sent the rack of drying dishes clattering to the floor.

"He'll do it better than you *ever* did. Just a nice, hard cock with no hidden agenda. I can't wait."

"I don't think—"

"No," she screamed, "let me say it! I'm not giving you the chance to break this thing off, you bastard. I'm doing it. It's over. We're over. I'm going to cry tonight, but tomorrow I'm going to be a new woman! Without you in my life!"

As the month of August neared, I made a conscious effort to reduce my options in preparation for a month in which I would have no choices whatsoever. I bought an answering machine, and as I didn't return any of the calls, it was like having the phone disconnected. I had my mail delivery stopped and held at the post office. With Margery gone, I went back to my routine, rising at 3:00 A.M., the hour the monks at New Citeaux started their day. My *labora* consisted of working in the garden, which was once again a lush and demanding cornucopia of rows of lettuce, carrots, broccoli, and beans, as well as more exotic vegetables—arugula and fennel, fine Italian small-leaved basil and bok choy. Tomatoes, peppers, and eggplant were also doing impressively, these seedlings purchased after I had killed off my own with the tainted monastery straw. I had so much produce in the garden that every few days I took full cardboard boxes to New Citeaux, quietly placing my offering at the refectory door, without waiting for acknowledgment.

But my *ora* was far less fertile. I could not concentrate. My mind wandered, careened: Aelred, Columban, Margery, Kiernan's pictures of the Haskins boy, Robert Trumbell, the voice of Peter Vanik on the phone that day, Polycarp. I was trying so hard to leave the world behind, but I was not yet anyplace else. I was deeply and aimlessly lost within the desert of the psyche, living in a confused world of voices and faces—alternately alluring, demanding, and terrifying.

Aelred was there with me in the hermitage, but in these

days he was hardly a compassionate old abbot. He told me
no more wild tales of his youth, those stories that allowed
me to rationalize my own failings. When I appeared at his
bedside, he never smiled; there was no small talk. He was
clearly impatient with me, questioning my seriousness, demanding more and more, ominously telling me that "No
one enters the various temples of God without death."
Death to my own wishes and needs. Death to my stubborn
will. "The higher experience requires greater purification,"
he said unequivocally.

Why I didn't put him aside in those days I'm not sure.
His words brooked no compromise.

And the man who had brought me from being an inquir-
ing smart-ass reporter to a seeker of life's meaning was
playing his part beautifully, exactly, withdrawing completely, purging me further still.

In the months before, at the sign of peace at daily Mass,
whenever Columban was on the altar, he would find me
and our eyes would meet for an instant. Those brown
eyes—at once pools to rest in and yet blazing with a profound intensity—gazing at me across that low wall of
smooth red bricks imparted enormous strength. His look as
the words were spoken: "Peace be with you"—his face
brimming with pride and confidence—this was a road sign
each day at Mass, telling me to go on. But after the confrontation over Margery, he no longer did this, instead smiling graciously to the priests on either side of him, holding
them tenderly in his arms, meeting their eyes with his char-
acteristically intense look. He was demonstrating—did he
know how dramatically?—the camaraderie that could be
mine, but only on *that* side of the wall.

When he distributed the Eucharist earlier, he had always
called me by name, and—why was this so important?—
looked directly at me before pressing the host into my palm.
I felt an amazing kinship with him and the entire Trappist community through that simple, personalized act. Now,
when it was my turn to receive, he spoke a toneless, per-
functory "Body of Christ." My face turned toward his, seek-

ing at least a glimmer of recognition. But his eyes followed the host from ciborium to my outstretched hand, where it was placed, as it was for every other communicant.

My scriptural *lectio divina* was no less an assault. "Leave all you have and follow Me." "O, ye of little faith, why do you doubt so?" "Place your hand into my side and then you will believe." "I am *the* way, *the* truth and *the* life."

Reeling from such unyielding demands, I tried in my three meditation periods each day to simply put myself in the presence of God and to open my mind to him. To be that blank page upon which he could write. My ear inclined toward him so that he might murmur his wishes. I tried desperately to be still and listen, but instead all I was able to do was to play back, over and over, what I had heard and seen in these past months.

Margery, with her characteristic clarity, had pinpointed exactly what I was: a spiritual dilettante. Would I repeat my past, spend my month at New Citeaux and come out with still another calling? Go back to New York and start the book, the movie, Mort knew all along I would write?

Yet there was Columban and his view. The opposite of Margery's. He had always expected more of me than was there. He was like Jay Gatsby, who infused his friends with the certainty that they were as good as he seemed to think they were. As I had come to know him, I so badly wanted to believe Columban. He sensed there was something deeper in me, something I had run from too much of my life, something that would not let me rest until I had faced it head-on. Isaiah. Saul.

Margery and Columban, both so clear, so certain of their vision—each of whom I could agree with. Depending on the day, on the hour. And then the others, static on the airwaves of the soul, confusing garbles, half-heard words and sentences, half-known facts. Robert Trumbell, such a good young man, so serious, so well intentioned, so aflame with the very quest and questions that had dogged me for a lifetime—and driven mad. The suicide of Kiernan's Trevor

Haskins—what role had Columban and New Citeaux played, if indeed any role at all? Polycarp, my enemy and, strangely and perversely, my friend. He saw through me, hated me for my shallowness, but could not—was this a matter of conscience for him?—would not, let the matter rest. This man named Vanik he had wanted me to meet. Vanik, Vanik, what was his story? He surely must have one.

Finally, one uncharacteristically steamy Vermont morning, still groggy after a restless night assaulted by the cacophonous chorus of voices, I listened to the only voice I knew I would ultimately have to trust.

I sat cross-legged, looking out at the green hillside, dotted with Mr. Standish's holstein heifers and finally, thank God, I *knew*.

The life of faith is always difficult, and seldom are its decisions made easily or without confusion. The Jealous Lover wants sacrifice and without it withholds his true love. Yes, the idea of a life with the Trappists was a little mad and certainly romantic, but then again, *that's what I was*. I wasn't a pragmatic civil engineer but a creative person, a writer, a dreamer, yes, a seeker. Merton, Aelred, Augustine—lusty, selfish, headstrong men, every one of them. And they found their rest and healing not in earthly pursuits but in a life devoted entirely to God. They were never comfortable in the world, giving God but a percentage of their time. Only when they committed themselves to his service did they begin to truly live. And they wondered and doubted right up to the moment they entered religious life. I had struggled to come to this point and now I was finally ready to give myself—for a paltry but crucial month—to a grand ideal.

Even Columban's rejection now seemed to make sense. Especially now on the eve of my entrance into the monastery. It was a stunning move. I knew that many postulants came to New Citeaux, taken with its beauty, attracted to the rural ruggedness of the life, eager to join the brave regiment of men, to pray and chant and fast, to do peasant's labor and eat spartan, vegetarian meals. To leave the crassness of the world behind, to live for something great.

And usually they would leave, disillusioned. For every ten who came—all of them men with the best of intentions and brimming with enthusiasm—nine eventually left. They found they had joined for all the wrong reasons. It could not be for companionship or aesthetics or bodily mortification but for only one reason. Only one: the unquenchable desire to try, in whatever hideously small way, to know God better. Whatever work one did was irrelevant, whether it be the erudite spiritual direction of Columban Mellary or the sweeping of the guesthouse by Brother Justus, who in the world would probably be considered mildly mentally retarded.

Friendships formed were equally unimportant. There was to be only one Friend. Father Columban was consciously withdrawing to see if my calling was nothing more than the symbiotic attraction of a worldly writer to the imposing man of the spirit he had grown to respect.

"Intention equals the act."

I kept repeating that to myself, a throwback to grade-school religion class. If I planned to steal a cookie, even though I met my mother on the way into the kitchen and made a detour for the backyard, I had already stolen the cookie. And likewise, if my intention was right—if I was truly seeking God, he would guide me, let me know if, to find him and know him, I should live as a cloistered Trappist monk, perhaps for the rest of my life.

What was it that brought me to this conclusion? A conclusion at once so simple and yet so necessary for my life. "I can trust myself." Many voices will be heard, but ultimately my own must guide me. And my own will be guided by his. Although the world looks at the monastic life as one of avoidance, escape, it is far from that. It is confrontation, facing straight on, and often in the most unflattering light, every part of myself. But I realize I don't have to hide in order to be holy. I could never do that very well.

The package arrived on the last Tuesday of the month, five days before I was to enter New Citeaux. Inside was a velvet-covered Tiffany box, its clasp sealed with a huge smear of red wax, and an envelope with a Price Waterhouse return address (they actually did exist outside those three breathless hours of the Academy Awards in Los Angeles). Price Waterhouse testified to me, by name, of the date and hour the seal had been affixed and then took four paragraphs to explain that if the seal had been "damaged, tampered with, or altered in any way" that they "could not guarantee the authenticity, completeness or the value of the contents."

I broke the seal with my pocketknife.

Inside, on top of carefully folded, scented pale blue tissues, was an envelope, of muted Wedgwood blue, bearing a monogram: *MAF*. Within, in a bold medieval Gothic on a matching card, Margery Addison Fowler had neatly printed:

> *This sacred vow here made,*
> *That virgin sweetness was not marred,*
> *Though soft summer winds did blow,*
> *Trust me, O dearest Abélard.*

The inner recesses of the tissues held a clamshell case of matching blue. Inside was her diaphragm, covered with a light dusting of powder.

She was at the store when I called. "José! I gave you up for lost," she laughed. "Not to the monastery—your sense of humor, Buster."

"I haven't been so good at getting my mail. I just picked up a bunch today, honest to God."

"From your lips I believe such oaths. Hey, look, even if we can't use that little piece of latex together, I wanted you to know your Héloïse was keeping her purity—at least until Abélard goes into Monkville. Seemed only fair. Sealed and mailed the day I got home. You know, we Waspy types believe in fair play, just like we believe in orthodonture and good posture, in clothes from Lord and Taylor, Laura Ashley—yes, Bean's too, wise guy."

"Margery, I never gave you a second thought," I said unconvincingly.

I saw her twice during the next few days, in the daytime, at the health food store. Our conversation was like that of two people who had been married for twenty years, had divorced, and who occasionally got together for a friendly chat over lunch. What might have infuriated each of us when we were lovers was now accepted with a maddening readiness to understand.

Margery talked about two old boyfriends she'd run into at her Manhasset yacht club, how handsome, suntanned, successful, and banal they were and how badly they wanted to get in bed with her. She had shopped at Saks, Bendel's, and Bloomingdale's, and had spent an afternoon at a new East Side Hungarian spa having every inch of her body pummeled, rubbed and mud-packed for a mere $375. It was not hard to tell how little any of this meant to her. She pointed to the tabouli-encrusted sandals she was wearing and giggled with certainty that $300 shoes had rarely been so abused so quickly.

I told her in some detail of the voices and faces that had haunted me while she had been away. She nodded and smiled, rather proudly. "See what happens when Ms. Right leaves your side? Chaos. And by the way, I never called you a dilettante, José, just a religious fanatic. Be careful how you quote me, even to yourself. But this Vanik guy, how could you not look him up? Give me the number, I'll find out why this Brother Polyester wants you to meet him. How can you resist? Did you have some sort of DNA transplant to subvert those reporter's genes while I was away?"

"I think I'm over that for good. And it's Polycarp, please."

"I *know* what his name is. Sure, it's out of your system. Just like the flu."

"There are a couple of days left and—well, I do have one notebook left."

Margery smiled that wonderful smile, her eyes glistening with anticipation.

She didn't touch me, nor I her, both of us living by an unspoken code as the last days of July sped by. At times I wanted, in the midst of all the rosy-cheeked customers of Nature's Bountiful Harvest, to grab her, hold her close one last time. She was so suntanned and beautiful, standing there in her neat shorts and tank top, her makeup perfect, her smell intoxicating.

Yet, as appealing as she was, I was afraid that something had gone from her. Something I had crushed that would never be whole again. Margery Fowler would never again appear at another man's door with such openness and two cold six-packs of Molson.

The last day of July was balmy and breezy, a perfect cloudless summer's pleasure. The gypsy moths had eaten their fill, gone into dormancy until next year's assault, and the tree had miraculously leafed out again. There was Bob Dylan once more gazing out at me, now from behind sunglasses that were lavishly trimmed with succulent swirls that would have pleased even the most outrageously flamboyant Miami Beach matron. Mr. Standish's upland fields were tall with corn and the pasture thick with grass after heavy rains. It was difficult to remember how barren that tableau—and my soul—had been in January.

Mr. Standish and his wife had paid a kind visit the day before—the first time they'd stepped inside my house—and joked that if the prayers of two bedrock Congregationalists counted, my month at New Citeaux would be a good one. They had promised to tend my garden as best they could and look after the house.

By midmorning, I was about ready to pack, but decided

I should call Margery and say good-bye. Then, I wanted my last hours in the hermitage to be unhurried and quiet.

Margery had other ideas.

"Can't bid adieu like this; a going-away picnic, José, wouldn't that be super? Full moon, too. But I promise to leave my fangs at home and also, holy one, to depart before the demons begin their nightly prowl."

I tried to beg off, saying I had nothing in the house to contribute and that I had last-minute details to take care of. But, of course, those weren't my major concerns.

"Oh, come on. I take a solemn vow not to be a near occasion of sin. I've got everything made anyhow. For old times' sake, Abélard?"

"I've got to say no."

"You've got to, but you won't. Anyhow, I want to hear who this guy Vanik is. What's in the notebook on this guy?"

"Never looked him up."

"Look, this thing is going to bug you every day up in the monastery. Especially with all that time—and no scotch to soothe you. What's the big deal—you sound solid about this thing; go for it. I'm dying of curiosity. And if you don't, guess who will? Okay, I'm flipping a coin, heads you look him up, tails I'm driving over right now." I heard a coin fall to the floor.

Well . . . we'd satisfy Margery's curiosity and not my own.

Peter Vanik's law office was in the middle of a small group of shops that lined the main street of Brewster, Vermont, across from the county court building. It was the prestige block—among its inhabitants were the accountant and investment counselor, land surveyor, the local congressman and two other lawyers. Vanik's smile was ready and his handshake warm when I entered, but at the sound of Columban's name, that changed. He took me to his office at the rear of the building and closed the door. He went to the opposite side of his desk, leaned over it, and glowered at me.

"I must be getting to the old boy; did he send you over?" he said with hostility.

"Not at all."

"Doesn't matter. Know him well?"

"Yes."

"Well, you don't. Not for a minute."

I wanted to get up and leave. I knew once again that despite my frequent vows to hand over my will to God I was hanging on to it tenaciously. "Perhaps we should just drop this, Mr. Vanik. I'm sorry I intruded. I really have no business—" To a lawyer such an unconvincing tone of voice must have been blood in the water before a great white shark.

He straightened up and leaned back against the shelves of thick law books, his arms folded in front of him. He was wearing striking red suspenders over an impeccably pressed shirt, one of a good Egyptian cotton, I would have guessed. His gray trousers were part of a suit I was reasonably sure was not sold in Brewster, Vermont.

"What brought you here?" he asked.

"I write. I'm writing about the monastery. I was given some names."

"By Columban?"

"No, not by Father Columban. I just wanted to get the fullest picture I could. I think it's a mistake. I'll be going. Sorry to have troubled you."

"Trouble?" He laughed. "My good man, I've been waiting for a guy like you."

I stood there stiffly.

"Sit—please sit down. It won't take long. A sad tale, but a short one. Sit."

I eased back into the chair.

"Harvard undergraduate, Fordham Law. Amazing, after being accepted at Harvard and Stanford, goes to Fordham. A newly minted Catholic. Vaguely Methodist background. Get the Catholic slant on things, the Catholic attitude, the

Catholic conscience, says the baptizing priest—so Fordham. Twenty-four years old. Graduates. With distinction. Law review. Ripe, eager, ready."

It was obvious he was talking about himself, but with such detachment it was as if he were, say, a radiologist explaining a rather routine X ray.

"Churchgoing. Daily. Read everything. From Merton to Graham Greene, Bernanos to Flannery O'Connor. Oh, he had a reading list for me and I plowed right through it. Turned into a great Catholic. You know what I am now?"

"No."

He put his hands on the desk once more. "I am a card-carrying, Church-baiting, agnostic atheist—how far out can I go? I'm testing the limits. I'm trying my damnedest, believe me. I think organized religion is no more and no less than a tax shelter for the clergy. Voodoo for all you saps. 'Turn the other cheek'? 'Empty yourself so you can be filled'? Buddy, have you ever heard such rubbish, such utter drivel anyplace else in the world?"

I looked at him.

"See those folders on the shelf? Two shelves? My name doesn't register with you, does it? Pete Vanik is Mr. Abortion. When the pro-lifers come after you, you come to me. State legislature giving you problems? Come to me. I've testified all over this great land to protect a woman's right to a legal abortion and you want to know something?"

I said nothing.

"I don't really care one way or the other. Fetal rights, women's rights? But after my wonderful days up there with Saint Columban Mellary, after having my head messed over, I couldn't think of a better way to do in his wonderful Church. A great crusader. I'm a damn hero. For something I don't even believe in. See what wonders the life of faith can do for a guy? See?"

"Exactly what did happen with Columban to . . . to make you this way?"

"Bitter?" His contorted smile was a mixture of triumph and pain. "Just ask him about it."

"That wouldn't be appropriate. I'm about to—"

"Oh, no!" he said, slapping his forehead with the palm of his hand. "You don't look like some country bumpkin. You have two or more brain cells to rub together. You're not going into that nuthouse!"

I was beginning to get irritated at this nonstop tirade. "I'll be at New Citeaux for a month's observorship," I said coolly.

"On a field trip or as the first step in joining them?" he said, laughing mockingly. "Just about got to that point myself. Believe this or not, I was ready to give up the law, submerge myself in the life of faith. Lost to the world. *Practice of the Presence of God, Cloud of Unknowing*, Thomas à Kempis. Sound familiar?"

"I have looked at some of them."

"Do I sound cynical?" He walked to the corner of his office and spread his arms out to grasp the shelves. His voice was so low I could barely hear him, but the intent of his words came through clearly.

"—sounded so right, so possible, so damn brave. Something to live for. Oh, God, it excited me. I looked at those pictures of the old Trappist life and was angry—angry, mind you—that they now had electricity, used tractors instead of horses, slept on cloth mattresses and not straw. But I was willing to compromise, I would go along with their new softness. I would go along." His voice trailed off.

"What happened?

"Columban pulled the rug out. That's what happened."

"And how was that?"

"Oh, he was so nice about it. So Goddamn nice. He put his hands on my shoulders and said, 'Pete, there are a lot of lives a man can live. This is only one of them. It's not for you.' Now, how the hell would he know that!" His voice had risen with the last words.

I sat quietly.

" 'Pete, get married, have a family. Enjoy your life. Go out and be a good lawyer. Help people. Stand up for the right causes. The practice of law is as much of a calling as the Trappist life. We are just another way to God. Not the only, and for most not the best.' That son of a bitch! I showed him.

"I have another appointment," he said abruptly. "I'll see you to the door." He followed me out into the sunlight of Main Street and nodded to passersby who obviously knew him. He looked at me. His eye sockets seemed to have darkened, or perhaps it was just the contrast caused by the splash of the sun.

"I assure you," he said, "Columban Mellary does not rest easily up there on Holy Hill knowing I'm out here."

Margery arrived at seven with a cooler and a wicker basket, wearing a peach-colored sundress with spaghetti straps. The dress was not cut low enough to be openly suggestive, but sufficiently so that a shadow of the cleavage between her breasts was demurely but surely in evidence. She had used the same sandalwood body oil she wore that first night she came over.

As we nibbled on crudités I promptly drank most of the first bottle of wine. Her tahini dip was extraordinary that night, but I tried to convince myself it was a shade salty— thus the reason for my thirst.

"Met him today," I said.

"Met who today?"

"The mysterious guest—Brother Polycarp's surprise."

"Knew you couldn't resist. And?"

"I never had a person open up like that in an interview. He spilled his guts in fifteen minutes. With no prompting. Very angry. An incredibly angry man."

"Why?"

"Just didn't work out for him." I opened the second bottle of wine.

"What didn't work out?"

"Wanted to join. They wouldn't let him."

Margery moved around in front of me. "Let's stop this cryptic Q and A. Tell me what happened, what you felt, what he said."

I repeated as much of the conversation as I could recall, and told Margery of Vanik's abortion work.

"Very, very angry man," she said. "Could you see him as a monk?"

Her question stopped me. I thought for a moment. "I guess I could. He had passion; he's after something in life. Just doesn't know where to channel it. But strip away that bitterness and at times I could hear myself talking. I left his office very confused, but right now, thinking about it—"

"Yes—?"

"I want to put it aside. I've got to, especially right now. If what he said means anything, I'll know this month. If it was nothing, it will fall away. I'm getting worn out, trying to figure out all the angles. I'm going in for the month; let's see. Okay?"

"Hey, okay with me, José; remember I'm just an orange-juice squeezer."

"I apologize."

"Forget it, I promised myself I wouldn't bring up any of that stuff. José, look at that sunset! Let's talk sunsets, for Chrissake. Tomorrow you're gone."

"He really got a bellyful of the whole—"

"Sunsets. C'mon."

"Sorry."

"Keep your promise; put it behind you." She stood, a huge smile on her face. "Let's find a place where we can see the sunset and the moonrise. In between two worlds. Like you, tonight, holy one."

Margery was backlighted by the setting sun, but it was wine as much as solar splendor that caused her face to go out of focus. "I think I know just the place," I said. "Hurry, the sun's almost down."

The southwest gate to New Citeaux is set back from the county road, buried in a stand of towering hemlocks, which—I had learned in one of my early interviews—had been planted during the Depression by CCC workers, three of whom eventually became monks. The gate was no more than a bar across the road, fastened by a snap hook. Brother

Boniface had been my guide up this road in early spring
when Father Columban had finally relented and allowed me
a short tour of the monastery property. As I undid the hook
the bell for Compline echoed through the perfect rows of
hemlock, each stroke hanging in the sun-streaked early evening dusk until relieved by the next.

On the northern edge of the trees, just as the road began
its climb, I turned off. I drove across a hayfield, which was
growing back after a second cutting, not for an instant
thinking of the track I would leave. Higher and higher we
wound our way, past the Vermont Historical Society's stone
marker commemorating the state's first major slaughter of
Indians by white men. Down the hill and up the next. I
parked the pickup in the long shadows between two huge,
gnarled cedars at the edge of the field and we walked the
last hundred yards to the crest of the hill.

The view was magnificent, exposed and high yet su-
premely private. Not a building of New Citeaux or any
other work of man could be seen; before us were just the
gentle folds of the foothills, cradling the blazing orange
ball, crowned by fine layers of purple clouds. And behind
us, the full moon, a ghostly, seemingly transparent sphere,
a pale reflection of what it would be when darkness fell,
was rising in the eastern sky. Brother Boniface had brought
me to this spot, presenting a monk's humble gift that even
the vow of poverty could not preclude.

How different it was then. He and I—our breath labored
from the long hike, foreheads damp with sweat, the smell
of perspiration radiating from our bodies—had stood there
silently. Margery and I did the same.

I spread out a blanket and Margery arranged the food on
it. Cold crab salad Louis, green and yellow wax beans
niçoise, curried rice, a small tin of caviar and Carr's crackers, stuffed eggplant topped with crushed walnut and par-
mesan cheese, and ears of fresh corn, still warm beneath
blankets of foil. Chilled Frascati, the third bottle of wine. A
boysenberry mousse. Red-checkered tablecloth and matching napkins. This was not an impromptu meal.

Margery sat upright between my legs, leaning back on me as we watched the sun flicker and disappear from the sky with a futile but fervent flare. We turned slowly about to take in the moon, now fully gold and rising far above the dense tree line.

"I love you, José," she said, patting my knee gently. "I just want you to know that. And thanks for talking sunsets and not religion tonight."

"I'm glad you got me off that subject and that lawyer. Bad dream, that's all. I love you very much, Margery," I said, running my hands over her soft, bare upper arms. "God, I love you so much." I smiled down at her. "Let me say that again. God. I love you, Margery, very much."

"It's so sad, isn't it?"

"Like some kamikaze mission. At dawn I fly. My timing was always rotten. I want you to know that leaving you behind is the hardest choice I've ever made."

"I know, José."

"Margery, I just don't want . . . well, what happened between us to—change you. You're so great and open and loving. Don't change because of me. I've not been the best."

"I've stepped on my share of necks. Oddly enough, I'm a better person because of you, José. Even this way. I finally finished *The Seven Storey Mountain* and *The Sign of Jonas*. How's that for vacation reading on Point o'Woods Beach?"

"It's not the way I would have wanted this to be." I kissed her shoulder lightly. "Maybe some other writer—a better writer—can fix this up with a rewrite."

She turned toward me. Her mouth was slightly open as if she were about to speak. Tears came into her eyes and she blinked vainly to hold them in.

We walked back down to the pickup, our arms around each other's waist, her head on my shoulder. The moon transformed the hillside of stubble into a shimmering, metallic sea. The warm earth's musky smell rose up to envelop us. I turned the ignition key, but got no further than the first notch, which started the radio but not the engine. WAFF, the Falmouth AM station, which specialized in old hits, knew exactly what kind of summer night it was. The theme song from *Picnic* embraced us in the fragrant air.

She looked across the cab at me.

I came around to her side and opened the door.

I was the rambler, William Holden, and she the local innocent, Kim Novak. The night air was perfumed with the smell of damp grass, hemlock, cedar, and millions of wildflowers. The music was too beautiful and sensual to resist—we danced on the smooth barren ground beneath those towering trees, her face resting on my chest, my hands pressed against her back. We were lost in our own world, where that song would play forever and the sun we had just seen set would never rise again.

She raised her head and I kissed her gently. Each of us watched the other for a sign of what to do next.

I put my arms more tightly around her. "Hail Mary, full of grace, the Lord . . ."

"What the hell are you doing, José?"

"What the nuns taught me to do whenever in near occasion of sin. And if I don't say the Hail Mary, I'm going to whisper the Hail Margery right into your ear."

"José, you still do have your sense of humor."

"And an excess of testosterone."

"I must confess it's not exactly ice water in these veins right now."

"Let me just hold you real tight and then we've got to go."

How long we were there I don't know. And how long Brother Polycarp watched us I have no idea. I'm sure he didn't quite know what to do as he came upon us. But he was charitable enough not to disturb us.

I saw him when I lifted my head from her shoulder, and then he was gone. There was no point in telling Margery.

"Thank you," I said when we were in the pickup. "Margery? Are you okay?"

"Just finishing my Hail Mary. The near occasion is still near."

We laughed and hugged one last time.

8. August

PACKING for my month at New Citeaux turned out to be a spiritual meditation in itself.

My instructions were to arrive at the monastery after lunch and before the liturgical hour of None at 2:00 P.M., which left me the entire next morning, that of the first day of August, to gather those items I would need.

I started at the top of my bureau and, in the first small drawer on the left, found a modest stack of twenty-dollar bills held together with a paper clip, some pressed white linen hankies and a maroon box of three individually wrapped Fourex natural lamb lubricated condoms. I closed the drawer softly enough not to disturb the angels.

In the right-hand drawer was a large bottle of Bentyl and a smaller vial of Tagamet, medicines to placate a duodenum whose inflammation and accompanying spasms could be counted on—unfailingly—whenever I was starting or finishing a book, finding or losing a girlfriend, generally when I was having a difficult time of life. Also, I found the Valium—still thirty strong—some plastic stays for the dress shirts that I never brought along and my address book.

The next three wide drawers were more carefully balanced between the prosaic and the emblematic. There were socks—gray winter wool and white summer cotton in front and a few, almost to the knee, for dress, in black, blue and brown, relegated to the rear. Underwear was next, and partially buried beneath the briefs were sturdy T-shirts and thermal underwear with well-stained underarms. Then, the Rugby and tennis shirts with designer labels representing a tidy income for some popular athlete or celebrity. Also there were some walking shorts and bathing trunks, the latter, from my days in the Hamptons, so immodestly skimpy that I tossed them into the wastebasket in embarrassment.

In the bottom drawer were sweaters, six of them, most still fresh from the dry cleaner's a year ago. Beneath were two pairs of Italian leather gloves, still encased in the plastic bags in which they had made their Atlantic crossing. They had journeyed from Venice to Brooks Brothers, from the soft underbelly of an unsuspecting calf to a hand-stitched work of art ready to protect my brawny hands while engaged in such arduous work as the steering of my Porsche along the rutted FDR Drive in New York.

The closet, which had been confronting me daily at eye level, was the most forthright. The tough choices had already been been made. In front of me were practical denim shirts and jeans, worn and respectably tattered by barbed wire and tomato stakes. To the right and left, pushed to the sides and still in their bags, hung the clothes of another man: garments of smooth fabrics and subtle colors, with tailoring that gently accented the shoulders or kindly understated the waist.

The top shelves of the medicine cabinet were crowded with an amazing array of colognes, skin creams, and nonprescription drugs, whose sanative powers I'd forgotten. On the lower shelf was a huge tin of Bag Balm to heal the painful cracks of the skin near my fingernails, calamine, various sprays to ward off insects or repair their ravages, a bottle of witch hazel—an honest after-shave and all-around antiseptic—and plenty of Band-Aids of various sizes. My toothbrush and tube of Aqua-Fresh stood alert in a chipped coffee cup on the sink's rim.

In the living room, stacks of books; in the hallway, a sweatshirt for cool mornings and a rubberized suit of jacket and trousers for the most inclement days; on a shelf, a pile of work gloves, most mismatched. In the kitchen, an apothecary jar of fresh-roasted mocha-java beans, a large box of

Nature's Bountiful Harvest specially blended herb tea . . . I
went no further.

I sat at my kitchen table with two postcards, the last and
best of a Monet collection I had purchased on a Paris trip.
The first went to Margery. "Thank you for the going-away
party. Love, José the Hopeful." The second went to Mort
Brunt, telling him that I was in New Citeaux, could not be
reached, and that I would pray for him. I took out a notebook.

> Last night, late, I read Héloïse's third letter to Abélard.
> She wrote: "Nothing is less under our control than the
> heart. Far from being able to give it commands, we are
> constrained to obey it."
>
> I must now listen to, and obey, my heart. Not my
> head. And such listening requires I write nothing
> about it.
>
> This is the last entry in these notebooks. Thank God.

A few minutes after noon I locked the back door and
climbed into the pickup. I was wearing a clean, relatively
unfaded pair of jeans and one of the newer T-shirts, bright
red in color. Jauntily stuck in the shirt pocket was my
toothbrush. That and the Orthodia Plus arch supports in my
sneakers—a concession to a pair of flat feet that even God
might not cure—was all that I took.

The modern world regards a monastery and finds, for the
most part, men cheerful in their work and deadly serious in
their prayer. I doubt whether it is much different today at
the original Cîteaux in France from the way it is at the New
Citeaux of Vermont, which is a mere babe in monastic
terms, having but a century's history. The monk in the New
Citeaux gift shop, on the tractor, in the guesthouse, going
into Falmouth to get the Sunday papers at Rondo's News-
stand or a rebuilt carburetor at Stanley's Auto Parts—each
is unfailingly courteous, patient, and always speaks in a

voice set to a lower volume than that of the rest of mankind.

Monks come from widely varied stations in life—at New Citeaux, for instance, there were, in addition to former factory workers, farmers, and computer programmers, a once very well known advertising agency creative director who had promoted Fords, lemonade, and pantyhose with equal success; a Jew who had graduated from Yale at eighteen and been a Rhodes scholar; an auxiliary bishop from San Diego who had resigned his office; and one of the stars of Eric Rohmer's early films. But to the public there appears to be a certain sameness about these people once they accept the Trappist life—a sameness not unlike that of neat rows of corn in a field.

It took no more than a few days within New Citeaux to see why some men, of best intention and perhaps with the real stirrings of a contemplative vocation, enter a monastery and are quickly disillusioned. They soon witness not only charity, moral excellence, and a profound quality of humaneness but also bickering and smallness, full-blown hates, selfishness, a thirst for power, and behavior that by mental-health standards would be classified as full-fledged neuroses.

And perhaps, as I did, they witness one single, shocking, and totally disorienting event that punctures their euphoric bubble. The incident occurred at Vigils on the Feast of the Transfiguration, a week after I entered. There, just a few feet in front of me, I saw Brother James-Edward turn around and slug Father Dominic squarely in the face, knocking him unconscious. It was the culmination of a de-cades-long feud, which started—so I was later to find out—with no more than a dirty look because of a dropped bale one day in the hayfields. In those days casual speech was prohibited, so the animosity was allowed to fester, and even when Trappists began to speak, the two men were so used to their silent standoff that they continued it. That feast-day morning Father Dominic tapped Brother James-Edward on the shoulder to render him a small service. The billowing sleeve of Brother James-Edward's choir robe had caught on a misplaced carved gargoyle that had been snagging Trappists for years, and Father Dominic was trying to make Brother James-Edward aware of the danger involved when he next tried to kneel down.

As for me—once recovered from my shock—I was encouraged by the sight of Father Dominic on the floor and Brother James-Edward standing over him, glowering. The men of New Citeaux were no different from me.

And it was not that Trappists had ever been as flawless as the world might have imagined, that somehow the monks now dead had been cut from some different cloth. New Citeaux had a legendary monk, Brother Pius, who every few months throughout his forty years of monastic life and under pain of sin and repeated threats from his abbot would cover his tonsured head with a stocking cap and hitchhike into Falmouth for the few shots of good rye whiskey and beer chasers he craved. And Brother Cyprian, who entered when he was twenty, suffered shooting pains in his neck for the next twelve years but found them gone the day he left the monastery for good. Homosexuals and drunkards, pathologic liars, and kleptomaniacs and hypochondriacs, men with their own private demons and mental static, struggling to be good. And failing much of the time. One of the adages that I'm sure has been around since the first two hermits decided to cook their humble broth in a single pot was to me the ultimate leveler: Only the weak come to monasteries. If a man was strong enough, he could live in the world.

Rising at 3:00 A.M. day after day took some getting used to, and for two weeks I dozed in choir and endured a faint but constant headache. But this passed, and although I neither woke up completely rested nor passed a day without fatigue, the wonderful balance among personal prayer, community worship, and physical labor that Saint Benedict had so wisely constructed was extraordinarily to my taste.

The first hour of the monastic day, Vigils, had a quiet, dreamlike quality. After all, who is more than half awake at

3:30? There was something both soothing and inspiring about those well-worn Psalms, which called out to an elusive but ultimately compassionate God in words that monks had used for centuries, and faithful Jews long before them. A period of private prayer followed, and although I had no Zen bench and hillside, a stark wooden crucifix on a plasterboard wall provided more insights than I felt I could assimilate. Even *mixt*, taken before Lauds and Mass, was an extraordinary pleasure. It was not only because of the organic peanut butter on fresh-baked whole-grain bread, but because of the collected way monks went about the meal, sitting quietly at the long refectory tables, sipping a cup of coffee, their minds upon God—or the south thirty acres of alfalfa ready for cutting that day.

Work—for me, cleaning the guesthouse or, when the need arose, helping out on the farm—was punctuated at midmorning and just before noon with the short hours of Terce and Sext. Whoever I was working with, priest or brother, even the abbot himself, who loved to be outdoors, would stand or kneel with me and pray. Then came dinner, the main meal of the day.

It occurred to me while I was there that a wonderful addition to all the motif restaurants on New York's Upper West Side, choked as they were with professionally tended plants and chrome and fiddle-backed café chairs, would be a place called The Monastery. There, simple, hearty vegetarian food would be served to patrons who would be seated democratically on benches at long tables. Talking would be prohibited and a book would be read aloud, as is done at the noon meal in Trappist monasteries. I'm sure the place would be mobbed.

Over huge salads and fettucine Alfredo (I don't want to leave the impression all the meals were as good, but the level, given the budget of four dollars per day per man, was most impressive), I listened to Daniel Boorstin's *The Discoverers* and Elie Wiesel's most recent memoirs. My digestive tract and soul had never been in such peaceful coexistence.

Between 1:00 and 2:00 P.M., the stronger men took walks. I was ready for the allowed nap.

The hour of None, said at 2:00 P.M. in the abbey church by all monks not already engaged in their afternoon work period, was the most beautiful fifteen minutes of my day. What was it about those Psalms, 126, 127, and 128, that so succinctly and surely linked man's work to his God, dismissed all matter of toil not devoted to a higher cause, and so gently gave courage to feeble humans paused at the middle of the day to consider if they were doing his will or their own? I daily saluted Benedict for his poetic insight. The words of those Psalms were exactly what everyone in the world needed to hear each day so that work neither possessed them nor seemed futile and demeaning.

Vespers and a sufficient but light meal called collation preceded what was gloriously called "holy leisure." No, it was not a Jesuit happy hour or communal watching of the nightly news on television, but a chance, near day's end, to read still more. The library had an appetizing array of books on spirituality as well as recent best-sellers. With the words of *Salve Regina* at Compline, all lights went off in the church and the Blessed Virgin looked down on her sons, her illuminated stained-glass face glowing with compassion and bidding us to take our rest. The Great Silence began, not to be broken until the next morning after Mass. We went to our cells. It was eight o'clock. I had no trouble falling asleep.

There was nothing in the day that lasted more than a few hours. The sharp rap of the abbot's wooden knocker in choir or the clanging of the tower bells gave no reason to linger. Everything would wait. A floor three-quarters polished. A prayer half made.

I found that such discipline was indeed relief, something I had unknowingly craved for a lifetime but had been too belligerent or frightened to embrace. My day was perfectly ordered and there was nothing to, in any sense of the word, *accomplish*. There were no calls to make or return, no concern about what to eat or wear. There was nothing to keep or carry in the pockets of my simple white alb except a handkerchief and a ballpoint pen. I felt like a carefree child. I even gave up the few choices that were mine, such as what books I might read. I simply asked the brother librarian for suggestions and blindly followed his lead.

The dullness, the sameness, of the days never bothered me. As a writer, I had spent day after day alone in my room in some transitory but seemingly grand enterprise; here I had companions for the most important pursuit of all. Even when my energy or attention waned, I had but to look to my right or left and immediately I would feel uplifted. How much of that did I have in the life I'd left behind?

Of course, there were the saints in our midst, those like the Chilean priest, Father Raymond, dying of a painful cancer, who never missed an hour of the Divine Office; and Brother Armand, who radiated an undeniable and pure holiness even while passing a piece of bread or holding a rake. But the rest were more ordinary men who saw the need to live in what Aelred called a "community of salvation" so that they might have the support of others in what they knew to be at once a noble and an impossible pursuit.

Such a life, lived in such restricted and close quarters, with little opportunity for physical or psychic escape, fostered a certain sensitivity that was almost uncanny. Late one afternoon I found myself with a spare half hour, so I went to the abbey church to sit in silent meditation. It was a hot, muggy day but the church was cool, its usual dampness now a refreshment. Although I had never had any special affection or affinity for the Blessed Virgin, I found myself in a small side chapel devoted to her. I stared at her impassive ceramic face and tried to envision her as truly my mother, concerned about my welfare, ready to take up my cause with her First Son whenever I asked her to do so.

I found myself strangely relieved with the thought, and delighted that I had found this new channel. My eyes searched the statue, as a man might do looking at an old acquaintance who had suddenly taken on a new and important role in his life. Her eyelashes and brows were sensual in

their exactness, the downcast eyes at once sorrowful and in-
viting, somehow asking me to make her smile. The white
veil covered a perfectly shaped head, its hem following a
jawline that was both firm and feminine. Her shoulders
were straight, not the least weighed down by the sorrow her
life had brought her. The color of her gown, a rich, deep
blue . . .

Rich, deep blue. Perfectly sculpted shoulders.

I got up instinctively and started for the door.

I walked, head down, through the cloister outside the
church at a pace slower than even the slowest monk's. And
I had the sense that someone was walking beside me. I
looked up. It was Brother Bertrand. Phi Beta Kappa at
UCLA and good-looking enough to have put himself
through college as a model, he had come to the Trappists
some ten years ago.

"Job, girlfriend, car, or cold beer?" he whispered without
looking at me. "Which one do you want right now?"

Of course it was Margery I was thinking of. It was not
the first time she had crossed my mind, but the striking
sensuality of that statue had weakened my libidinal fortifi-
cations, so much so that my mind had quickly taken off
that blue gown and run my hand across that fine jaw.

"It's nothing," I said.

"Sure," he whispered. "Bullshit."

He put his arm around my shoulders. "It hits us all. Hey,
look, if it gets tough, we can talk. Okay? And if you get
real thirsty, I got a stash of beer. Later, good buddy."

Community spirit was one of the great attractions of the
life. We—I could use that pronoun for those blessed thirty-
one days of my life—were infinitely there for one another,
holding up the weak when they faltered, carrying their load
as they gained strength, or just—most important of all—
staying around when temper or age or ennui or the align-
ment of the cosmic bodies caused a single false step, or the
latest in a series of false steps. Where else in the world
could I find this? I had played sports. But this was neither
a game nor an enlistment; theirs was a lifelong commitment

that made mere marriage between man and woman seem but a tepid and selfish alliance.

Brother Steven, a burly young man who'd played nose guard for Michigan State, hated to be indoors—everyone knew that—but each day he worked in the steamy laundry without so much as a long face. Father Marian, a graceful painter of museum-quality still lifes and seascapes and a shy, introspective man, cheerfully tended the gift shop in the afternoon, listening to the gushy homage of purple-haired Rosary Sodality ladies and answering the same questions from assorted tourists who bought factory-produced copies of artworks that in no way resembled the originals. Brother Pontius, a fastidious young black, and Brother Anthony, a redneck Southerner, whose personal hygiene and politics were both scandalous, worked side by side, day after day, in the huge vegetable gardens.

The monastery was a place where you could obey quietly without feeling you were a victim, where you could show unabashed love and enthusiasm without having your sexual preference questioned, where you could live in a confined place without feeling in any way a prisoner. Here you could act in simple goodwill, yet not be considered a simpleton. Everyone knew what the ideal was, why he was here; the ethic of the place was obvious. And yet, there was nothing sanctimonious about New Citeaux. These still were men, human beings, and it was obvious that their nature or inclination was not always to be good and kind. But regardless of their virtues or failings, they were loved and accepted, not only by the invisible God but by the visible monks before them.

A few days after the assault in choir, Father Dominic came to Brother James-Edward to ask his forgiveness. His eye closed and purple, he acknowledged that he should not have touched Brother James-Edward on the shoulder, allowing he could have transmitted the same information by a simple whisper. Without mentioning the punch he had landed, Brother James-Edward accepted the apology, gave Father Dominic a fraternal hug but warned him not to do it again. Or else, he made it clear, he might well mete out the same response.

The brethren at New Citeaux, with two exceptions, were unfailingly kind to me. I felt more like someone returning home after a long absence than an "observer" coming into their midst to sample their life. Some of the monks knew me and many knew of my writings, and of the parallel life I had attempted. They confessed that over the months I had earned the nickname of "Brother Joseph Outside the Walls."

Only Brother Polycarp and Father Columban kept their distance, averting their eyes when I passed them in the cloister or stood opposite them at the cafeteria-style serving table for breakfast or the evening meal. But to their credit, neither did anything to dampen the spirit of those who showed so much eagerness to welcome me. When I did catch a glimpse of Polycarp's face, I could read only one emotion: disdain. His chin bunched up, like a sponge being squeezed of its moisture.

Of course, I wondered if Polycarp would tell what he had seen that night on the hill. All he would have to do was to mention it to a single monk and within hours the entire monastery would know. The Trappist grapevine was an awesome means of rapid communication.

Polycarp's attitude toward me was actually easy to offer up. One of the ultra-pious books that came into my hands restated that old Catholic saw about seeking scorn rather than running from or fighting it off. During my month at New Citeaux, I tried to live that way. I never let Polycarp pass me that I did not smile at him or, if the occasion was inappropriate for doing so, offer a prayer for him. I prayed not that he would grow to love me but that he would fulfill that particular monastic calling that God had designed for him. Certainly, I never prayed that he keep my indiscretion to himself. Perhaps, I thought, I even needed additional scorn. I had almost committed a most untoward act on the eve of my entrance into the monastery.

I could live with Brother Polycarp's shunning, and live with the mystery of his note-writing, but it was not so easy to deal with Father Columban's avoidance of me. I hungered for him to speak to me, to merely show he knew that I was there, to acknowledge that, as he had finally allowed and then encouraged me to do, I had come to experience the Trappist life.

I was reading two or three books a week and my voraciousness must have amazed the brother librarian, whose name was John Peter. One evening he looked bemusedly over the top of his smudged reading glasses, received the books I was returning and asked me if I had any favorites among spiritual writers. In my new state of humility and docility, I said no. My face was meant to present itself as being as open as my mind. "Do you have any suggestions, Brother—something that would be good for me at this particular point in my observorship?" I inquired.

He nodded and handed me Squire's *Aelred of Rievaulx*, a basic text that I'd read twice.

"Oh," I began, ready to boast of my knowledge of my old friend Aelred, but I quickly changed my response. "Thank you very much. I'm sure he has a lot to teach me." I proceeded back to my cell, confident that the tough, arrogant shell of the old Joseph showed at least a hairline crack and, secondly, that through the book given to me by this Trappist monk, who had joined New Citeaux even before I was born, God might speak to me in a new way.

I was ready to be uplifted.

I closed the door, kicked off my monastery-issue work boots and swung the straight-backed chair around so I could put my feet on the bed. There was but a half hour or so before chapter, our weekly community meeting. That night a Gustav Weigel scholar from the University of Chicago was to address the community. I opened the book from the back, letting the pages flip past my thumb, waiting for gravity, the tensile strength of the paper, the elasticity of the binding, and the hand of God to stop them.

The pages stopped. I opened the book fully. My eyes were drawn to the bottom of the left-hand page. And there, at the end of the paragraph, were the words—at once familiar and suddenly so haunting.

Aelred wrote triumphantly of the monks of Rievaulx, as always, praising with soaring hyperbole their steadfast adherence to monastic observance. Then, abruptly—and I could almost feel the white-hot anger boil up in him—he left the twelfth century, soared across the centuries, and entered the very room where I so slothfully sat. He concluded leadenly:

> You are a novice, and so I attribute what you have said to fervor rather than to vainglory. But I should like you to be on your guard, lest you should suppose that there is in this life any profession that does not have its frauds.

My hands began to shake.

How long I stayed there, I can't remember. Bells may have sounded, but I didn't hear them. All I recall is a series of scenes from the walk that I must have taken, stop-action moments frozen like randomly halted film streaming through an editing machine. It must have been after Compline, for the abbey was empty, the monks having gone to bed.

On that cloudless night the glazed tile floors shimmered in the moonlight streaming through the cloister arches. In the enclosed courtyard, the flowers of summer had all turned a sickly gray; Our Lady's peaceful granite face was blotted out by a black shadow. The carved Stations of the Cross within the cloister hovered menacingly over me: pained and vengeful faces not reliving some past events but moments as fresh as if Pilate had that day handed down his judgment, the soldiers had just scourged, a Mother had received the lifeless, bloody body in her arms.

At my feet, the prickly arms of crown-of-thorns plants reached out from their stone urns, ready to ensnare me in their stinging clutch. Their normally red flowers were a ghastly purple color, their thorns, bleached white, long and needle-sharp. Out beyond, the cemetery loomed, the crosses seemingly swaying ever so gently in the cool night breeze. The sturdy wooden markers, statements of a life faithfully pursued to the death, had been transformed into fragile reeds just by my gaze.

The great Roman staircase leading down to the refectory—with steps wide enough for a horse to keep its footing—appeared unending. It seemed as if I could follow them forever and never arrive anywhere. When I finally did come to their base and entered the high-ceilinged refectory, the long tables and benches were empty. There was a feeling and smell of staleness and death. The odor of a burial vault.

When I came to the abbey church, I found the fine stained-glass rose window was yellow and blemished, no longer a riot of praise to God but a sickening patchwork of burnt scourings, soiled, diseased colors. The choir stalls were dark and still, upright coffins awaiting their fill of rotting flesh.

I crept back to my room and threw myself on the bed. I was freezing cold. My face was covered with perspiration.

I loved the life I had been living for the past few weeks; it perfectly agreed with me. The services were transcendent, my individual prayer time peaceful and comforting, my few talks with the novice master, Father Methodius, a tiny Nigerian priest, illuminating and helpful. I had thought little of my life before New Citeaux; my days melted into one another, one blissful blur of reading and chant, the dutiful scrubbing of the guesthouse floors, cleaning toilets as if surgery would be performed upon them, emptying wastebaskets with reverence for each crumpled piece of paper, each crusty Kleenex.

But now in reading Aelred once more, I had discovered what a parody all that had been. How, in my smug calmness, I had committed the greatest sin of my life.

Was I ready for the desert? For a life of devotion to God?

No. I had found nothing more than an escape, a medieval reprieve from the daily concerns of survival and self-worth that plague mortal man, from Margery and a career that seemed even less than "middling," as Columban had pronounced it. Unable to cope with the world outside, I was gladly ready to leave it behind. A cozy sinecure. A damnable and pathetic escape. A room of one's own. A quiet place to read. Hero? No, and not even a man. I was the fraud Aelred knew me to be.

The next morning I stumbled toward the church for Vigils, dazed from lack of sleep. My head was beyond pounding, the ache knew no rhythm—there was just a solid mantle of pain. I knew, as agonizing as our meeting would be, that there was only one man who would understand.

When I stopped Father Columban outside the scriptorium and asked if I might see him privately, he smiled graciously and said, "Of course." He suggested "our room" in the guesthouse as if nothing had transpired between us and we were the best of old friends about to take a walk along a familiar country road we'd always cherished.

He was waiting for me; two glasses, a bowl of ice cubes, and a pitcher of lemonade sat on a tray. "About time for me to treat, isn't it?" he said. "Sit, Joseph, please."

I sat across the table from him, saying nothing for some time. I stared openly at him. He did not look away. Although I had requested this meeting, I expected him to begin, to somehow see in my face the difficulty I was experiencing and, with his first words, begin the healing I craved.

"I don't understand you, Father," I finally said.

"And how is that, Joseph?"

"I put my spiritual life more or less in your hands, come into the monastery, and now that I'm here, you act as though I didn't exist. You even seem to take some kind of pleasure in avoiding me. We had a horrible fight, we seemed to make up, then you act as if I'm not alive, and now it's as though nothing happened. Frosty lemonade on a hot August afternoon. 'Our room.' This is too saccharine for my taste. And for you, it's slightly ridiculous."

He took off his glasses and polished them with his handkerchief. Then he raised himself for an instant, releasing the back of his scapular from the seat of the chair. He pleated it neatly behind him and sat again.

"May I pour some for you?"

"No, thank you, Father."

"May I, for myself?"

"You don't have to ask a one-month observer. Yes, dammit!"

He poured a glassful, without ice.

"You appeared to be doing so well, Joseph; you looked like the perfect young Trappist. What happened?"

"Nothing."

"Such rage isn't the product of a man who hasn't seen one of his faces. And, if my instincts serve me—recently."

"If I need more Jungian analysis, there are, as I've told you, people better trained and in a more convenient location."

"Joseph," he said softly, almost pleading with me to stop my posturing. "Just tell me; it's the best way."

I could face him no longer without bursting into tears. I turned to the window.

"If a man ever came with the right intentions, it was—no, dammit, I don't want to start off with some sanctimonious prelude. I'm sick to death of that part of me! At the beginning of the year I didn't have the best intentions. False pretenses. Reporter in mendicant's clothing. But then it happened. God reached out to me. I don't know why he did. Isaiah and Saul didn't know either, I'm sure. But he did. He showed me somehow that this was possible. For me, the phony, the day-tripper I am, the rationalist, the escapist. And I love it here. Absolutely! Let's start with that. Everything *was* right, frighteningly right. Then Aelred—" I fought, oh, how I fought those tears. "Aelred, Aelred came right into my room, stood there and said that . . ."

"Take your time, Joseph; there's no hurry."

When I had finished my slobbering tale of smug dishonesty and the ensuing apocalyptic revelation, Columban, uncharacteristically, responded immediately. And I felt, when he began, that he was slightly off the mark, as if he had a stock response to any postulant's doubts and had not heard my particular story.

"Egypt—inhabited Egypt—follows us all into the desert. I'm sure even Benedict and Bernard looked over their shoulders. Perhaps you're not in the desert, yet. Maybe you're just whizzing about the belt parkway running through the Cairo suburbs. And perhaps, unconsciously, you're going round and round, wondering which exit to take: the one that leads back home or out to where the road ends, where you have to leave the car behind. None of us gives up a good night's sleep, the morning paper with a cup of coffee, a loved one"—he hesitated—"friends, without a sense of loss, of longing. That's what makes us human; that's what makes the embrace of this life all the more real.

"Or"—he tapped his fingers on his lips—"it is more subtle. In a moment of silence—and in our life, there are more than enough of them—we sometimes come to the conclusion that the bondage of Egypt wasn't so bad. Not unlike the Israelites. Certainly preferable to what is touted as this 'freedom' experienced in the desert. With this life, there are no markings, mile after mile of sand dunes and the sun beating down continually upon us. Walking, wandering, because to sit is to burn up and die. Thirsty, exhausted. No, there is no one to trouble us. But freedom? What price this freedom? I have escaped, but to what?

"Our minds play games with us, the world does not easily release us from its grip. But deep in the desert, my friend, God waits, ready to comfort—no, not the strong, but those of us weak enough to fall at His feet with a plea for mercy on their parched lips. Years of wandering, years of wondering, and only then . . . then, Joseph. The relief, the release is so sweet. And it may be for just an instant, but that instant is worth everything. After that, you are forever changed. For God was there all along on the journey. Waiting, wishing to bring us into the promised land. Many men—many monks—are not willing to suffer so. Only a few. And God does not find the rest of men lacking. No, he loves them completely.

"Consider this: had Saint Francis of Assisi been a successful merchant like his father, buying and selling cloth; if Dorothy Day had been an influential socialist editor or Merton another excellent secular social critic; Saint Peter, the owner of a fleet of fishing boats—would God have loved them less? But they saw something else was to be made of their lives. And they had no choice. God would have loved them either way, but each of them would have awakened in the night, howling with misery. They could never have loved *themselves*. The desert called, and they could not deny it."

The glass before him remained untouched. Columban was spent. That rich—though misguided—lesson had been constructed and imparted at great physical cost. In talking about the desert, he had reentered it. He was speaking from his own painful experience. I jammed my teeth together, trying to say nothing, trying to make his commentary apply to my life. But I couldn't.

"Father," I said softly, "forgive me, but it's not a choice between Egypt or the desert. Did you listen to what Aelred said to me? I love the desert. But I'm floating along, my feet haven't touched the ground. The sand isn't hot, it's pleasantly warm. I feel as if I've answered some religious Club Med ad. I find the life agreeable, pleasant, not at all demanding." The words were coming faster and closer together. "How many Goddamn synonyms do you want me to come up with? Get me a thesaurus; I'm sure I could find twenty more! I'm a phony, a fraud, a monk manqué. I've been a writer so long I don't know whether I'm really feeling something or I'm just feeling it so I can put it down on paper."

"Joseph," he called out softly.

I was anything but spent.

"You guys have a great life of it up here. No woman to nag at you, no kids yapping, three good vegetarian meals a day, fine incense—oh, I love that incense, by the way! Nothing too taxing. A little prayer, a little work, a little sleep. Never bored. The best-kept secret in the Western world. Don't worry, I won't blow it for you guys when I leave."

He started to rise from the chair.

"Well, what do you have to say, Columban?"

"I think it best to leave it for another time. You're upset. We can talk again before the month is up. There's time."

"Don't play those games with me, Columban, leaving me thrashing about. I am not upset! And I don't appreciate stupidity masquerading as temperance one little bit."

He was standing, staring down at me.

"All right, my friend"—he leaned over the table—"here it is."

I have seen men rise to anger, but Columban's ascent was all the more terrifying because of both its speed and what then issued from his lips. He was consumed with anger at me for what I had said, and somehow this passion was magnified a hundred times over by what I had inadvertently forced him to relive.

"There are levels of this game, like any other. As in art, writing, music. There are those who are hacks. There are emotional cripples all over the world and we have our share—fewer, let me add, Mr. Hotshot Reporter, than you'll find in most other walks of life. Middling writers, middling monks; yes, you could fit in just fine here.

"You want to paint by numbers? Or do you want to be Van Gogh? Just remember he hacked off his ear in one frenzied moment of creativity. Pulp fiction or Dostoevsky? Muzak or madman Mozart? You cheater! You pathetic Goddamn cheater!"

The tears flooding his eyes could never have been mistaken for a gesture of sympathy or concern. They were the outpouring of fury now beyond his control.

"Turmoil, pain, struggle, conflict—that's what produces great literature. And great monks. And you, you pip-squeak, you want to find Christ in peace? The Rod McKuen of the Trappists. 'Listen to the warm. Listen to the heartbeat of God.' Oh, God, you'd sell millions! They'd love it: the new, no-pain religion. You're just right for your generation out there working out on their exercise machines, with their headphones on. Maybe that's exactly what you came in here to find. It'll sell like hotcakes. Oh, Joseph, another in that proud lineage of your kind of writer: lose a husband, get cancer—live the pain and take notes while you're still bleeding. Helicopter in and helicopter out. Don't stay long enough to really know or understand anything. Once over lightly, use some strong verbs and move on. Better story, different brand of pain down the road.

"All this pious drivel we see coming out between book covers—priests and pastors and 'reverends' and nuns who think they are people of faith, and all they amount to are crummy, second-rate writers. Not even 'middling,' mind you. And those alleged monks over at Wakefield Abbey, wailing for Jesus, selling those pathetic albums, sounding like a poor imitation of—what's his name?—yes, Barry Manilow. That's the level you want, Joseph. Drip-dry, low-maintenance religion! Go down the road to those Benedictine nuns at Mater Dei. Old-fashioned—up at two A.M. for the night office; we've already slipped to three, and some monasteries aren't up before six! Those grand ladies still do the office in Latin and maintain a strict cloister that makes this place look like a college campus. Smiling faces, every one. But take a trip through their ovaries, up and down their fallopian tubes, into their uteruses. Ravaged! A gynecologist could spend full time over there, for Christ's sake. Why, little Joseph?" He leaned still farther over the table. "Because they *care*.

"Travel through the neurological passages of the monks of New Citeaux; feel the short circuits, the overload, the blowing of fuses. Why? Because they *care*. They care enough about God to offer themselves up, burnt offerings. Go dry out with the alcoholic monks who've been boozing on that altar wine for years, stealing and sinning just to get some relief. Go ahead, if you have the guts; which you don't."

I reached out to touch his hand, but he pushed me away. I began to mutter some apology.

"You, you, Joseph," he breathed. "I thought—I thought you were different, an exception in a generation whose moral compasses are shot. But you're not willing to be an adventurer, a discoverer, a pilgrim. You want a guided tour, all-inclusive fare, baggage handling and tips included. You are afraid to get out of the tour bus, Joseph; afraid you might get lost, somebody might touch you. A reporter! Read back over those books of yours—as I have in recent weeks—and you'll find you were nothing but a poseur, nothing but another disingenuous poseur.

"Out there"—his fingers stabbed at the air in the direction of the window—"is a world out of breath, searching for meaning. They try this guru and then TM, they meditate, they try to levitate; oh, let's be Buddhist this year and Unitarian the next. Sufi? Islam? Let's eat cottage cheese and get thin, let's jog a hundred miles a week, keeps the pulse lower, you know. Move on to the next fetish! Their God: diversion! You and all of them worship at the altar of that tin god, that contemptible false idol.

"You're not ready to be a foreign body, Joseph, to be incomprehensible to people, even to yourself. You want everything to add up, neat little columns. You don't have the courage to wager on what is uncountable."

He sank into the chair, exhausted. He put his head in his hands. "Forget everything I said," he said, his voice muffled. "But know this. Nothing is more worthwhile than the pursuit of God. Nothing. And here, we wretched men who call ourselves Trappists try to know him. It hurts, Joseph, believe me, it hurts." He looked up at me, his eyes milky and bloodshot. "Deprivation, sensory deprivation of all things familiar. Only then is God made clear. When you have nothing, you find him.

"I must go."

"Father?"

There was nothing left of me in that word. I was between one life and another, at a moment of judgment so exacting as to preclude any semblance of volition or hope.

He nodded tiredly toward me to proceed.

"Father, I came to Falmouth to see the face of God—okay, so I could write about it, to find out how men sought God, what paths they took, why they persisted, why they left. But we both know that's past now. I'm trying to see the face of God for myself. I can't go back knowing I didn't follow through. If you walk out of this room and I drive past those gates with no more than what I have now, I go a broken man. With no hope of a cure. Help me, Father, I beg of you."

At my supplication, his fingertips dug into his scalp, gouging frighteningly at his skin, leaving behind a pattern on his forehead not unlike a crown of thorns.

"You pathetic creature!" The anger of moments ago had been only a tepid sampler of the true wrath of Columban Mellary. His eyes flamed and his lips quivered in an uncontrollable spasm. " 'Came to see the face of God!' Where did you learn that *fervorino*? When are you going to get a clue about simple honesty?"

"Now." The word choked me.

" 'Now,' the great impostor says. Are you ready, God—Joseph is ready," he screamed to the exposed-beam ceiling. "Oh, you lucky, lucky God to have such a declaration of intention. Rubbish! Crap, shit and rubbish!"

"I want to. Please, Father, help me." My eyes were dry and clear. To have cried then would have been just another facile ploy in a life laden with such contrivances.

" 'You *want*.' That's just the problem. You haven't a clue. Our Lord is mine—Our Lady, the sweetness of a mystical communion with the saints, is mine, mine, mine! And do you know why, Joseph? Because it is only by not wanting anything else that you gain them. Putting your face to the ground and telling God how wretched you are and that you do not even deserve to draw the next breath. Want! When you want to possess one particular thing, you get nothing. Nothing, you hear me! You can have it all, but you can possess nothing; everything must go. And it takes a man to give it all away, not some two-bit writer from New York."

The bell sounded for morning work period to end, and outside, in the circular driveway, a tourist called for his family to gather closer together so that they and the church rising behind them would fit into the viewfinder of his camera.

"I guess I deserve all this," I said hoarsely. "God, it hurts!"

His lips were moving; Columban was praying, of that I was sure. He kissed the top of his hand, the way a peasant does after making the sign of the cross. Then he spoke. "Perhaps we have both overdramatized this situation." He was completely calm.

He continued: "Again we—I—have not given God his due. You have been a worthy monk. Even for a few short days. If you are serious, when your month is complete, you should go back to your home, your hermitage, and continue to live the life you've begun there. And if, by the end of the year, you still feel God calling, you should enter as a postulant. Wait upon him and no one or no thing else. That you must do. Strictly, Joseph, or else we will have this same, terrible confrontation again. But be sure in your own heart that you are being honest. Is there anything in the secular world you still cling to? A lust for fame? Look deeply, Joseph. Or is there any *one*?"

I could have and probably would have uttered "no," but my face told him otherwise.

"Your work or the girl, Joseph?"

"Father, I have tried to keep her out of my mind and for the most part I have been successful. Honest to God."

"I believe you. Nothing can keep her from entering your

mind, but, equally, nothing forces you to dwell upon her or to see her. That is an act of the will, not the unconscious."

"I think I can do that this time, Father. I'm sure, it's—"

"José?"

"My name is Joseph," I said firmly, "and I almost had sex with her the night before I entered. I confessed placing myself in that situation, did my penance and I've put it behind me. Is there anything else? I want to look ahead. Soon I'll be returning to the world. I'm sure it hasn't changed. How should I live? Should I do something more, or different? Different schedule, more fasting, more prayer?"

"Nothing heroic. Please. Just calmly live these days within the cloister and then, upon returning to the world, avoid her and, if you're serious, all those who would divert you on your way. The Devil is as jealous a lover as our Lord. He has had a good companion in you for many years. In these days he will plant all sorts of things in your mind, put people in your way who will make this life sound foolish and vain."

"I know." My voice gave it away. Mine were loaded words, not a simple acknowledgment to keep the rhythm of a conversation.

"Joseph?"

"Yes, Father."

"Say the rest."

"My friends in New York—they won't know what to make of it," I quickly replied. "My sisters and brothers— they think I'm weird, but not this weird. But I think I can handle all that."

"Joseph? Please?"

"Well . . . the two men I met," I said, my tempo slowed, "my shadow sides, as any first-year shrink intern would point out. Robert Trumbell you know about; there's another, a lawyer named Peter Vanik."

He looked at me blankly, as if he had never heard those names before. The room was silent. He closed his eyes and then spoke. "You have found another one. How, may I ask?"

"For Trumbell, as you remember, I had to do a bit of sleuthing. Vanik came recommended. In a note. I have a good idea of who did this, who wrote it."

" 'Did this' implies you have no control in the matter."

"I didn't exercise control. I tried. But I ultimately gave in. But, Father, those days are past. I am no longer doing investigative reporting on the life of the spirit. I am trying to live it."

"And Peter—as you must know, I know him. How is he doing?"

"It's a tragedy to see so much talent so misguided."

"In the abortion business?"

"The outward sign of an inward disposition. It's scary to see someone working as he does, with so much hate for the Church and—"

"For me. Is that what you were going to say?"

"Yes, I was."

"What did you take away from meeting him?"

"Only that he was hurt so deeply when he was told he did not have what it took to be a Trappist. And how it warped him."

"Did it frighten you or give you a moment's pause?"

"A moment, yes. But frighten, no. It wasn't right for him; or so you said. He could have gone elsewhere; the Trappists aren't the only order in the world. Or just gone on, doing something that would make him happy. Believe me, this is not making him happy. Revenge sours quicker than warm milk."

"Would you feel as he does if you were told the same thing?"

I thought for a moment, studying Columban's face. "Perhaps. But I wouldn't make a life out of paying back you, the Trappists and the Church. I think I'm on more solid ground than that."

"And so do I."

There was an awkward silence as we both reached for the closing words.

"Father, before I leave," I said as we both rose, "if I could have your blessing?"

He came around the table. I bowed my head, but he took my face in his hands. He pressed his cheek against mine and held me tenderly in his arms.

Where they had gotten the pepperoni pizza and that much beer was a mystery to me. And the magnificent multicolored crêpe-paper streamers. The sheep barn had been cleaned and its inhabitants banished to a distant pasture. Fresh dried hay covered the floor, and by the time I arrived, supposedly as part of a work crew to stack firewood, at least half of the New Citeaux brethren were there.

Brother Pontius got a little tipsy and insisted I open their present immediately. It was a beautiful hand-bound volume, with messages from each of them, a few pictures of me—one scrubbing the guesthouse floor on my knees and another, my very serious profile at prayer, with a halo painted in—and the Psalms of None, my favorites, in Brother Martin's faultless calligraphy and illuminated by Father Theophilus.

"You guys!" was about as eloquent as I could be. They applauded the speech and hugged me. They asked me to read one of the Psalms. I began the familiar words of 127:

> "If the Lord does not build the house,
> in vain do the builders labor;
> if the Lord does not watch over the city,
> in vain does the watchman keep vigil."

I returned to my room to change into the clothes I had brought with me a month before. The clothes were lying on my bed, where I had left them, fresh from the monastery laundry, neatly pressed by Brother Steven. On top was an envelope.

"To be opened only in the comfort of your own home. *Ipse dixit.*" This much Latin I knew; the proper translation was "He has said it," but often it was freely translated as the imperious and authoritative "Rome has spoken." The writing seemed to have been done in haste, this time in script, not block letters. The lines seemed thicker than I'd remembered. But it was the same green ink.

Perhaps Polycarp was using a new pen. And was he getting a sense of humor?

9. September

WHICH were the powers—human, natural, supernatural?—
that tended my garden with such generosity and balance
while I was away, wrestling with my paltry soul? Some
force conspired to send moisture to the roots of the chosen
plants and to cast out intruding weeds, which would have
usurped precious nutrients and sunlight. Or was it a pair of
human hands on my Rototiller keeping paths wide and clear
or on a hoe that put an end to the malicious hopes of bur-
dock and witchgrass? How much had it rained during the
month of August? I remembered great haying weather at
the monastery. But my garden hose looked in place; the
sprinklers were still where I had left them on the porch rail-
ing. Who or what had been at work?

The corn was green and thick and over my head. Huge
ears bulged within their shucks, begging to be taken. Stalks
laden with tomatoes strained at their stakes; eggplant and
peppers were so abundant that many were already resting
on the warm brown soil. Potato plants and onion greens
were properly wilted, these phantoms of once-lush growth
luring me to pull their buried treasure from just beneath the
earth's crust. The handiwork of God and man—or woman?—had blessed me a hundredfold. How could it be? The
Standishes had barely the strength to tend their own farm
and small garden. Margery?

There was a great lesson in this unbelievable abundance
and it centered on what I had been struggling to believe:
that only in letting go would I receive.

My first week back in the hermitage was an orgy of

picking, digging, washing, sorting. Besides spiritual reading and meditation at home, daily Mass, Compline and Vigils at New Citeaux, I gave myself over to a harvest that would have made the purveyors of seed catalogs—those roseate publications that strike every gardener's fancy in the bleakness of winter but rarely deliver on their promise—blush with envy.

I was in that most enviable of mystical states, of having so much to give and so little need. The only job was to gather this opulence and distribute it. I went about it with a joyfulness of which I didn't know myself capable. The bed of my pickup laden with boxes of fresh produce, I traveled to churches, Protestant as well as Catholic, within a twenty-mile radius, asking pastors and ministers to use what they might and distribute the rest to the needy. If they asked my name, I just waved them off and thundered on to the next stop.

Upon my return from the month at New Citeaux, I had concluded that I would have Delight Bliss—yes, the real name of the Falmouth postmistress—send back all the mail that had accumulated in my absence, but her welcoming smile and the huge stacks that she had so neatly arranged tempered my fervor for abstinence.

Mort had tried by regular, express, and special-delivery mail—return receipt requested—to reach me. I opened only the most recent letter, knowing that such a frenzy could mean only one thing. For years I had waited for the phone to ring, for a letter to arrive, and here were a half dozen telling me that while spending a month in a Trappist monastery I had—potentially—become a richer man: one hundred thousand nonrefundable dollars for merely signing my name, signifying the intention to write a book "about a modern-day man's search for himself at a monastery." An additional one hundred and fifty thousand dollars, in thirds, would be paid out to write the book. And should I exercise the option to write the screenplay, I would receive another unholy amount of money. And, by the way, Jeremy Irons had said a resounding yes to a nonexistent script.

Mort, Mort. My life had changed. If the next few months went as I hoped they would, there would be no full-screen credit with my name, no trips to location for last-minute polishing and perhaps an interlude with one of the ladies who would play a character into whom I had first breathed life and who might feel disposed to return the favor. No book-publishing parties, no whirlwind fifteen-city promotion tours. All of those things that I had sought, with my modicum of talent and excess of zeal, now meant nothing at all.

I selected a beautiful postcard showing the New Citeaux cloister at dawn, and wrote Mort, telling him that in a matter of months, I would join the Trappists and, hopefully, spend the rest of my life as a monk. I asked him to neither ask for nor accept any more work for this client. He knew of my friendship with Father Columban, and Mort being Mort, he had already parlayed that into a rather substantial offer for a second book, one on which Father Columban and I would collaborate. It was to be called *Finding God, Finding Yourself.*

Columban would turn beet-red laughing at that.

It was about the middle of the month, on a Wednesday, after a morning's harvest and a lunch of gazpacho and fresh corn, that I readied myself for the customary prayers for the hour of None. Usually I simply read them from a small loose-leaf notebook of daily prayers the monks used, but that day I wanted to recapture something of my days at New Citeaux, so I took out the bound volume the monks had given me. I read aloud:

> *"If the Lord does not build the house,*
> *in vain do the builders labor;*
> *if the Lord does not watch over the city,*
> *in vain does the watchman keep vigil."*

My voice faded into a whisper.

"It is vain for you to rise up early,
Or put off your rest,
You that eat hard-earned bread,
For he gives to his beloved in sleep."

My mind held on to that line: "For he gives to his beloved in sleep." The effortlessness of it all. No, the pursuit of God was not a pursuit at all. But a rest in him, a confidence in him. I sat there for some time, overwhelmed by the thought.

When I returned from that meditation, I paged slowly through the handcrafted book. There I was, ankle-deep in cow manure. There, with a mop bucket at my feet in the guesthouse. There, standing next to a tractor. Pictures of my work and a life dedicated to God. Not bad at all.

Between the last page and the back cover was the letter. Okay, I was in the comfort of my home as I was supposed to be, so I opened the envelope.

I read the contents once and then a second time.

It was puzzling. Why, after saying nothing to me during the entire month, would Polycarp have done this? Why was he persisting?

I drove by Nature's Bountiful Harvest only once, diverted in my rounds of distributing my vegetables by the laying of fresh asphalt on Route 114A. I must admit I was tempted to walk through that front door, open to the soft September air, and to whisk Margery out to the bench at the rear of the store and tell her about the month at New Citeaux. Héloïse-and-Abélard style. But I would be fooling myself. I knew I couldn't do that, both because of my promise to Columban and the sure fact that if I saw her, all the sanctifying graces might easily have been overtaken.

I also wanted to talk over Polycarp's latest note with her. But, thinking about it, I realized that what I really wanted was having her know my reaction. She knew well of the insatiable reporter's curiosity that had led me to Robert Trumbell and Peter Vanik, and I wanted to prove to her that something inside me had changed. I was not going for the bait this time. No more would I buy the lottery ticket, sign on for the mystery cruise, go on a blind date. I was finally in control of myself.

Throwing Polycarp's note away would be firm testimony that I had broken the chrysalis and emerged anew. That act would surely have made easier my entry into New Citeaux in January.

Two simple incidents at a morning Mass turned my life in a direction I could not have imagined.

The first happened at Communion. Father Columban was distributing the hosts and Father Methodius the chalice to visitors in the guest chapel opposite mine, on the other side of the altar. I always remained kneeling at that time, focusing my mind on the precious gift that would soon enter my body. The God of the ages, through a Son who instituted with his friends a simple ritual of remembrance, would soon be with me. As real as he was to Peter and James and John. Flesh and blood; the Real Presence. I cherished that moment.

I raised my head slowly as others in the pews began to move toward the low brick wall, where we would receive. When I looked up, Columban and Methodius were not yet there. Some overeager visitor had risen and begun the movement. My eyes focused beyond the wall on the line of monks waiting to drink from the cup, which they did at the main altar after receiving the host from the principal celebrant at the low marble steps at the foot.

All the monks' heads were either bowed or their faces turned toward the altar, except for one.

Polycarp was staring directly at me.

How is it possible that a momentary look can carry so much meaning, be so clear in intent?

It was a question from Polycarp, brusquely put, to be sure, insistent and even impatient for an answer. He was not a man who could ever be politic in those everyday dealings that tact and even a trace of deviousness made so easy for many of us. He had given me the names—one, now a second—for some reason, at first baffling to me. But now it was becoming clear that Polycarp, in his own strange way, and for his own reasons, was trying to point out to me the dark side of life in the cloister. He wanted to make sure I had consulted other sources—as he must have known that any good journalist would do—before making my decision.

And then, moments later, the second occurrence: Columban's words as he pressed the host into my hand. He had never said more to me than the customary "The body of Christ," adding my name in good times and knowing the sting of withholding it in the bad. I was the last communicant that morning, and with the host in my hand, I hesitated for an instant. Columban looked behind me, and seeing no one waiting to receive, he whispered, "Have no fear, Joseph. Hold your heart and your mind open to God in these days and he will guide you." He made the sign of the cross over me.

I returned to my seat and bowed my head.

But it was neither God who was on my mind nor Jesus in that upper room. It was that young man in his neatly pressed jeans telling me that he was the Mother Teresa of his asylum. And that lawyer with his wide suspenders who with his own venom had poisoned himself. I had not wanted to meet either of them, but through fate and Polycarp I had. And, strangely, each had been a source of grace to me. I had seen that thin, thin line between derangement and holiness; I had seen where misguided passion for God can lead. With each man, my mind had been open—and opened—and through each of them I had been brought closer to a life at New Citeaux.

But now I was sure I had seen enough.

I did not want to spend my lifetime with such horror stories so that I could—again and again—know that, with all my faults, I was on this side. And they were not. No, Polycarp, I wanted no more. I might or might not become a Trappist monk; I might or might not be able to make it my commitment for life; but my days of field research were over. It was now up to God.

When I returned to the hermitage, I went to the bound volume the monks had given me and took out Polycarp's note. I was ready to tear it in half. I hesitated. I turned the envelope over. The flap was attached once more, this time with the lightest brush of September's humidity. I turned it over again and my index fingers and thumbs came together at the envelope's middle, ready to rend it.

My hands seemed frozen.

Why? Why couldn't I do this? What was holding me back?

I put the envelope down on the butcher-block kitchen counter. And I knelt down on the linoleum. I tried—successfully—to offer a wordless intercession to God. My mind was blank.

It was perhaps no more than two or three minutes later—it actually could have been no more than thirty seconds—that I opened my eyes and saw the envelope lying there before me on this ersatz altar, at eye level, its flap now ungainly erect. So many signs and symbols had guided me throughout the days at Falmouth. I had suffered; I had learned. I was still here. I must not close down now.

I was still kneeling when I reached for it.

The questing heart must know all. Before you go further. A visit to Robert Bellarmine. 25 Church Street, Brattleboro. *Ite, missa est.* Go, you are sent.

By the time I reached the address it was after five o'clock and the office of the *Brattleboro Journal* was deserted, another day's paper having been produced. In the reception area was a sign, ALL DELIVERIES TO GUARD ON DUTY, but there was no one in sight. The only noise was the gentle purr of a printer somewhere at the rear of the lobby. I saw a sign for the newsroom and began to climb a winding set of stairs, past displays of old typewriters, a linotype machine, the fonts of movable type that had served so well until, virtually overnight, electronic images condemned most of them to scrap heaps and the chosen few to such museums.

I hesitated at each outdated relic. Perhaps it was the memory of those sweet and innocent days as a daily reporter, when I was so excited each day to see my name anew in print. I would go to the back shop and run my hand over the byline in raised type, rubbing it for good luck so that it might be seen and I'd get a job on a major newspaper—say, in Buffalo or Syracuse. Albany was too grand even to imagine.

Or was it that those trusty, worn pieces of metal represented another era in my life? A time when three visits to the church of the right saint on the correct day merited a plenary indulgence, the wiping away of all punishment for sins forgiven in confession but still deserving years of scorching fire in purgatory? Waking up the next morning to receive Holy Communion, aware that my soul was as pure as it had been when I was baptized. Longing—if it ever had to happen—that I would be run over on my way to church. The sure formula of the Baltimore Catechism, that wondrously comprehensive book that held all reasonable questions about *the* authoritative religion and straightforward, unflinching answers. To memorize it was to possess the fullness of Catholic theology, to *know.*

A key pressed on the linotype, through a series of visible, mechanical movements dropped a matrix containing that letter onto a waiting rack. A line completed, it was swept away to receive a rush of molten lead that would form the words exactly. Equally, there was nothing complex about hand-set Bodoni or Garamond, no mystery in an old Royal typewriter.

Now the modern machines were covered with pale gray enamel and dotted with lights. They emitted unearthly sounds, ominously prodding when the user had erred and never deigning to show cause and effect. Letters on a page were no longer the product of a piece of metal pressing through an inked ribbon. No, now the images were sprayed on, a series of minute dots, seemingly random, that eventually formed perfect letters.

The spirituality that Columban had encouraged me to embrace was not like this. Nothing simple, straightforward. Somehow if you allowed this great nozzle called God to spray, he seemed to be saying, the words would be printed eventually—clear, clean, sure.

At the top of the stairs I walked by the spotlighted bronze Pulitzer Prize and the scores of brightly lithographed but gratuitous state awards—I had won so many local certificates I stopped having them framed—and toward the only man in the newsroom, seated inside the rim of a horseshoe-shaped copy desk.

Technology had changed, but this man had not; he had been an American newspaperman before indoor toilets became common and he would be here when lasers and not newsboys bring the paper. He was bald, and wore a red-striped rep tie, a blue-and-white-striped shirt—still crisp after a day's wear—and garters to take the slack from his sleeves. The ashtray beside his video terminal was full of butts, and the skin on his first two fingers looked charred.

I mentioned the name. He glared at me suspiciously.

"Who? Never heard of him; never worked here," he finally snapped in a gravelly voice. He reached for his pack of Lucky Strikes. "Sure of it. Been around for fifty years. More or less," he tacked on just in case I doubted the depth of his knowledge.

"Must have something mixed up," I muttered. "Sorry. Bad lead." I thanked him, more profusely than necessary for his abruptness and paucity of help, and headed back toward the stairs. I found I was sweating, although the office was comfortably air-conditioned. I also felt enormous relief. I wanted to be back in the hermitage, preparing some dry-fried string beans or a zucchini soup. I wanted to be sitting in the cool darkness of Compline at New Citeaux, think ing now of my God and ahead to my life as a Trappist monk. I had given in to my stupidity, my pride once more, but, thank God, I had come to a quick dead end. In a half hour, I would be home. And in a few months, at the monastery for good. Yes, that's what it would be—for good.

"You there. Hold on."

There was a certain fatigue in his voice, that of a weary veteran scientist for whom the breakdown of the chemicals had finally occurred but who didn't trust the results.

"That wasn't his real name, of course," he said, tauntingly holding back the precious piece of information his encyclopedic mind had just released. "You a reporter on this? National? Thought they put this one to bed months ago. Looked pretty straightforward to me. That's the way we reported it. What else could you say about it? We did a couple pieces. Ugly business." He got up from the desk and started toward the reference library at the back of the newsroom.

"Well, you coming or not?" he snapped.

Microfilm spun dizzily on the screen before me. I had to look away.

"See, right there. 'Refer to Haskins, Trevor B.' Did you know that was his real name?"

"No," I said, exhaling. "But that name I know."

"He called himself Robert Bellarmine only for a year or so; fell in with one of those kooky religious communes. Crazy bunch. Set up shop up around Killington and the kids couldn't get there fast enough. All of them took on names of famous Catholics, saints, intellectuals. Hell, we even had a Cardinal Newman and a Catherine of Siena. I don't know what they were about. Look at the background on Haskins; what the hell happened? Such a promising kid."

Trevor Haskins was the only son of an obviously wealthy New Hampshire manufacturer, a graduate of Notre Dame who had studied briefly at Louvain, as—as I had now dredged up from my junkyard of once-heard facts—had his idol, the seventeenth-century cardinal Bellarmine. The file, before the suicide, was as plentiful as any young man who was not an athlete could merit. He had gone to St. Callistus Priory, a prestigious local prep school run by the Carmelites, had won every academic award there and was a National Merit Scholar. In the words of his headmaster: "Trevor is the young man for all seasons; he has the highest average in the 125-year history of the priory school. He's a gifted person who can chart his own path in the world. To quote Cicero, *'Qui summam spem civium, quam de eo iam puero habuerant, continuo adulescens incredibili virtute superavit'* [Who as a young man has surpassed the highest hopes the citizens had entertained throughout his boyhood.—*De Amicitia*, III, 11]."

My lips moved and I read aloud the name of the headmaster who had spoken those words. It was an old habit, something I did when I could not believe what the words were telling me.

"P. Octavius Kiernan?" the editor said. "Knew him slightly. Quite a Latin scholar, wasn't he? With a name like that, what else could he be? School had to close down; I don't know, three, four years ago. Even Catholic parents didn't want that kind of old-fashioned education for their kids anymore. By then the priory was already finished. You Catholics and your Vatican Councils. Cleaned that place out. What an operation they used to have up there."

At St. Callistus Priory, the old monk in his stained black habit told me I would have to inquire at the parish house in town. He wasn't supposed to give out any information. About anything. And certainly not about former students or staff. He complained about the amount of work he had to do as watchman and confided that the Vermont Department of Corrections was interested in taking over the old sandstone buildings and turning them into a minimum-security prison. It would have made a fine prison, turrets and all. St. Callistus had been built at a time when calling a school an institution, a place at once formidable and forbidding, was considered a compliment.

The two priests at the parish house, in black trousers and sleek synthetic shirts stretching to cover sagging stomachs, looked both tired and annoyed. I had interrupted their

watching of a 7:30 celebrity-interview show, and I could
see from their faces that life itself had become a burden.
They were the remnant cloth of St. Callistus, Carmelite
monks given a dying parish that needed little tending, just
a morning Mass and an occasional funeral. Effectively, they
were retired. Both were in their mid-sixties. One of them
sighed heavily, as if merely listening to me demanded great
exertion. He then sent me back in the direction from which
I'd just come. I was not to go any farther than a small
house near the priory entrance.

I parked a distance away so I could try to gather my
thoughts, the first of which was: What was I doing here?
What did I expect this man to tell me? Had Brother
Polycarp intended this to happen? Had he led me here, and
if so, why? This man, so intent on telling me, in gory detail, about Trevor Haskins's death—what would I unleash
by now showing interest?

The front lawn of the house was a tangle of matted
weeds and grass grown tall and gone to seed. It had once
been a beautiful little fieldstone place, but huge hunks of
mortar had fallen out and the windows were badly in need
of caulking and painting. I assumed it was the gatekeeper's
home from its location just inside the high wall that had remained intact.

I stood on the tiny wooden porch for a moment, the rotted timbers straining under me. I raised my hand to knock.
I wished I was still a smoker. I would have loved a cigarette. I needed time.

Just days before—hours, really—my life had been so
simple; finally I was on track. I was ready to enter the
Trappists, to join that proud and select line of men, to become part of fifteen centuries of quiet monastic heroism. To
live my days and march toward the necessary death with
my eyes on God, trusting in His goodness and mercy. And
then, like a headstrong fool, I had again taken the bait.
Prayer? An openness to God? Signs and symbols? What a
common fool. The inquisitive reporter wouldn't die.

I had been exposed to three lives driven by a hunger different only in surface affects from the one that gnawed at me. Three lives, brought to madness, the death of the spirit, and, finally, the death of the body. Three men informed, influenced, and inflamed by Columban Mellary's spiritual vision. Had they sat with him and drunk coffee in the retreat-house parlor? On Wednesday mornings? Had they lived nearby, attended Mass, prayed, meditated, read Aelred? I shook my head violently, trying to make the questions stop.

I could hear someone moving inside the house. I had to knock. I didn't want to be caught on Kiernan's porch, my mouth hanging open, my arm paralyzed in midair. He was not the kind of man I wanted to meet from a point of weakness any more pronounced than mine already was.

I banged on the door twice.

At first he eyed me cautiously, as if he couldn't make out who I was. He'd been drinking. The light was fading fast now, the sun setting behind me, so I must have initially appeared black and faceless to him. "Ah," he said, taking me by the arm. He ushered me across the threshold. "I knew you'd look me up, mister. Eventually." His voice was weary, but he was pleased. *"Pax Intrantibus."*

He led me through the kitchen of his house, which struck me both with its neatness—he was such an unkempt man— and its sterility. Plastic curtains hung rigidly in place, never having been pulled back. A yellow colander served as a fruit bowl for a few wrinkled apples and a forlorn brown pear. A toaster, still in its box, sat on a kitchen chair. He was obviously a bachelor, or a widower, without any knowledge of how to make the space between four walls an actual home. There was an immediate sadness about the place.

In a small pantry at the back of the kitchen I could see a small selection of canned goods. Part of one shelf was devoted entirely to bottles of Canadian Club. The other shelves were bare.

The living room was even more of a curiosity. I have seen old women occupy such places—Eastern European widows, for the most part, in the neighborhood where I grew up. Torn from their villages, their husbands dead and children gone, they were frozen in time, waiting to die. Babushkas on their heads, rosaries in their hands, they surrounded themselves with a gallery of old friends who would not forsake them.

He motioned me to a chair and was about to ease into a well-worn recliner.

"Maybe you'd like a drink," he asked.

"I need one, yes, please."

"With ice or straight?"

"Straight will be fine."

"Make yourself comfortable."

On the mantel were various statues of Our Lady—at Lourdes, at Fatima—the Infant of Prague, the Sacred Heart of Jesus (an especially graphic depiction with a bleeding heart that looked like a piece of fresh liver), Saint Christopher, Saint Francis of Assisi, Saint Joseph, and a family of other saints whose trappings were not immediately familiar. Behind the statues and on his walls were dozens of holy pictures, the kind I remembered from my youth but which had been banished from most churches and homes long ago: the Immaculate Heart of Mary, the Virgin's eyes uplifted toward heaven; Saint Sebastian, a well-arrayed cluster of arrows in his heart; Pope Pius XII, in a state of emaciated saintliness, almost swallowed up by full papal regalia.

The table beside his recliner was stacked with books. From where I was sitting, I could easily read the titles. There was Thomas à Kempis's classic *Imitation of Christ*, the trusty *Rule of Saint Benedict*, and other old, worn books of spirituality: Dom Marmion's *Christ the Life of the Soul*, Faber's *All for Jesus*, and several titles by Tanqueray, Rodríguez, and Alphonsus Liguori. In their midst a few paperbacks with startlingly bright, glossy covers seemed misplaced. The artwork and technology that had gone into their presentation was modern, but the message was decidedly Old Church. There were a number of books about Padre Pio; others by assorted unproclaimed visionaries; and one, entitled *Is the*

Virgin Mary Appearing at Medjugorje?, about another in a seemingly endless series of her appearances, this one in what had been Yugoslavia. They were remnants of a religious faith now considered overly pietistic, one that was theologically suspect to most—except for gentle old souls, the furthest reaches of conservative Catholicism, and, obviously, P. Octavius Kiernan.

He returned with two mismatched juice glasses filled almost to the brim with whiskey and a yet-unopened bottle of Canadian Club.

"Wash?"

"Excuse me?"

"Would you like a wash for your drink? A little water? I've got a couple cans of ginger ale in there."

"This will be fine." I took a long swallow, as did he.

It was a bonding of sorts between Kiernan and myself, a ritual as old as that first meeting between primitive men when each voluntarily gave up a portion of his rationality to create a space where they might begin to find agreement. The whiskey went right to my brain. I had not eaten much all day. I don't know what immediate effect it had on Kiernan—or if his brain needed further deadening—but all the hostility of that morning when we had confronted each other at New Citeaux dissolved before our glasses were half empty.

It was obvious we knew we needed each other.

"Well, I guess I should tell you why I'm here. If I can figure out for myself, Mr. Kier—"

"Octavius would be better. My father was also a Latin teacher; a man with a love for the language, as am I, and a rather wicked sense of humor. Patrick was my baptismal name, but he put that out of the way the same afternoon."

"I was at New Citeaux for the month of August," I said. "As I was about to leave, I got a note with a name on it. Unsigned. I'd gotten another before. This one had Trevor's name on it. Not exactly—it was the name he took when he was part of the group at Killington."

"Robert Bellarmine! He was such a clever boy, so well

read. Only he would have chosen such a moniker. Oh, he was so wonderfully Catholic. Bellarmine had no stomach for the Anglicans, neither did Trevor. Bellarmine writing about their stupidity in a past century, Trevor in the twentieth. Did you ever see his column in the *New Oxford Review* and the great series from the Holy Land in *The New York Review of Books*? He was no more than twenty-four years old when he wrote it. Caused quite a stir. Absolutely first-rate. He was going through a phase up at Killington. I knew it wouldn't last. The other name?"

"A lawyer named Peter Vanik. And before him, I'd found out about a younger guy, Robert Trumbell."

"And?"

I told him what I'd found.

He pushed himself upright in the recliner, emptied his glass with a thirsty sailor's swallow. His eyes were gleaming. He filled both his glass and mine. His sallow skin seemed to take on new vitality. His labored breath was now regular and even.

"Now we have a Columban Mellary fan club. Whoever led you did so with the grace of the Holy Spirit. Poor souls. There are more of them, I'm sure of it. They say you're a writer. You should have great insights about all this, I should think. Some story, eh?"

"The first two troubled me," I said, careful to talk slowly so I would not slur my words. "Troubled me, yes, but I chalked it up to what was apparent: Trumbell had had a breakdown; and Vanik the lawyer was an overachiever, I guess—couldn't cope if everything didn't fall into place, and when it didn't, he turned against Columban, the Church, the whole business. But Trevor? Tell me about him and how he got—involved at the monastery."

" 'Involved'! What a sanitized little term! Don't use words like that with me, mister!" His face was flushed with anger; he ground his poorly fitting false teeth together while speaking as if he wanted to chew every word before he spat it at me for this insult.

"That boy killed himself, hanged himself on a self-made

cross so that the world and Columban Mellary could see he cared enough to make any sacrifice, any! 'Involved'! *Deus in adjutorium meum intende!*"

"Sorry. Let's get past it. Please go on."

He leaned back in the chair. "There is one woman in a man's life, and for the teacher"—he closed his eyes, speaking slowly as if to conjure up an image—"there is one student. Mine was brilliant, witty, kind, and wonderfully capricious. You know, one day he sneaked into the sacristy and starched my alb—we senior lay faculty vested with the religious community on major feast days. I was like Frankenstein in the procession. He had the whole school howling.

"I loved those rituals. Wanted to be a priest myself, but they said I was too scrupulous. Put me out of the junior seminary just for following rules. To the letter. Called me a 'scroop.' I was probably the only one there with a true calling. So I took a job at Saint Callistus. . . . It's a long story.

"Back to Trevor. He was deeply spiritual, and even though he was just a boy, he was a dear, dear friend, someone I could bring my problems to. Yes, and he was frail, terribly, terribly frail, as all great spirits are. Do you think Jesus was strong? I don't for an instant. His range was spectacular. Quantum physics and metaphysics; he played the piano, recorder, guitar; oh God, anything he picked up, he could make beautiful music with it. While the other boys were thumping their way through the standard texts, he was on to Maritain and Teilhard de Chardin, the new ones even, Schillebeeckx, Rahner, Küng, although I warned him about their modernist tendencies.

"But that didn't matter. I could forgive him anything, because he never held on to a theory or to knowledge selfishly or righteously. He took it all in and, with his marvelous mind, filed everything away for later use. His was the most capacious mind I'd ever encountered. He was never dogmatic."

His rhapsody of praise stopped. "Not until he discovered Columban Mellary."

"How did he come to meet him?" I asked.

He went on as if he hadn't heard me.

"Merton. I was never much of a fan of his. Ended up a Buddhist, didn't he, fawning over those pagan idols over there in Asia someplace? And Mellary was in the same vein. Conventional religion wasn't good enough for him— bored him, I think. But, but"—he exhaled heavily— "Columban Mellary was *alive*. That made it very difficult. Master of men's souls! The way, the truth and the life! *Via, veritas et vita*. No, not God! Columban Mellary painted *himself* that way!"

He held his glass in front of him the way priests offer the chalice at the Consecration, one hand grasping the side, the fingertips of the other hand gently supporting the base. He stared into the amber liquid, raised the glass still higher, then brought it down to his lips.

"He was searching—been to see others. Jesuits, Carthusians, the diocesan vocation director. But they all could see he was flailing about. But Columban listened to him, took him seriously. And then Trevor would come back with all kinds of cockamamy stuff. Jung, Freud—pagans and Jews; what did they ever offer the world?—meditation, contemplation, all that rubbish. What ever became of the classical tradition? Aquinas rolls over in his blessed grave at such stupidity. 'Divine mercy.' 'A loving God.' God, it made me sick! But I couldn't reason with Trevor. He saw Columban Mellary maybe a dozen times—that's all—but he defended whatever he told him that day. 'Father Columban thinks I might have a Trappist vocation.' I sat him in the very chair you're sitting in and tried to tell him he was being led astray. By a demon, an Antichrist! Trevor raised his voice at me. He had never, ever done that before."

We sat in silence for a while, as I tried to sound the depths of the old man's pain.

"Did you ever confront Father Columban, tell him what was going on?" I finally asked. "Maybe, just maybe, there's another side to this."

"Mister," he glared at me, "I only went up there to the

monastery to investigate, for Trevor's sake. I never said a word to the man and I don't intend to. Until he's in his casket. And then I'll offer a prayer to God that Satan who had possessed him left his body before he died. Yes, possessed! Does that sound like too strong a word, mister?" He leaned toward me, his eyes widening.

"A little stronger than I've heard. Since grade school."

"If you could have seen what came over Trevor, how he just unraveled right before my eyes, you wouldn't doubt me one bit. How about you? Didn't you think you were going off sometime?"

"I've been doing that on and off most of my life, Octavius. I'm not a good litmus test."

He leaned toward me and put his hand on my knee. "All right, that's all behind us now, history. I want your help, mister. Please. Something for Trevor. A memorial. I think it's only fitting."

The whiskey made his face blur, although he was no more than a few feet in front of me. But there was something distinctive about his mouth that I noticed as he smiled at me, asking my cooperation. The middle portion of his lips were thin, but formed. The edges, the part that turns up or down to show emotion, didn't exist. It was as if a plastic surgeon had neatly cut them away. Or, through a life of Old Church piety and abnegation, they had atrophied from disuse.

"I feel bad for the boy. But he wasn't a boy, was he? Must have been—"

"He was twenty-seven. Good, good," he breathed, "I knew you'd help. We can get started right now."

"I've got to get something to eat."

"No, mister, it's exactly the right time."

"For what?"

"To begin our planning, our strategy—"

"I don't understand."

"—that will lead to the indictment, trial and conviction of Columban Mellary. *Homicidii causa!* For murder! That lawyer's name? Vanik, was it?"

10. October

HEAVY frost struck early in the month at Falmouth. Viciously cold nights with innocently clear skies caused even natives who had seen decades of summers abruptly snuffed out to search their memories for a more brutal autumn. There was no gentle easing, with temperatures just below freezing for a few nights. The weather changed with a hammer's blow, definite and unyielding. It was 15 degrees one morning when I awoke. A weather-bureau mark that had stood for over a century was broken.

My winter squash lay on the ground, burned, the bloated oozing fruit not even fit for the rapacious raccoons and woodchucks. Kale survived, but the leaves were bitter and coarse. A normally sturdy strain of spinach lay in damp, thick piles, festering with brown rot in the midday sun. Cabbage and broccoli were black and mottled with death. Why had I planted so much—in faith—and harvested so poorly, without discernment? The bounty was there. Like a partygoer at a wonderful affair, I didn't know when to go home. October was not a month to be trusted.

Mr. Standish's arthritis was giving him more of a problem with the early onset of cold weather, so he asked me to help him with his fall plowing. It was the only blessing of what turned out to be the cruelest time of the year at Falmouth for me. Thank God I had some real work to do.

I traversed the fields high above the house, which commanded views of the already snowcapped mountains of Vermont and New Hampshire and, to the south, the thick pine forests and open farmland of Massachusetts. In front were frostbitten clumps of alfalfa, splayed out on the grass, and thick knots of weeds that had begun to choke the planting. Behind were thick brown rolls of broken earth, studded with rocks and clods of torn sod that had so valiantly produced year after year, even as the clusters of grass were being strangled to death.

Sacrifice, always, sacrifice. Always death so that life might rise anew. Frankly, I was sick of it. Any remnant of a symbolic, transcendent way of looking at my life was gone. I yearned for the static, unchanging, straightforward, venal, ordinary—my old life. My Egypt had not been so bad; why was I so eager to leave it behind? And for what? This?

My love affair with suffering and sacrifice was over. I was beginning to see a new side of religious commitment.

Aelred, Saint John of the Cross, Bernard, Augustine, Merton—I put them all aside and, for some reason I still cannot fathom, concentrated on a new spiritual mentor. I was soon obsessed with him; I sensed his hunger, felt his pain, knew his intensity. But instead of inspiring, as so many wild-eyed seekers had before, he confirmed the dementia—kindly put, the darker side—of the mystical quest. Why hadn't I seen this before? Why, before Charles de Foucauld came alive on the pages of those three books, had I rationalized and turned my eyes away?

As a cavalry officer in the 1880s, de Foucauld helped conquer the Sahara for the French—before the desert, in its turn, captured him. Somehow, the stark beauty, uncompromising justice and purity he found in that barrenness resonated in his soul. He didn't want to wander in the desert, he wanted to *live* there. He joined the Trappists, yearning to spend his days in simplicity and peace, but even they were too lush and lenient for him. His God was out on windswept plateaus, where sand slashes the human face and the tongue swells for lack of moisture. Too intense, this de Foucauld, his spiritual betters concluded. Heartbroken that he had not found his calling, confused about how he might live his life, he went back to the desert, alone, to be among the nomadic Tuareg in the rugged Hoggar mountains of Algeria.

As best he could determine, there was only one way: to live in poverty, to pray, and to serve these wretchedly poor Arabs. He built a tiny stone hut, receiving as the Christ whatever visitor came to him. How wonderful, this man, how giving, my Church would say, how Christlike. He might have starved himself to death, but that would have ruined his chances for everlasting greatness. No, Charles de Foucauld let himself be killed by the very people he helped. The Tuareg butchered him no differently from the way they would have killed any other old goat. Rome will make him a saint someday, guaranteed.

This fanatic lived on harsh grains and dressed like a tribesman himself, following his personal vision of God, eagerly yielding to the beckoning of the desert so that he could truly find him. Why, I was finally acknowledging, should such derangement be honored? The way of the pilgrim? Why was this Church of mine so edified by such excess? While supposedly in pursuit of God, it seemed, any sort of outlandish act, any stripe of aberrant behavior, could be written off as grace, a special gift.

After that trip to Brattleboro and the evening with Kiernan, and with de Foucauld running through my mind, I couldn't look upon the monks of New Citeaux as I had before.

They became different people, alarmingly so. But equally, something within me—a deep yet somewhat preconscious belief in God and in his ability to help me through this crisis—would not allow mere retreat from the monastery. There was more to know before I headed back to New York. But, for sure, I was no longer the willing, supple neophyte; my eyes had been opened. Monks I had come to know more intimately during my month at New Citeaux, in whose faces I had found inspiration and in their demeanor, hope, I now saw differently. No, it wasn't every monk into whose heart I could now see more deeply, but I understood enough of them that it sent shivers through my body just to watch them.

Father Joachim, who I had thought looked at the world impassively from behind Vermont's bushiest eyebrows, came clear as a scowling, raging man. His hands were always balled into fists. Why hadn't I noticed that? And just the way he marched onto the altar on the days he was the principal celebrant, the way his heels dug into the thick red carpeting, made him look like a goose-stepping Nazi, on parade before his Führer.

Father Thomas, the lone Asian in the community, had always appeared to be so mild-mannered. His face never changed as he walked toward the altar. But when his turn came to receive Communion each morning, he snatched the host out of the priest's hand, allowing it neither to be placed on his tongue nor in his palm. I thought he would crumble the fragile wafer with such a mighty swipe. What was roiling about beneath that placid surface? Why did he never concelebrate Mass with the other priests?

Brother Boniface was effeminate, to be sure, and what was behind that seductive leer—it could never be called a smile—he imparted to the priest offering him the chalice? A look like that couldn't be interpreted as anything other than an invitation. What liaisons were there within those walls; what illicit acts behind closed doors? Brother Pontius, Brother Marcellius, old Brother Januarius—why did they never take Communion at all, choosing instead to lurk in the shadows at the back of the monks' choir? What pact had they made, what sin committed, what belligerence perfected?

Father Vincent Ferrar, a short, grossly overweight man— the author of a handful of devotional books that had found a wide following among the charismatics but were so embarrassingly gushy that they were rarely reviewed in monastic publications—always seemed to be onstage. The way he lifted his eyes and raised his arms to heaven at the Our Father. The way he extended his two fingers toward the altar at Consecration when he was a concelebrant, mimicking

Michelangelo's depiction of God at the Creation. Delivered in a rich baritone voice, his inappropriately dramatic inflections at the recitation of ordinary prayers cast him as ludicrously overstated, pretentious, and vain.

Then, there was Polycarp. And Columban.

This perverse pair, situated as they were in choir where they had no choice but to exchange the sign of peace, feigned such overwhelming affection for each other. Who was the Jekyll and who the Hyde? And on which day?

I could see so clearly now that Columban's serene countenance, which had so attracted me, was no more than a grotesquely peaceful mask, seemingly expressing acceptance and love and compassion, but in reality being nothing but an ingeniously fabricated disguise. Polycarp's stony exterior was an equally fine pretense. Such a face continually solicited others to seek his good graces, to hopefully eke a smile from his turned-down lips. Polycarp, who had dragged me through the trash heap of souls. Columban, who had taunted me with my weaknesses to go farther and farther into his desert. What was he hoping for, an intellectual soul mate—the son he would never have—someone to share his declining years at New Citeaux? Someone to talk over the new translation of Antony of the Desert, an exciting new Catholic author, a new book on contemporary morality, the lead review in the Sunday *Times*, or an excellent bit of analysis in *The Economist*?

These were men of God? Keepers of the eternal flame?

Octavius Kiernan, whom I had so easily labeled as deranged, suddenly looked almost normal compared with them. He began to attend Mass more regularly, and when I saw him outside the church the second week of the month, he pressed into my hand with a knowing smile an article from what at first appeared to be a scholarly journal. "The Cloister: Vision or Pathology? Followers of God or the Devil?" The tone was decidedly biased, produced as it was by some rabidly anti-Catholic group called Keepers of the Flame, whose address was a post office box in Virginia.

But as I read through the tirade, parts of it now made perfect sense to me.

Kiernan appeared in even better spirits a few days later as he rushed to head me off before I reached my car after Mass.

"Mister, mister!" He was out of breath, and positively elated. "Vanik will handle the case for us. For free. Sees it our way. Oh, boy, does he! He's ready to take affidavits from you and Trumbell, and me about Trevor. The first step, but down the road there's a grand jury, a trial and—"

"Hold on. Right now I don't know how well any of us would stand up in a grocery line, much less in court."

"Insignificant details. We'll find more people like you. I'm sure Columban's bodies are strewn all over."

"Mr. Kiernan?" a voice said.

There were two of them. Vigorously healthy, trim and tall. Their rosy cheeks looked absolutely cherubic, but their eyes were unblinking, clear and cold. They wore dark suits of a fabric that would not tolerate wrinkling. When Kiernan protested the handcuffs, they grabbed him more roughly than I thought necessary, and when I tried to intercede they were not inclined to listen. They shoved him into the backseat of their unmarked car.

"Malicious trespassing with criminal intent. That's the charge. The folks up there"—the taller of the two plainclothes Vermont state troopers nodded toward the abbey—"are tired of his monkey business. Now step away from the vehicle. We're just doing our job."

I was stunned. What to do? Follow them? Go up to the abbey and find out exactly what had brought this about and, more important, who had notified the state police? I watched the car turn around in the circular drive and speed down the road toward the gate.

I looked up at the massive bell tower, at the golden cross atop the church roof sharply outlined against the dazzling blue sky. I looked at the tiny windows of the monk's cells, and then at the huge leaded windows of the chapter room, where the community gathered for their meetings. At the puff of smoke coming out of the guesthouse chimney, the sign that the parlor fireplace was in use. A rich benefactor having coffee with the abbot? I looked out across the monastery fields, gently sloping down to the trees, to the barns, all painted the standard New Citeaux shade, a murky, practical brown.

I put my hand on the door handle of the pickup. I was shaking.

I needed a while to cool off, to think this through rationally, to put Kiernan's arrest in perspective—and certainly to spend some quiet time alone in prayer. At least one habit I had cured over the year was impulsiveness. In a strange way, Kiernan's arrest helped me test myself. I tried to convince myself of that on the drive home.

But back at my house I was hardly a study in reason. My intention was right, but what was welling up in me was much too strong to be controlled by a mere act of the will.

I added wood to the stove, burning my finger. I slammed the lid, cracking the cast iron.

I chipped my coffeepot while washing the morning dishes. I flung it across the room, shattering it against a wall.

Changing into work clothes, I dislodged a shirt from its hanger. I cleared the rack with a sweep of my arm.

A piece of wood wouldn't rest straight on the sawhorse, so I kicked it into place. The pain in my foot was so great I bit the inside of my lip. I didn't know what to do first, stop the bleeding in my mouth or do something about my foot. I wasn't sure if I'd broken it.

I soaked the foot in cold water. As the toes turned a pale purple, I clutched at the side of the tub to help diffuse the pain. Then, trying to ease the bruised and swollen foot out of the tub, I bumped it against the faucet. That released me.

"Columban! It's you, Columban!"

I had, for that hour or two, smothered my rage, but I knew who was behind this. Only one person needed to have Kiernan removed. Columban Mellary's neat little kingdom had been violated and he wanted the intruder banished. Ah, charity! The good and gracious Christian monk having to call upon the Roman centurions to do his dirty work.

Anyhow, it was time. What a propitious moment to confront Columban and tell him that his soaring allegories of monk and prisoner might someday soon be grounded in reality.

I heard a noise on the wooden deck outside the sliding glass doors.

My heart began beating rapidly. The pain in my foot was instantly gone.

I crept into the hallway, keeping my head down so I couldn't be seen through the windows. There was a rap on the glass. A second knock, soft, disarming. Scenarios flashed through my mind. Where was my ax? Why hadn't I bought a gun? The voice outside was muffled at first. Then it registered.

"Joey! Hey, Joey, you in there? Lox and bagels from Zabar's—fresh, Joey. Pastrami from Katz's. Katz's, Joey—remember 'Send a salami to your boy in the army'?"

He had two huge bags with him and a recent Bennington graduate who was working part time at his office while doing advanced studies at Princeton. She was well scrubbed, attractive, and terribly earnest.

"Joey, I tried everything to get through to you. You even got Uncle Morty praying. Why don't you have a fax up here? Listen, we got to get working on this. The publisher wants it yesterday. Bentley-Weber—high-class house. Spring list, fall list; they'll make up a special list for you. Metro wants to go into production ASAP. They got Jeremy Irons, Joey, even without the script. Joey, eat, eat, while we're talking. This Nova will take your breath away. Courtney, get the rest of the stuff from the car. Joey, I got Perugina chocolates and Dom Pérignon and some beluga caviar. I want to love you, Joey, but I can't get you on the phone! Is it working? Courtney, check the phone. Order a new phone."

"Mort, you sweetheart." I kissed him on his glistening forehead.

"Now, don't say you're not going to do this, Joey. We're looking at big bucks here. Six figures. *Well* into the six figures, just for openers. I got more since I wrote you. You could retire on this one."

"Everything's up in the air right now," I said weakly.

" 'Everything's up in the air,' he says. Let's bring it down. On the table. Contract. Simple. Look, you need help? Courtney, honey, put all that stuff over there. Joey, this girl is the best researcher you ever saw. Types like a whiz, smart, easygoing. Takes dictation. Imagine, Joey, a Phi Beta Kappa who takes dictation. Courtney, call a motel—closest one. Get a room. Best they got. Rent a car. I'll send up your clothes. Hell, buy everything new." He pulled out a roll of bills and peeled off at least ten hundred-dollar bills.

"I'll do anything I can to help," Courtney said. "Mr. Brunt has told me so much about you. What a fascinating idea. You're so brave. I've read everything you've ever written."

She smiled. Just as Polycarp's look had told me so much, so did hers. Courtney would stay at the motel a few nights and then, if so required or requested, she would stop wasting time commuting back and forth.

"Right now, I'd like to—" I began.

"Good, let's eat. Then we'll sign the contracts. Got a bathroom in this place? Don't do anything rash, Joey. Don't join up, please! Call Uncle Morty when you feel bad. Call your shrink. My shrink. Courtney, do you have a shrink?"

"—but I can't," I said.

"Joey, don't say words like 'can't.' Uncle Morty doesn't understand 'can't.' *'Can.'* 'Can.' Think 'can.' You're hurting Uncle Morty's feelings! Courtney—you're hurting Courtney's feelings too!"

Was it Brother Polycarp's compassion for my limp or did he see a man he had beaten so badly there was nothing left but pity? He opened the guesthouse door while I was still some distance away. His huge, unblinking eyes seemed almost painted on his thick lenses: Oriental enamel, impassive, all-seeing. Eyes that no longer needed to smolder in their sockets, for they had subdued their prey.

He allowed me in without saying a word. "Can I help you?" he inquired as properly as a new clerk in the menswear department.

"Is Father Columban in?"

"Oh, I'm sure he's *in*. After all, this is a cloistered—"

"Might I see him, then?"

"I'll ask. Did you hurt your foot?"

I stared at him. He blinked nervously at the pause. I hobbled over to the windowsill, where a box of old library cards that were used for notes was kept.

"Yes?" he asked tentatively, a nonquestion, to be sure.

"Yes, what?" I confronted him.

"Can I . . . do you . . . what are you doing?"

"I thought I'd give you a message to take to him. In case he's forgotten who I am."

"I'm sure he remembers you, Joseph," Polycarp answered brusquely. "Wait in the parlor, please."

I waited the better part of an hour, constructing both simple and complicated lines of argument, only to find some fault with each of them. When I heard the familiar shuffling footfall of his monastery-made sandals, I still had nothing ready. All I could do was mutter a quick prayer to the Galilean who promised his shaky and anxious disciples that, in whatever situation they found themselves, He would inspire them in what to say.

Columban knocked gently, and entered the room.

He smiled and patted my hand across the table. "Should I get us some coffee? Brother Polycarp says you've injured your foot. Is it serious?"

"I'm fine, Father. And you?"

"Oh, nothing much different here, Joseph. Some new young men. Many letters from prospective applicants. Seems to be a lot of interest in New Citeaux these days.

For some reason, a national group of vocation directors thinks I have something to do with that. Isn't that silly? They want me to go to New Orleans to address their convention. Imagine, New Orleans. What would I possibly say? Perhaps that spiritual revolution you talk about is here. Is there something wrong? You haven't been attending Mass as regularly. But then, I respect your need to be alone, to think this decision through on your own. To pray for God's guidance. Your reading, Joseph—what is it now?"

"I'm reading about a madman. In fact I'm rather . . . rather preoccupied with him."

"Really?"

"Charles de Foucauld. He took the desert seriously. Didn't want to leave. Even you wouldn't advise that, would you?"

"Ohhh." He shook his head slowly from side to side. "Don't be quick to judge de Foucauld. God calls each man in a different way. And each man in his own heart knows if he is true to that call as best he can discern it."

My foot was throbbing and my face must have shown it.

"Joseph, are you well? It's unlike you to just show up."

"Just thinking, Father. About discernment. Paths in life. Vocation. Not only an individual's task—now, is it? He can have help along the way."

"Yes, of course."

"From a holy and wise soul. A spiritual director. Someone—like you, perhaps."

He folded his hands in front of his mouth, the signal he would not return such a feeble volley. He would wait until I hit and hit strongly to his forehand. He was not a man who wanted his first stroke to be anything less than authoritative.

"But that's a tricky business, I'd say," I continued. "Discerning for someone else, as a spiritual director must try to do. Perhaps he's leading the person in exactly the wrong direction. Or, God forbid, toward something harmful. But"—I tossed my head back—"that couldn't happen. Heavens, no! But let's just posit. A very fervid young man, a bit immod-

erate and intemperate, but a real seeker after the truth.
Thinks he wants to become a monk. Now, he could turn out
like a Merton or . . . a Mellary and pour all his energies
into the quest for God. Or—and now it gets interesting—
the young zealot is just a shade unbalanced. Nothing you
might have noticed if he were an accountant or a man re-
pairing vacuum cleaners in some back room. But this awful
rowing toward God is more than his circuits can stand—a
mixed metaphor, but I wanted to employ your analogies,
Father, if I quote you accurately—and he goes off the deep
end. Now, who's to blame, would you say? Hypothetically,
of course."

Columban took a deep but inaudible breath. "Joseph,
what is it you're driving at?"

"I'm not being clear? Sorry, Father. Let me cite some
cases, mention a few names—good men, to be sure. Unher-
alded as yet. But they gave it all for God. Ready? Robert
Trumbell. Peter Vanik. We've talked about them, right?
And now Trevor Haskins, may he rest in peace. Three persons, a sort of trinity, no?"

Columban lowered his eyes and then, as if that movement had lowered a fulcrum point, slowly bowed his head.

"Too bad about them, isn't it, Father? But don't worry;
after all, you have so many fans out there, hanging on
every line you write them, thirsting for ever so tiny a drop-
let distilled through the mind of such a wise spiritual master. And another batch coming up. Ah! Thousands of new
converts to the Gospel according to Columban—"

"So your search for new material goes on, Joseph." His
voice, so low and injured, stopped me for an instant.

"A good friend wanted me to know a few of these fellows before I went any further with my Trappist vocation,"
I continued.

"I would imagine your friend must dislike me a great
deal to go to such lengths."

"I consider it a blessing."

"I weep for them, you know that, Joseph. I can't tell you
how much. Such good young men, so determined, so seri-

ous about their journey. And so . . . so fragile at the same time. Robert—" He paused as if to bring a face vividly to mind. "Peter, Peter. And poor Trevor—to lose sight of God's mercy like that. Just this morning I offered my Mass for him. I feel so—"

"Guilty? Would that do?"

He mouthed the word as if it were in a foreign language and he was trying to decode its meaning.

"I wouldn't say 'guilty.' "

"Then what would you say?"

"Joseph, why are you badgering me like this? Three young men I tried to help, three young men in enormous pain who sought guidance in their life's journey. I did what I could. Obviously, it was not enough."

"To help them?"

"Yes, to help them."

"And how exactly did you go about that, Father?"

"I don't think that's an appropriate question. As you would expect our conversations to be between you, me and God, so are theirs confidential."

"But it interests me, now that I've seen all of them. Or at least two of them—but I know something about Trevor. Did you encourage them to join? Help them figure out the faces in their trees? Give them the standard reading list on pain and privation?"

"That it *interests* you isn't enough, Joseph," his voice edged louder. "Can't you ever leave the reporter at home? I told you I would say nothing about it. Why are you doing this? What do you hope to gain? What's wrong with you?"

"*Wrong?* What's wrong, the great one asks me. One of them strings himself up with a piece of liturgical paraphernalia. Another is in the loony bin saying, 'Columban is so invested in me.' And the last guy is a shell of a man, thriving on hate. Oh, nothing's wrong, Columban. God's in his heaven, the Trappists are safely ensconced at New Citeaux and peace shall reign upon the earth!"

"Joseph, please, you're disturbing the other retreatants."

"How do you explain it? Just bad luck? Three strokes of bad luck?"

"We are weak; the road is long. The gate narrow."

"Lovely quote, Columban. You've used it before. Many times. Let's just call it what it is, goddammit—spiritual hysteria, cultivated by you!"

"*You* are becoming hysterical, Joseph; it doesn't suit you."

The tone of his voice, so rational and uninvolved, so bled of emotion, was suddenly more than I could take.

I lunged across the table.

The seventeenth-century French parlor chair crumbled into a pile of elegant kindling beneath him. We tumbled onto the Persian rug. I could hear the seam giving way between his scapular and hood.

I had a man's flesh between my hands and I wanted those hands to meet. A manner of praying, of sorts. I wanted to press the last drop of life out of him, to snuff out this perverted, deceptive beacon by which so many had steered their ships of soul, only to be dashed upon the rocks of their own limitations. Why wait for Kiernan, for legal relief? Justice was in my hands.

I might have killed him, had he fought me.

He lay there, the very breath being choked out of him, and Columban Mellary did not so much as reach for the hands on his throat. What a tribute to Trappist discipline and to his years of renunciation including, at that moment, his will to sustain his life.

I slowly released my grip. Thumb-sized reddish welts formed on either side of his larynx.

"Father? Father, is everything all right?" Brother Polycarp's voice called through the door.

"Yes . . . fine," Columban said, his voice raspy.

He carefully moved the remains of the chair out of the way and brought its mate to the table. He rearranged his garments and repositioned the buckle on his huge leather belt to the side.

"Can we start again, Joseph?" he said, as if nothing had happened.

It took a few moments and a series of deep breaths for me to calm myself enough to talk.

"Columban Mellary, I have no way of knowing if what you do is intentional or not. Frankly, I don't care. But what you are doing is nurturing a flock of cripples to believe that someday they can run the marathon. Ordinary, pathetic human beings who think that someday they are going to be Trappist monks. With you as their guide, their inspiration. Me, I'm one of them, no different; I just have a better rap. That's what'll probably keep me out of the nuthouse and off the limb of a tree.

"I believed you and you led me on. Oh, God, I believed every last drippy bit. 'A love beyond telling.' What seduction! Who could resist that? You dangle the beauty of a Trappist life in front of them—me!—and drive all of us wild. You should be in jail for this. Murder, that's what it is. You murdered Trevor Haskins!"

The only trace of emotion on his face was in his eyes, which narrowed to a squint. Was it pain he felt?

"And then you have Kiernan dragged off. For what? For knowing the truth about you? Good God, look at what you're doing."

"Do you still want her that badly?"

"What are you talking about? Don't try to lead me off with your smooth sophistry."

"The girl. Margery—is that her name? José?"

"Don't you dare call me that! She has nothing to do with this. Those cadavers, living and dead; that's what we're dealing with. Margery is the last—"

"Shut up!" He slammed both fists on the table and glared at me. "You've been playing games so long, you don't have an idea what's truth and what's an artistic moment! Yes, it is horrible, absolutely horrible, about those young men. If their souls have been lost because of me, then God will be my judge and may I burn in hell. But do you think for an instant that by conjuring up all these excuses, by setting up these paper soldiers to blow over, you can fool God?

"Fool me? That's easy. I'm a professional fool. It's part of my vows. 'I vow to become a fool for Christ and to take the abuse of anyone who chooses to do so.' But I warn you. Don't trifle with *him*. For if he wants you for his own, you'll never be happy in the arms of a woman or a career or a reputation. At some moment in the waking hours of every day of your life, you'll know. You'll be driving along a beautiful country road, alone—and it will be there. It will haunt you in your dreams and eat at you. That you tried to delude the greatest lover the world has ever known."

"You're so fucking facile," I said. "You can take whatever anybody says and turn it around. It sounds so religious all of a sudden. Not ugly and murderous as it really is."

"Joseph."

He waited after calling my name, to make sure that the air was absolutely clear before he made the final pronouncement.

"I may be a devil or an angel to you. Only you can decide. But in God's divine plan we cannot ask why certain things happen to you or me. Only what each of us must do with our life. It's your choice, Joseph. Do you wish to live by faith or feeling? Do you want to be a good journalist and get the whole story? An intellectual and understand all that's happening about you? A man with a woman? Or, Joseph, do you want to trust in God's mercy and become a saint?"

11. November

THERE is a vivid blood-red circle made with a thick felt-tipped pen around the date on my calendar. I circled the date, the twenty-fourth, the Feast of Saint Columban, long in advance of the day—and not after it. That is important to remember.

I marked the twenty-fourth during one of those green and fertile periods when I loved Columban Mellary so much and wanted more than anything to please him. Trappist monks not only leave behind all material possessions, but also turn their back on family and friends as well as those yearly events that mark the turning of their lives and their station within those lives. Birthdays mean nothing to the monks, their own or anyone else's. There are no Father's Days or normal secular anniversaries to celebrate. Everything is taken from them, their clothes, their name, those signal days. They are pottery broken into shards, and hopefully, in faith, formed anew.

And so, monks take on new celebrations, commemorative of their new life, such as the anniversary of solemn profession or ordination. But the one day each year that the monastery especially rejoices with them—in fact, the entire Church on earth—is their feast day.

The Feast of Saint Columban this year also happened to be the day Vincent Mellary entered New Citeaux thirty years before. The abbot at the time, a grumpy old Frenchman in office too many decades, looked at the bright face before him—one of the many young men of the time inflamed by the Trappist ideal—turned to the church calendar and, without consultation or hesitation, pronounced his religious name.

"Ici nous n'avons pas un frère Columban. Pourquoi pas vous?"

For months, I had wanted to make this November 24 a truly memorable day for Columban, as I realized it could be the last time as a secular man I would have such an appropriate occasion to bring delicacies from the outside world that were denied to him. Cold pressed duck, champagne, croissants, a wonderfully ripe Brie, steak tartare, crisp Calvados from Normandy, wonderful herb breads, dry Alsatian wine. I had a menu concocted that would have taken a week to consume. I also wanted him to remember me in the simple, restrictive days yet to come, those we would share together as monks of New Citeaux. So I created a list of presents he might, in good conscience, be able to keep: a pair of warm sheepskin slippers, a soft cashmere sweater easily worn under his white house robe, gloves, an imported beret.

It saddened me that I had left for church that morning with nothing for him in the pickup. The best I could do was to vow still another of my many promises: my Mass and prayers would be offered to God for him, regardless of what harm he had done to others. Or to me.

Because I knew, in turn, he had done more for me than anyone I had ever known in my life.

The twenty-fourth dawned cloudy and bitterly cold, the temperature hovering around 5 degrees. The wind, from the northwest, was only a mild breeze when I left the hermitage, but by the time I arrived on the monastery hilltop it had become stiff and biting. As I walked around the half circle of the driveway, I remembered those early days when I thought the Vermont winter an apt metaphor for the state of my frozen soul, and when my body rebelled at such assaults. The seasons had turned once more. Warmth was a distant memory. The cold weather, which inevitably forces a man inward, this year had asserted itself authoritatively, allowing no quarter. Yes, in certain ways I was a stronger man than the one who came here a year ago. But the God whom I sought—his face, presence, mind, whatever quality I variously and vainly attached to him as this year sped by—had evinced awesome power in the most concrete way. From All Saints' at the beginning of the month, as frigid day followed upon frigid day, it seemed as though God had commanded nature to enter a new ice age. His hand was upon the earth, glaciating the soil he had so graciously allowed to thaw months before. Displeased with what had sprung up on this planet this particular year, he had unleashed those winds and gases, the whirling stars and planets we have yet to discover, the unfathomable mix of Creation. He had angrily struck a blow against mankind.

Frost plunged through leaves already too clotted to be raked and stabbed into the earth's crust. Mantles of ice were cast over the shallow lakes of Falmouth. Waterlines burst in homes where screen windows had been frostily welded onto their casings. Fuel trucks worked from before dawn and into the night. Mr. Standish, not a man to be grim in the worst of times, gravely nodded and said that perhaps this spring another man would have to plant his corn and alfalfa. Would I be available? The Vermont National Guard was placed on alert; there were rumors of old people dying in their frigid homes.

My pickup was only one of many vehicles whose gas lines, filled as they were with the merry moisture of warmer days, turned solid. I imagine I could have called a service station for help, but my problem seemed so small. I had missed Mass not a few mornings.

My morning meditations during this month—longer, given that I had more time—became an even more disquieting time of picking and sorting, going through the year I had spent in this house, and considering some of the companions who had walked with me part of the way.

Aelred, first and foremost, had beckoned with his croaking voice, soothed me with his own confessions of guilt, and then, when I was close to his bed, grabbed me by the throat. No, he said, the spiritual life was not merely so many hours on a Zen bench, the humble recitation of past sins, a few convenient good deeds. Not at all; it was a building upon that shaky and pathetic foundation an entirely new way of living, disciplined and alert. Ever watchful, never yielding. Awesomely difficult. Unsure. Painful to the end.

Saint John of the Cross, de Foucauld, the four writers of the Gospels, Cassian, Bernard, Stephen Harding, Robert of Molesme. Sometimes they were too zealous and rhapsodic, but each, relentlessly, absolutely sure of his insight and convictions, pointed me toward an ideal of earthly perfection that could be gained only at great cost.

Father Raymond and Brother Armand were among those uncrowned saints at New Citeaux who seemed to have come closest to achieving it. Robert Trumbell, Peter Vanik, Trevor Haskins—holy men in their own right—driven mad in the process. Then there was that contingent of monks who had looked so holy and yet, viewed with my now practiced eye, seemed to be impostors. It was all so confusing.

Polycarp. Columban. Which were they?

Then there was Margery.

The thought of her was so frighteningly alluring that I tried to blot her from my mind whenever she entered it. She had never deceived, only given love. There was not a hint of guile in her, no hidden agenda. Here was true, unvarnished goodness.

But I realized if I gave in to her now I would know for the rest of my life that I had, ultimately, not allowed God's grace to work. I had not permitted him to bring forth the good fruit—as the first Psalm proclaims—"in due season." Whatever that fruit might be.

And, of course, there was P. Octavius Kiernan.

He had been in the background for much of the year, but now he was foremost in my mind, a crusader battling in a Holy War. He wanted desperately for me to wear his colors and to send a lance through the heart of a man I had thought of as a great spiritual master and he believed to be Lucifer incarnate.

Kiernan came to the hermitage on two occasions before I saw him on the twenty-fourth. On the first visit he was triumphant that he had been released without bail, and assured me he not only would be acquitted but would successfully sue the monastery for defamation of character.

He had been to see Trevor Haskins's parents. They were not enthusiastic about his campaign, but, he was sure, "They'll come around once we start getting the evidence together. When they see what Columban Mellary has been up to, we're going to have to hold them back."

On his second visit he was even more visibly exercised, citing Vermont cases and Supreme Court rulings. He had even looked into British common law. I tried to tell him I'd decided I didn't want to get involved with bringing charges against Columban, but he never heard me.

"Mister, do you realize how famous this will make you? And what a book it'll make. A movie too, I bet. You write those, don't you? True life, every bit of it, and you're right at the center of the whole thing. A Trappist has never been brought to trial for something like this before. You'll go down in Church history."

"I've got my life to work out, Kiernan," I said, somewhat limply.

He was perspiring profusely, although he'd been in the house only a short while. He had been wearing the same shirt for days; that much was obvious by its stained appearance and the odor emanating from it.

"So he can go on and do it to others? Right now they're probably lining up to see him. You want a bunch of them hanging from those trees? Look! Look at this and then tell me to count you out!"

The photographs were by now battered and crumpled from too many of these quick draws from inner recesses of his topcoat or jacket. How many people had he shown them to? The police; Vanik; who else? Were there others like myself he was talking to? Had he convinced them? Nevertheless, the shock was no less.

His face fractured into geometric patterns by the cracking emulsion, Trevor Haskins looked like the crucified Christ in an old Russian Orthodox icon. His eye sockets were dark, sunken, as if in death some inner force had sucked them in toward his screaming brain as it felt the full force of what he had done to himself. But his mouth was slack. Perhaps, after all, he had not cried out in pain but had died uttering a final prayer.

Kiernan was talking, but my mind was wandering; strangely, all I could think about as he rattled on were two somber words, words, like "abortion" or "divorce," whose very sound sends chills to every Catholic heart.

Presumption and despair. These were the only unforgivable sins. I had learned about them in a hushed fourth-grade religion class. One expected too much of God; the other, not enough. The pastor of St. Procopius, Father Theodore, who visited our room each week to terrify us with the mandates of ours the True Faith, left us to quake in the aftershock of even the thought of these offenses, so serious that even the merciful God was powerless to pardon them.

"Was it despair?" I blurted out in the middle of one of Kiernan's invectives.

"No, no," he shook his head, knowing full well the weight of the word. "He was sick, made sick by that man. There is no sin without reason, and at that moment his reason was gone. He was a loving, beautiful, brilliant young man. With only the brightest of futures. *Tamquam ovis ad occisionem ductus est.* Like a lamb, he was led to the slaughter."

Kiernan turned his back to me. I knew he would use any device to have me help him, but it was also clear that he would not share the true depth of his grief with anyone. Trevor had meant too much to him for that.

"I'm sorry. But I've got to do this my way," I said finally.

When he turned back to me—I will never forget his face

as long as I live—I saw a Kiernan I had not witnessed before.

His moist eyes glistened. He was smiling. It seemed as though a profound riddle, no less than the secret of life itself, had just been revealed to him.

"We cannot journey together," he said softly. "I know the path I must travel, mister. *Pax tecum.* Peace be with you."

I couldn't say that my soul exactly soared the morning of the twenty-fourth as the Mass unfolded on the other side of that squat brick wall at New Citeaux. The priest celebrating his name day usually offers the Mass, but Columban was not on the altar. Why I thought this I can't explain, for there was nothing logical about it, but I immediately and foolishly took his absence as a personal statement directed at me. Columban would not even allow me to share this one hour on his feast day. He was sequestered in the security of the cloister, where he knew I could not reach him. Undoubtedly he knew I had been thinking—and not favorably—about him.

I mouthed the familiar prayers, knelt, stood, and sat at all the right places. After all, I had been well trained as a soldier for Christ. Even if the state of my soul was confused, I still had a firm grip on the externals. As the Consecration approached, I tried even harder to clear my mind. The Consecration was usually the cutoff point I allowed myself for self-pity or rummaging through the dusty bins of my mind. This was now the most serious part of the Mass—the holiest of sacred mysteries was about to happen. I folded my hands in front of me.

"This is my body which will be given up for you. . . ."

The host, glistening in the overhead spotlights, was elevated above the altar. The bell rang three times.

And three more. And again, three more.

Father Athanasius, the celebrant, looked to the side aisle where the bell-tower rope hung. His hands, resting on the altar, tapped impatiently on the cloth. Trappists can tolerate most of the petty annoyances of life, but when their liturgy goes awry, they have little patience. He refused to say another word of the Consecration prayers until the foolish brother, whoever he was, stopped.

Three more times the bell tolled. And three more.

Suddenly, I realized the bells were not coming in series of three. The bell was ringing continuously.

I leaned forward to look down the side aisle.

Brother Polycarp, his face smudged, the white sleeves of his tunic blackened to the elbows, his eyes bulging with panic, pulled the rope again and again. He wouldn't release it on its upward path, so the momentum of the bell rhythmically yanked him into the air. Priests on the altar and brothers in their stalls stared at him.

Brother Francis, the sacristan, finally grabbed Polycarp's legs and pulled him to the ground. Polycarp's voice pierced the stillness of the great abbey church. "Fire! Oh, my God! Fire all over the place!"

Their enormous choir robes flapping behind them, the monks ran from the church. Priests spilled from the altar, pulling off their stoles. Only Father Athanasius stayed behind, a lone figure on the altar. I had to admire his presence of mind. He knew his assignment and that was to complete the Mass.

When I reached the hill adjoining the retreat house, I could see that the sheep barn beyond the cheese factory was smoldering and the chimney on the new brick kiln was belching uncharacteristically thick black smoke. The two barns in the valley to the east, which housed the various pigs, goats, horses, and cattle the monks kept more or less as pets, were already engulfed in flames.

High in the clear Vermont air, I heard the sound.

It was the first of what would be a chorus, as fire apparatus from the surrounding communities converged on New Citeaux. The lonesome wail brought back a chilling memory of the siren I'd heard that January morning when Trevor Haskins was still hanging from the tree.

Down in the asphalt yard near the tractor barns, the monastery's old fire truck lurched out of its garage.

I must have stood there for a few minutes before I snapped out of my daze. The barns in the valley were lost and the fire could spread no farther there. The cluster of buildings beyond the cheese factory were next. With the wind blowing from the northwest as it was, the fire could destroy them all.

I ran down the hill.

"Axes, you guys, five of you, over to the pond and break through the ice. Over here, bring the hose over here! Dammit, Brother, stop looking at me, pull the son of a bitch off the reel."

Brother Martinus, whose monthly fire drills had been the laugh of the community for years, was suddenly in charge, a new abbot demanding unflinching obedience. He wore a fine white plastic hat with "Chief" emblazoned on the front and he measured up to his high post immediately, though his crews were better schooled at fighting fires that were eternal rather than temporal.

I grabbed one of the axes and helped pull the hose toward the lake beyond the outdoor Stations of the Cross. We ran along the cinder path, with Jesus, Mary, and Simon of Cyrene, those mournful, weather-beaten figures, our honor guard. At the lake, Father Joachim blessed himself, hoisted the ax over his head and landed the first blow.

After a half-dozen hits, we were through the ice. I was sent back to the fire truck to report that the hole was made, but as I ran along the path the hose was already swelling with water.

"What now?" I hollered to Brother Martinus over the noise of the pumper engine.

"Secure the church and the cloister," he barked at me, sounding very much like the marine sergeant he had once been, a winner of the Silver Star who had led his platoon on a daring assault at the Chosen Reservoir during the Korean War.

"Secure?"

"Goddammit, Joseph, this is arson. Smell of gasoline all over the place. Now, go secure that area. You know the terrain. Take one of these firefighters with you; he'll know what to look for. My ninnies would start looking in the holy-water font. You there, Vernon number fourteen. Follow this here man and check for arson. Ring that bell like crazy if you find anything."

The figure in a heavy rubber overcoat turned toward me and flicked up the helmet's protective visor. "Chief, we're taking a couple of hand extinguishers just in case. Okay, Buster, let's go."

"I don't believe it," I said, catching up.

Margery looked magnificent in her Vernon Volunteer Fire Department rubberized suit, and even wearing hip boots, she moved faster than I could.

"What happened?" she called over her shoulder as we ran up the hill.

"Who knows? I was in church, guess it was maybe a half hour ago, and Polycarp starts ringing the bell. The animal barns are gone. They'd better contain it down there or else the whole place is going up."

"What's this about arson? Who the hell would do something like that?"

"You always said it was a nutty place."

She looked over her shoulder. "Hurry up, will ya?"

We entered the visitors' chapel. The glow of the two candles, which Father Athanasius had failed to snuff out, cast a pale gray canopy over the main altar, but otherwise the body of the abbey church was dark. We climbed over the low wall and made our way toward the faint light coming through the leaded windows of the doors that led out into the cloister.

"I'll check the church; you look around out there," she whispered, motioning toward the cloister.

"Why are you whispering?" I whispered.

"If somebody's doing this, I'd think it'd be better if they didn't know we were here, you jackass. Meet you right here in ten minutes." She took a few steps and was lost in the dimness of the choir stalls.

I left the church and tiptoed along the shimmering tiles

of the cloister, ducking in and out from behind the vaulted arches. The enclosed garth was a ghostly white at this hour, devoid of direct sunlight; the Virgin and her adoring court of sculpted bushes seemed like objects cast adrift on a steely sea.

Something moved.

I forced my back against an arch, banging my head on the stone toes of a statue of Saint Benedict. I peered across the garth through the Plexiglas that enclosed the cloister. At first I could see nothing. Then, a figure emerged from behind a brick column. I put my hand over my mouth. I was out of breath, gasping, and I sensed the noise probably sounded like a howling wind in the quiet of the abandoned cloister.

The figure disappeared behind a column. I made the first of a series of quick moves, from arch to arch. When he reached the corner near the abbey church, I wanted to be there to surprise him.

My heart was pounding as the footsteps came closer. He was in no hurry. He had planned so well, skillfully diverting all the monks away from the very places they spent most of their day. He reached the corner. I could hear his labored breathing.

I grabbed him, pinning both of the long white sleeves of a Trappist tunic behind a monk's leather belt.

"Columban!"

"Joseph, what are you doing in here?"

"I have to ask you the same thing."

"I have the flu. Went to the dispensary for some aspirin. Nobody's there. What's going on anyhow? Let me go!"

I released him and he turned toward me. His complexion was waxy and his lips were dry and parted. He coughed, wearily leaning against the column.

"I'm sorry, Father. There're fires all over the place. Brother Martinus sent me to make sure nothing gets started up here. He suspects arson."

"Oh, my God, who would do that? You suspected me, Joseph?"

"No, no, of course not. I didn't know who you were. Everybody's got the jitters."

"I may be evil, but—" He smiled.

"Joseph!"

The whispered voice sounded softly through the cloister, like the first, faint rumble of distant thunder. Margery stood in the doorway of the darkened church, visible only because of the three slashes of reflective tape on her rubber coat. She held her finger in front of her lips. I passed that message along to Columban and we moved quietly toward the door.

"He's in here somewhere," she said hoarsely. "I made a wide circle and heard him. I think that way. What's up there, Father?"

"It's called the jube. It's where we read the Gospel on major feast days."

"What's kept there?"

"Oh, just a wrought-iron stand, a—"

"Flammable, what's flammable?"

"Flammable? We wouldn't leave the large Bible out there, you see it's quite an old one. A low stool. The organ pipes are metal."

"Not much. How do you get up there?"

"A set of stairs behind it. Rather narrow."

"Joseph, you go down the main aisle toward him. I'll circle around and get to the back of the church. Start counting and let him begin to hear you when you hit twenty-five. Father, you count to fifty, then turn on as many lights as you can. Joseph, pull these damn boots off me and take off your shoes."

I did as I was told and, at the count of fifty, was twenty yards from the stairway leading to the jube. I could make out Margery about an equal distance on the other side.

With the first set of lights going on, directly overhead, I instinctively recoiled into one of the monk's stalls and dropped to my knees. Slowly, the rest of the church lit up. Margery was waving me on. We both ran toward the steps and peered up to the jube.

"Friends, looking for me?" The voice echoed through the church, the "me, me, me," holding on with chilling effect.

"He's up here." It was Columban's voice at the front of the church.

Octavius Kiernan hoisted two large red gasoline cans onto the altar, placing them precisely behind the candles. His sacristan's duties completed, oversized cruets in place, Kiernan, now the priest of this mad sacrifice, took his place at center altar.

"Just stay right where you are, friends; I don't want you to be hurt. Only the Devil must be denied his lair. The Lord shall avenge ye, Evil Spirit, and demons shall flee like frightened doves in his path. Oh, foul one! These purifying flames shall burn thy evil heart and death will be thy due for killing the innocent of my flock. *Exsurgat Deus, et dissipentur inimici eius; et fugiant qui oderunt eum a facie eius.* Let God arise, let his enemies be scattered; let those who hate him flee before his face!

"Lord God of Israel!" Kiernan cried out, looking up to the crucifix. "You have delivered him into my hands, and at your bidding, justice shall be done!"

I was stunned by the quickness of his next move. Kiernan bounded off the altar, grabbed Columban around the waist and dragged him up the granite steps. Slowly I started moving up the main aisle toward them.

"Octavius?" I called out, trying to keep my voice calm. "Come on, now. Let's call it a day before someone really gets hurt."

"Stay back, I warn you! The mighty sword of God shall fall only on the guilty!"

Columban had little strength to resist and Kiernan was empowered with might beyond human telling. Kiernan was wearing an old-style cassock, the type popular years ago, with buttons from neck to waist. Where he could have gotten it was a mystery, but as he stood there officiating at the middle of the altar it was obvious he had prepared for this moment. He was also wearing a Roman collar.

His face bore a strangely exaggerated smile. Now that he had us for an audience, he wanted to be sure we knew how pleased with himself he was at that moment. But it was a grotesque mask, poorly applied makeup on an old, tortured face.

"Let him go, you bastard," I screamed and was about to run at him when Margery grabbed my arm.

"Careful, Joseph, we've got to talk him down. Look behind the altar, for God's sake!"

Kiernan had been the lone laborer, but in the austerity of a Trappist abbey church he had assembled the makings of a substantial bonfire. Stacked against the huge Venetian tapestry that hung at the rear of the church were stools and chairs, choir books, vestments, a pair of enormous wooden candlestick holders. In the air was the sweet, noxious odor of gasoline.

With a swift backhand, Kiernan felled Columban. Grabbing one of the gas cans, he doused the priest.

"I baptize thee son of Satan and condemn thee back to the fires from which thou came. Ashes to ashes. Dust to dust."

I started running.

Kiernan emptied what remained in the can over himself.

I careened from side to side like a drunk. My stocking feet slipped on the smooth marble floor of the main aisle. Margery was screaming behind me: "No, don't! No!"

Kiernan dragged Columban down from the high altar and tossed him like a rag doll onto the heap. I was still some thirty yards away.

He scooped a candle off the altar and, holding it before him with both hands in proper liturgical fashion, turned toward his unfinished work.

Why, in his methodical effort to accomplish his goal, he didn't see that step, I don't know. Visiting priests in a state of reverie had done it for years, I'd been told, stumbling foolishly just after they had received Communion and, with their heads bowed, were returning to their seats in the main church. Maybe it was the intoxication of the moment, or his haste. Or the hand of God.

The noise emitted was no greater than that of an oil burner lighting. A soft *whoosh*.

I raced up the steps.

Kiernan's body was enveloped in flames. On hands and knees he crawled in the direction of the saturated funeral pyre, a human wick burning toward the explosive payload. He was within an arm's reach of Columban.

I dived for him.

I skimmed over Kiernan's back, but it was enough to knock him off balance. He tumbled down the steps on the far side. I pulled off my coat and jumped on him once more.

As I tried to put out the last of the flames, I could feel his skin move in strange ways beneath the cassock. I beat at his cuffs and wrists with my bare hands. Finally the fire was smothered.

His face was a radiant red color, and already starting to swell. He opened his blistered eyes.

"Mister, mister," he rasped through his seared throat, "why did you forsake me?"

"I'm sorry, Octavius. I . . . I just didn't know how serious you really were. Now lie still. I'll get help."

"Where's the nearest phone, Father?" Margery said urgently.

"Out those doors, to the left; past the scriptorium," Columban said, slowing rising to his feet. He stood over Kiernan for a moment, then hobbled to a small niche in the wall and opened a tiny carved wooden door.

"Father Columban," I said, "you'd better change those clothes. It's pretty dangerous. Your leg okay?"

"That can wait." He unfolded a purple stole, kissed it, and placed it around his neck. He brought back two small vials containing water and oil.

"Mr. Kiernan," Columban said gently, "if I might, I would like to anoint you."

"Don't let him touch me, mister," Kiernan said, turning away from the priest as best he could. "*Vade, Satana!* Get thee behind me, Satan!"

"It's all right, Octavius," I said. "It's God's will. His blessing, not the blessing of any man."

"Yes, please, let me," Columban said, kneeling down beside the smoldering form. He blessed himself with the sign of the cross.

"You! Filth of all ages! Demon possessed!"

"Please, Mr. Kiernan, for eternity's sake, not mine, let me—" Father Columban said gently.

What then issued from Kiernan's mouth would benefit no one to know. Nor would I feel I had done this poor soul justice as it struggled in those last painful moments of life. With all his religious background, Kiernan had to be in mortal terror of the judgment that awaited him in the next world and aware of his need for the last rites. Nonetheless, convinced of the unremitting evil of the man who hovered over him, Kiernan's shrieks accused Columban Mellary of the most graphic forms of bestiality, and questioned his priestly orders, sexual preference, the legitimacy of his birth, and his mother's state of purity.

With each new verbal assault, Columban turned his face away as if he were being slapped.

Kiernan was relentless. "God blind your eyes, pluck out your tongue for your life of sin!" he croaked, barely able to catch his breath.

"You are right, Mr. Kiernan," Columban said quietly. "He should."

Kiernan eyed him suspiciously.

"I am a wretched sinner and what you have accused me of is only a fraction of the evil I've done in this world."

Kiernan's chest was heaving now. He tried to moisten his lips with his tongue, but all he did was flake off a thumb-sized hunk of skin onto his chin.

"Help save my soul by allowing me to save yours," Father Columban said.

Kiernan closed his eyes.

"Step back," Columban said softly to me. "Let me hear your confession, Mr. Kiernan. In the name of the Father and the Son and the Holy Ghost, Amen."

Columban knelt beside Kiernan and leaned over him.

There was a phlegmy rumble in Kiernan's throat. His eyes opened a slit to take in the face just inches from his own.

Then he spat.

Columban, who had recoiled at the man's words, did not move.

"Happy name day, Father," he snarled. "I wanted to make it extra special for you. A last little tribute to the memory of Trevor. A boy you killed." His charred, leathery flesh was quickly dulling in color, but those bloodshot eyes glowered. He had fallen short of his goal, yet no one could ever say he was not giving his all to this final act.

He exhaled loudly and closed his eyes.

"Octavius, lie still, don't—" I said.

Columban stopped me with his hand.

He blessed himself again silently. Opening the vials of water and oil, he began: *"Asperges me, Domine, hyssopo, et mundabor: lavabis me, et super nivem dealbabor."* (Sprinkle me, O Lord, with hyssop, and I shall be purified; wash me, and I shall be whiter than snow.)

They were familiar, soothing words from that ancient, dead language Octavius Kiernan knew so well and loved so much. Outdated and hardly used as they may be, they were etched in stone for him, unaltered by the ephemeral preferences of ordinary men.

"Adjutorium nostrum in nomine Domini." (Our help is in the name of the Lord.)

Kiernan's chest slowly swelled. And then, without a sound, the air was released.

"Qui fecit caelum et terram." (Who made heaven and earth.) His lungs were seared, his mouth swelling shut, but Kiernan's pronunciation was impeccable.

Rhythmically, effortlessly, he breathed in and out. His hands relaxed at his side.

"*Introeat, Domine Jesu Christe, domum hanc sub humilitatis ingressu nostrae felicitas, divina prosperitas, serena laetitia . . .*" (As I enter here with a sense of my own unworthiness, O Lord Jesus Christ, let abiding happiness enter with me; may the blessings of God and unmixed joy accompany my visit . . .)

As he intoned the prayers, Columban gently made the sign of the cross on Kiernan's eyes, his ears, his nostrils, his mouth. He reached for Kiernan's swollen hands and turned them over.

"*Per istam sanctam unctionem et suam piissimam misericordiam indulgeat tibi Dominus quidquid per tactum deliquisti. Amen.*" (May the Lord forgive you by this holy anointing and his most loving mercy whatever sins you have committed by the use of your sense of touch. Amen.)

Kiernan took a deep breath. He, above all, was well aware of the symbolism. Only priests were anointed on the back of the hands. Tiny tears formed at the corners of his closed eyes.

There was noise in the cloister as Father Columban finished the prayers. Heavy boots, shouts, running—uncharacteristic intrusions even now. Then there were a half-dozen people with Margery, including two burly, red-cheeked country boys carrying an aluminum stretcher and a small tank of oxygen.

Columban stood.

"The doctor's here, Mr. Kiernan," Margery said, bending over him, "we'll have you out of here in no time at all. Helicopter's coming. Take you right to Boston. Best place for burns." She was crying. "How about that for service? Ever flown before?"

Columban rose from the floor, took the stole from around his neck, and kissed and folded it.

"He was a pilgrim on the face of the earth, like all of us," he said. "Praise God, he died peacefully in the state of grace.

"Now, we must pray not *for* him but *to* him."

12. December

"HOLD the calls, Miriam. Sit down, Joey. No, let me sit down. Cancel the lunch, Miriam. I don't give a good Goddamn who his mother is. Then tell him to go have lunch with his mother!"

Agents, it seemed, came in two sizes and two distinct packages. There were the tall, lean, elegant men with wonderfully melodic names like Prescott Dodson, Slade Winfret, and Jackson LaRue. They were well educated, able to quote Homer and Rousseau and toss off pithy, appropriate lines from not only Cicero but Theophrastus, who in reality was the brains behind Cicero. Their offices were unfailingly done in period antiques. They were the gentlemen of the industry, who never really appeared to be doing business. They were "bringing a remarkable author to a wider public," not having a paperback auction. They never "did deals" but "reached agreements."

"You're kidding, right, Joey? Look, I can take a joke. Tell me you're kidding, Joey. Feel okay? Miriam, get my doctor on the phone! I know he's in Palm Beach. A thermometer—do we have a thermometer, Miriam?"

And then there were the short men. Their huge offices were testaments to their success; their furniture, changed seasonally, was a paean to contemporariness. Their patron saint was Elmer "Lefty" Frank, who was exactly five feet one inch tall. Huge horn-rimmed glasses, elevator shoes, large diamond rings, and Cuban cigars were their hallmarks. They were unabashedly in love with their work, and regardless of where they were on this earth or in the most

227

intimate recesses of their sprawling apartments and homes, they were reachable, within seconds, by phone. Deals and phone calls were oxygen to them; without either, they would quickly perish.

"Say it again slow. No, don't say it. I've got it! Beau-ti-ful, Joey. Won-der-ful! I see it now. Hold the thermometer, Miriam. Hold all calls. You're going in for a while to get the real inside stuff, the atmosphere, the drama. Brando going to live on the waterfront. To smell it, taste it. Fab-u-lous! I can get you another hundred thou for this with one phone call. Just for the book. On the movie, you'll get another two hundred, full-screen credit, boldface in the print ads, two, maybe three percent of the gross. The gross, mind you. Remember Jeremy Irons, Joey. Bankable."

Mort Brunt was, of course, a member of the second legion, a tiny, well-dressed fly buzzing about his chrome-and-white-leather office, a man so convinced of what he was saying he needed no confirmation. His was a corner office in a brand-new concoction of a building—Nouveau Bauhaus in style, so the architect claimed—with floor-to-ceiling windows and a magnificent view of Central Park. The park that day was basking in stagy sunshine, its snow-covered meadows and dappled stands of bare trees edged by buildings—dull and tall for the most part—shouldered together so that as many people as could pay ever-escalating prices might daily have this visual feast.

"I can have new contracts in a couple days. This afternoon. Now! Don't drive me nuts. Pleeez. Your hands? Can you type? I'll get Courtney; you don't have to type. You hurt that girl's feelings, Joey. Miriam, some Perrier. Two Perriers. Lime? Put some lime in, Miriam. Coffee? Maybe you want some coffee? Tea? Herb tea; I got anything you need."

"Mort, if I could do this for you, I would. But it's just not working out that way." The excuse sounded flat to me, too. I tried again. "It's one of those times when if I don't go with this thing that's been at the back of my mind for years, I'll regret it forever. I just can't go through life with a notebook in my hand."

"You're the best at it, Joey. Nobody can feel stuff like you do and then put it down on paper. It's a real talent."

"Thanks, Mort. If that's true. I don't know. But maybe I've been abusing it. A lot of cheap grace and cheap thrills. Too many books and not enough thought."

"Thought? Schmought! You sell. You're good at this."

"Really, I'm sorry."

He had been facing me all this time with that look that had worn down many before me. He put his cigar in the ashtray and turned toward the window. "Here's the problem with this one," he said, his voice flat and suddenly tired. He reminded me of Columban when I had disappointed him.

"Yes, go on."

"This wasn't just a deal, Joey. I felt real good about this. Look, I'm into buying and selling. Hookers, politicians, murderers, movie stars—they got a name or a story and I can get top buck for it. This was different. I knew it right from the start. You're different. I think you have something to say to people. Something they need to hear."

I went around the desk and put my bandaged hands on his shoulders.

"Joey, I've sold my share of human potential hucksters, the hereness, nowness, whenness school," he said, looking down. "Everybody had *the* answer. And nobody had the answer. I'm a good Jewish boy from Flatbush Avenue. I'm old-fashioned at heart. You're on to something real important. Something that would last. I believe in you, Joey."

I pulled him close to me. He leaned his head against my chest.

"Somebody else, one of those monks up there, said I might have something to say to people. And you know what, Morty? I believe you more."

Robert, the custodian, and Jimmy, the day-shift doorman, were elated to see me. They threw their arms around me as some new tenants walked by, not recognizing who I was

and, I'm sure, wondering what had prompted such an untoward display of affection from their normally reserved and
proper employees. In my apartment I found a note from my
novelist friend. "Hey, you praying for me up there or something? Me and Peggy worked it out. I'm back home. I owe
you." He had left a fine Stetson hat as a present.

I plopped it on Robert's head as he wheeled in the hand
truck and a huge rolling laundry basket, and soon we were
hauling my life's belongings over the fine pile carpeting of
the lobby and out into the street.

At first, the people walking by looked suspiciously at us,
a man with gauze-wrapped hands in a tattered parka and a
Puerto Rican in a Stetson depositing the entire contents of
a five-room apartment at curbside on West 10th Street. Perhaps we looked like sheriff's deputies carrying out an evic-
tion. Whatever, I didn't want the passersby to feel guilty.

"He died. Put it in his will to get rid of everything. Help
yourself. He would have wanted it this way. Take anything
you can use," I told them. "Come back with somebody to
help you."

Sadly, Robert was too small and Jimmy too big for any
of my clothes, but there were the contents of the liquor cabinet, some lamps, tables and kitchenware they could use, I
said. They surprised me by asking for autographed copies
of my books.

The well-groomed lady in the real estate office on Sixth
Avenue at first thought I was trying to sell her the Brooklyn
Bridge, but when I produced the deed, she treated me most
courteously.

"But that's only a fraction of what it's worth! Why do
you need the money today? We have to do a title search,
get approval from the co-op board; these things take
months. If you insist. Don't be so impatient. You're throwing tons of money away here. I'll have to get a counter signature. Wait here. Give us till tomorrow morning to cover
the check. Promise? Make it out to who? Why do you have
to complete this transaction today? Can't it wait until tomorrow?"

"Tomorrow's the Feast of Saint John of the Cross."

"Er . . . of course. I see."

There were no more than the usual number of cars in the circular driveway outside the abbey church at New Citeaux. It had snowed the night before, but with typical Trappist efficiency the asphalt had been scraped clean and the walkways shoveled by the time I arrived for Mass. There was no one in sight under the portico as I approached the left-hand door to the guest chapel, through which I always entered. When the figure suddenly moved, seemingly emerging from the snowbank at the side of the church, it startled me.

A monk, dressed in a white choir robe, rubbed his hands together before pulling back his hood. It was obvious he had been waiting for some time.

"I knew you'd come today, Joseph. Thank God." Brother Polycarp's nose was bright red; his chin quivered from the cold.

"You fellows have your fraternity in there and we outside the walls have ours," I said. "Octavius was one of us, I guess."

"Are your hands healing?"

"Coming along fine. Surface burns, miraculously. Won't even leave scars, the doctor tells me. Yours?"

"Not even as bad; my clothes protected me. Joseph—?"

Polycarp blinked. For certain, he was not a man for whom such idle talk came easily. The transition was even more difficult.

"Joseph . . . I . . . want to ask your forgiveness. I beg you—" He began to kneel.

"Don't be silly," I said, stopping him.

"No, it's very important to me. Before I go in there to pray for the soul of Mr. Kiernan, I need to do this. I must remove the beam from my eye before I can approach the altar. Scripture tells us."

"Of course, Brother. But it's hardly a beam."

"Yes, it is. I've been terrible to you, Joseph. I don't

know if God will ever forgive me. If anybody tried to stand in the way of your Trappist vocation, it was me. How can you ever forgive me?"

"Brother, you did me a favor. And I thank you for it. I needed to know about those people. You helped me."

"People?" He thrust his ear toward me as if he were not sure that he'd heard what he had.

"Vanik the lawyer, Trevor Haskins. Without you, I wouldn't have known what happened to them."

"I don't understand."

"Your notes. I followed up on them."

"Notes?"

Brother Polycarp stared at me. I told him what I had found.

"I didn't write them," he said. "My sin is far worse than that. I hated you. I coveted the close friendship you had with Father Columban and I secretly hoped—even prayed—you would go away and never join our order. I did everything I could to make your life difficult. I beg your forgiveness."

"Who wrote them, then?"

"I wouldn't know."

"Why did you hate me? What did I do?"

He pulled his hands farther inside the long, ample sleeves of his choir robe. His head was down.

"Father Columban was the reason I became a Trappist. He's the reason half the community is here. He's magnificent at spiritual direction. Maybe it doesn't give proper credit to God, but Columban has had a great impact on this community. In the beginning, we had wonderful talks. My own father died when I was seven. Father Columban was everything to me. I joined when I was eighteen. And Columban moved on. I don't know what I wanted of him, but there always seemed to be someone new. I know that's his job. But I wanted a special friendship with him. You see, it's very difficult for me to make friends. He wouldn't allow it. 'For God alone.' He kept telling me that, but I wanted to possess him in some way. I should leave. I'm such a selfish, unworthy man, unfit to be a monk."

"Brother, I think you're a great man. I couldn't have done what you just did."

His thick glasses steamed with his tears.

"And, Joseph," he said, pausing to withdraw a handker-chief from within his robe, "I want you to know that what happened that night will never be told. I promise that."

"Thanks. It was kind of a rash moment."

"I thought it was beautiful. I could see you dancing as I came up the hill. I was the watchman that night; your tracks led me to you. I didn't look for all that long at ... at ... you both ... together ... but I knew in my heart that there was nothing sinful whatsoever. Regardless of what we're taught. You see, I've never—"

The Mass for the Dead that morning took no more than the usual hour, including Father Columban's homily. The entire service was all the more powerful because Patrick Octavius Kiernan's name was never mentioned. Yet no one could have the slightest doubt he was the object of Columban's short, masterly talk.

It was about the Dark Night of the Soul, Saint John's well-known concept, and how painful it is to feel God so distant. "Despair is too soft a word to describe what the soul feels," Columban said, and with a slight smile added, "for those of us who have experienced it.

"Some live in that horrible darkness for weeks or months, and some, those whom God blesses with the great-est trials, may be there for years. It is a purgatory with suf-fering beyond anything merely physical that we might experience in this life.

"God allows that darkness for only one reason." His eyes sweeping over the monks before him, Columban paused to embrace any of the brethren who might still be holding on to any judgments against the man who had burned down a quarter of their monastery. "So that the moment of illumination can be so serene, so beautiful, so complete and so reassuring.

"Those of you who have been blessed with such an experience"—he paused—"and those of us, not having experienced it but who have been privileged to see such a moment in others, forever know that the God to whom we dedicate our lives is indeed merciful, forgiving, just, and loving."

He folded his page of notes and looked out over the community. "Merciful. Just. Loving. And forgiving. Can we do any less and call ourselves his children?"

What struck me most about his talk was his use of the words "you" and "us," clearly revealing that he himself had never felt the divine presence of which he spoke so eloquently. Columban Mellary, OCSO, I knew now, was on the road himself, perhaps still journeying through the Dark Night.

I walked up to the retreat house and went directly to the guest parlor. There was no appointment, but he knew, as did I, that we had to meet that day.

He appeared a few minutes later. He walked in, closed the door silently and sat across from me. We looked at each other for some time, trying to find words to begin.

"A wonderful sermon, Father; you should be proud."

"Oh," he said as if someone had gently woken him from a nap.

"It was very charitable to Octavius and very open about Columban."

"I hope so. About him, at least. I can't remember exactly what I said. Funny thing is that I had prepared an entirely different homily. I don't know where this one came from."

"You never mentioned his name."

"Really? What a terrible oversight."

"Everyone knew."

"How are your hands, Joseph—were there any other burns?"

"A couple of weeks and I'll be as good as new. And then, Father . . . I've made my decision."

"I feel you should approach the abbot directly," he said quickly, "either way. I want to make this as easy as possible for you."

"Something like this past year?" I smiled.

"It has been a roller coaster, hasn't it?"

"There's only one thing I can't figure out," I said. "I thought it was Brother Polycarp who sent me on the trail of Peter Vanik and Trevor. I saw him this morning and he says it wasn't him. Who else could have done that? Who would want to?"

The air was so still in that room I could hear Columban inhale and exhale, and even the soft rustle of his skin beneath the garments he wore as his shoulders and chest rose and fell to the cadence of his breathing.

He spoke softly. "I would."

He stared at me, then his eyes dropped away. It was hard to tell if it was a penitential look or merely one of embarrassment.

"That doesn't make sense, Columban. To lead me to the very people whose lives—and death—make you out to be some sort of mad Pied Piper."

"You have been most difficult for me, Joseph. I have never so hoped and prayed that God would touch anyone with a vocation. It was just so clear to me that this life would be right for you. I don't honestly know why I was so obsessed. I spent long hours in prayer before the Blessed Sacrament.

"Then, oddly enough, it came to me one day when I was helping in the refectory kitchen. I was dumping a huge box of macaroni into a boiling pot—isn't it strange I can remember the moment?—and I knew what I must do. If I had in any way lured you into this life, praising its glories and what you might become, I had to show you the other side. My mistakes, if you want."

I could feel tiny neurological charges detonating behind

my eyes, in my upper lip, high on my cheeks. I opened my mouth, but was dumb.

"It was only fair. Men with the best intentions can end up either way. I had to show you what can happen; how some men come through the desert and others perish there. And, I think, due to no fault of their own. It is a harsh and dreadful love that we live to practice. For some, those blessed with more simple minds, it is not always so. But for you—for me—it is a constant struggle, maddening at times. But ultimately, I pray, fruitful."

"Thank you, Father"—just getting out those few words was a tremendous effort for me—"for being honest."

"If you looked to me, Joseph, you had to look beyond me. Am I your angel of deliverance from your current life? Or nothing more than a tempting devil, asking you throw yourself off a mountain so that the Lord might bear you up before your foot touched a stone? Am I your transit into the Trappists—or the best reason why you should *not* enter? I wanted the choice to be yours, Joseph. Yours and God's, not Columban Mellary's."

I shook my head. "I thought I had a pretty good idea about you, this life, and now it's all gone. Poof. Up in smoke. I don't understand this at all. Why is it so convoluted? If God truly loves us so much, why does he make it so hard to reach him? Why not just give us the peace that passes all understanding?"

"Oh, I could easily say 'original sin' and be theologically correct, but it's more than that. It bridges all faiths, really. We call it in our language the Dark Night of the Soul; for the Sufi it is *dahash*, bewilderment. Buddhists, our friends in Islam . . . all seekers go through it. For none is it easy or simple or sure.

"But that is the nature of God. A lover, who in turn, craves to be loved. And what lover doesn't want that love proved? By grand, insane gifts, by enormous struggle. Wearing the scarf of the lady beautiful, the knight goes into combat, knowing if he dies she will love him forever, and if he lives he may—just may—be able to kiss her hand. Bad odds, I'd say."

"But what else can a man do with his life? Or so they say," I added with a slight smile.

"The desert, the scorching desert, where what I want means so little. And where God's will can be worked wondrously in my life, to provide water and food. To be what God wants of me, not what I would have for myself. Ah," he sighed, his mind drifting momentarily away from the point. "There it is. It took me only a year to get it out."

"Who's counting, my friend?"

He looked down at his watch. "I'm sorry, I must go. I'm to lecture to our novices. About Aelred, strangely enough. On fraternal love."

"Can we talk again—next week perhaps? There's still so much that's unclear."

"I think not, Joseph."

"But—?"

He said nothing.

"You're probably right."

He nodded.

"The ink. Polycarp used that guesthouse ink."

"Guesthouse ink?" Columban smiled. "We have gallons of it. Everybody uses it. Our trademark. One of our benefactors manufactures it. Insists we use just that shade."

"One more thing," I said. "How, Columban Mellary, did you know I'd go for the bait? And the Latin? It flashed across my mind that dear Octavius might have been my pen pal."

"I get to use Latin so infrequently, I just couldn't resist. A badly done dramatic flourish, I suppose. *'Ipse dixit,'* indeed! Just a middling writer, myself. As for the 'bait,' I knew you would take it, Joseph." He paused and smiled. "Because you were a reporter first. And a seeker after the divine truth second. This time they went together. Simple, really. And maybe because I wanted to see what you'd do with the clues—clues to the other side of the story."

He rose from the table and extended his hand. His eyes

held that clarity I remembered from our first meetings, a quality that made Columban at once man and pure spirit. He was looking at something I could not see. At least, not yet.

"I've always enjoyed our talks, Father," I began. "I learned from them. But beyond that, what you did for Octavius was ... well, it was the most profound lesson in charity I've ever experienced. A man cursed you and you saved his soul."

Our hands met across the table and he took mine in both of his.

"Pray for me," he said. And Father Columban left the room.

I drove directly from New Citeaux to Nature's Bountiful Harvest. Margery was working at the juice bar.

"Anything on the bitter side, young lady, for a Catholic who's temporarily left his hair shirt at home but still wants to do some penance."

She turned and, with that enormous grin on her face, replied, "Special on cactus juice today. For you I can leave in some of the prickers. Or sauerkraut? I've got some really ripe stuff at the back of the cooler that should do it."

"Or can I buy you a beer?"

"Sir, it's just noon."

"A woman of principle?"

"You buying or am I getting stuck with this?"

"I'm buying. Actually have a few hundred thousand on me. Will that cover it?"

"I'll pick up my principles later," she said, taking off her apron.

We went back to that wonderful roadside bar and played the same old fifties hits and ordered Molson. It was smoky, strangely enough, even at noon. I wondered if they piped the smoke in. We were the only customers.

"I'm going to do it," I said. "Entering New Citeaux the first week of January."

"José, I guess I never had a doubt. Hoped otherwise, I must admit, but never had a doubt. Catholic intuition."

"You probably think I'm nuts, don't you, Margery."

"Actually, no. Well, yes. You are nuts. We could have had a beautiful life together. Now I'll have to think of you as my very own laboratory specimen, safely in a bottle of formaldehyde on a shelf up there. If I can't touch you, nobody else will. Some satisfaction, Margery. You going to turn into some kind of Merton up there?"

"I'm not going to write anything. I just want to get swallowed up in the place. Be a silent monk, never to be heard from again."

"Right, José, right. I expect a publishing party within the first two years. I'll turn on *Good Morning America* and there will be your holy puss."

"Don't condemn me before I even go in."

"You'll do great, either way."

"You've been a wonderful friend, Margery."

"Sounds like you're eulogizing your dog who just died."

"Seriously. I love you, Margery. This is not easy."

"Okay. I know. I love you too, dammit. Now stop this soppy crap or else I'm going to cry right into my Molson's and the bartender will think we're breaking up or something."

"Pray for me."

"I will."

"I'll do the same."

"José, look. If you make it, let me know. I want to come to your profession or ordination or whatever they do in the post–Vatican Two Church ... and ..."

"And?"

"And if you don't ... I wish I could be the good Catholic girl and say 'Look me up; I'll be waiting.' But I'm not that good. This Catholic girl forgives, but she doesn't forget. I'll never feel about anybody the way I feel about you—even right now—so I don't want to see you again unless you're wearing a cowl. Now let's have another beer and hit the road."

"Last dance?"

"My quarter, please."

"My selection. Theme song from *Picnic*."

"Risky, wouldn't you say?"

"Are you going to be a near occasion of sin?"

"I'll try my damnedest," she said.

ACKNOWLEDGMENTS

Between the first draft and a finished manuscript is a journey that some writers successfully navigate alone, while
others falter and need help along the way. It is often
achieved less by the tenacity or talent of the writer than by
the good fortune of finding people with patience and insight
who will read and comment on the various versions. First
of all, I wish to thank Sam Vaughan, my editor at Random
House, who is old-fashioned enough to read—and reread—
continually making suggestions and never wavering in his
support or sense of humor. Olga Tarnowski and Joe Fox
also carefully read earlier versions and pointed the way.
Mark Edington is to be thanked, both for his grasp of the
English language and for his firm but kind nudges.